# GALVANISM AND GHOULS

MANNERS AND MONSTERS BOOK 2

TILLY WALLACE

Print edition ISBN: 978-0-473-48812-3

Published by Ribbonwood Press

www.ribbonwoodpress.com



To be the first to hear about new releases, sign up at:

www.tillywallace.com/newsletter

# 1

A wraith feasted on the carcass of an innocent soul as Hannah watched from the doorway.

She placed a hand over her heart to steady her nerves before venturing forth. If she attracted its attention, it could turn on her and rend her life in two. With careful, deliberate steps, she eased into the breakfast room.

She might have indulged a slight sense of the melodramatic. The black shadow sucking down the life force of a soft-boiled egg was Viscount Wycliff. But they were practically the same thing in Hannah's mind.

"Miss Miles." The viscount looked up and half rose from his seat to acknowledge her presence.

Hannah stopped in her tracks. The man was bordering on civilised, but she wouldn't be fooled. He still had the wariness of a wild dog used to fighting over every scrap, and she would make no sudden movements that might provoke him.

"Good morning, Lord Wycliff." Hannah kept her eyes averted as she took her seat diagonally opposite the viscount. It was as far away as she could sit while still remaining in the same room, and it removed him from her direct line of sight. She fussed with her napkin before reaching for a piece of toast. Next she poured a cup of tea, the sound of liquid hitting the bottom of the china cup overloud in the silence. Given what she knew of the man, she doubted he would entertain light conversation about the weather.

The viscount had been in residence at Westbourne Green for a week now, and Hannah thought it an experience comparable to a malevolent poltergeist deciding to haunt their gothic mansion. He had been given a suite of rooms on the first floor—mercifully at the opposite end of the hallway from her own. A study on the ground floor near the library had been allocated for his use. A leggy black mare had appeared in the stables, and a glossy top hat adorned the stand in the entrance foyer.

It was all far too much for Hannah to bear. If her mother were playing some jest, it had gone too far. Whatever would she be forced to endure next—his smalls on the line outside on laundry day? A glimpse of him in a state of undress as he shaved?

The image her mind conjured made Hannah snort and inhale tea at the same time, which resulted in a coughing fit.

The man in question looked up and arched a dark brow. Now she had disturbed his morning perusal of the newspaper. He flicked the paper as she caught her breath and muttered an apology.

"What news is there today, my lord?" She braved a conversation starter, since she had inadvertently attracted his attention.

"Salacious nonsense about a monster roaming the fields around Chelsea." He spoke to the newspaper.

"A monster? How intriguing. It could be possible—there are many different types of Unnatural creatures. Perhaps one has moved to the area. It would be quite affordable for a monster of means." Her father would love to examine a genuine monster. If he heard the rumour, he might take to stalking the fields himself at night, hoping for a chance encounter.

"It is most likely a drunk who lost his way home." The newspaper snapped rigid and the viscount was hidden except for the long fingers curled around each edge.

Hannah wished her mother would appear in the breakfast room. Not that Lady Miles needed to eat with the family; she only held an empty cup for the sake of appearances. But Hannah longed for her mother's quiet conversation to settle her nerves. She also needed another body in the room to create a barrier to the viscount's dark presence.

Hannah cast around for a metaphoric shield when she caught sight of Mary out of the corner of her eye. The maid crept past the half-open door on tiptoe.

"Oh, Mary," Hannah called.

The maid froze, glanced at her with wide eyes, and then retreated until she was hidden by the door.

"Mary, where is Timmy this morning?" Hannah addressed her question to the panelled door, since it did not appear the maid would emerge from where she sheltered.

"Tucking into his breakfast in the kitchen, miss. He's like a feral kitten, that one, and doesn't seem to believe he's allowed in the house." Her voice came from offstage.

"Thank you, Mary, that will be all." Hannah held in a sigh. Neither the maid nor the young lad would be standing between her and the wraith. Even her father was absent, which was decidedly odd.

Then she remembered it was the first Monday of the month, which meant he had his regular meeting with his fellow scholars investigating Unnaturals in general and the Afflicted in particular. He was probably packing his bag with notes and materials he wanted to share. How she wished she could accompany him, but the presence of women was frowned upon, especially if the group had a cadaver to autopsy. While Hannah assisted her father in his home laboratory, some men clung to the old-fashioned belief that the weaker sex was unfit for such study.

Then, as though summoned by her thoughts, a voice boomed along the hallway. "Hannah! Where are my samples?"

Should she shout back? Family members yelling up and down the halls might send the viscount scurrying away, horrified at their uncouth behaviour. Except she couldn't bring herself to yell. It was such an indelicate thing to do. Despite the autopsies she attended, she held to some of society's rigid rules about manners.

"Excuse me," Hannah murmured as she dabbed her lips with her napkin and rose from her seat. "Father is attending a SUSS conference over the next two days and needs to prepare."

"Suss?" One black brow shot up and the opposite eye narrowed.

Hannah paused at the door. "The Society of Unnatural Scientific Study. They are a group of scientists, surgeons, and theologians at the leading edge of studying Unnaturals and the Afflicted."

"Ah. I have heard Sir Manly refer to that group. He thought it might benefit me to attend their meetings to keep abreast of their discoveries, but it sounded like a load of empty rhetoric to me." His implacable expression seemed to suggest he had more to say about his opinion of the group, but for once, he held his silence.

"Quite the contrary. There is no *empty rhetoric*, but keen minds sharing their work. I'm sure they would welcome an open mind eager to discuss their research." By sheer willpower Hannah managed to keep a smile on her face. Why had Sir Manly suggested he attend when he patently didn't want to, yet those who did want to attend weren't allowed? In that instant, she decided to tackle her parents about the subject, so that she might attend the second day of the meeting.

The viscount grunted and returned to his newspaper. Hannah took that as a dismissal and slipped away.

Her father stood in the foyer next to the side table as he burrowed into a large black leather bag balanced on the narrow table's top. A pile of papers tied with green string waited next to his hat.

Hannah patted his shoulder. "I will fetch your samples. Mother was adding a magical shield to their cage to ensure they didn't escape."

"Oh. Good girl." Her father looked up and beamed at her before frowning at his bag and muttering into its depths.

Hannah walked to the library and approached her mother, who was working at the large desk. The mage had always seemed otherworldly to Hannah, with her strong magical abilities. With the morning light bathing her from behind, Seraphina appeared the embodiment of a supernatural creature, draped in cream fabric that covered her from the top of her head to where her legs stopped at the knee.

"Papa is ready to leave." Hannah rubbed her arms to dispel the gooseflesh raised by the magic chilling the air.

"All done. I have cast a web so that if a mouse jumps out, the net will capture it." Seraphina held in her gloved hands the metal box that contained the Afflicted mice.

"Thank you, Mother." Hannah's fingers tightened on the handle and a tingle ran up her arm as she retraced her steps. She carried the doomed mice into the hall and placed the cage on the table by her father's bag.

A white muzzle pressed to an air hole and Hannah resisted the urge to stroke the velvet nose in case she startled the mouse and it bit down on her finger. "Do be careful, Papa."

Sir Hugh let out a puff of air. "Of course I will, my dear—can't have a plague of Afflicted mice descending on London. We would need the Pied Piper to lead them all away."

Hannah held his hat as he donned his Garrick coat, the heavy layers around his shoulders adding more bulk to his already large frame. Despite the calendar's insistence that they were moving into spring, the weather stayed stubbornly chilly.

Mary stood at the front door and peered through the decorative glass square. "Carriage is ready, sir."

Hannah placed the hat on her father's head and then stretched up to kiss his cheek. "I do hope the conference is productive. I look forward to hearing all about it tomorrow morning. Perhaps I can attend tomorrow's proceedings and we could compare our thoughts afterward?"

"We'll see, Hannah. The others think it no place for a gently bred young woman."

That made her screw up her face. She had assisted her father at many autopsies and helped weigh and examine internal organs. That alone should have been ample proof she was no fainting damsel.

Sir Hugh laid a hand on her shoulder. "I will raise

it with the others, Hannah, and point out how much work you do at my side."

"I would appreciate your trying to get them to admit me, Papa. Viscount Wycliff also expressed an interest in attending the meeting."

"Ah! Two more eager attendees. I shall do all I can and regale you on my return." He picked up the metal box and black bag.

Seraphina wheeled herself to the hall and raised her face to him as he kissed her cheek through the muslin veil. With a final wave, he strode through the front door.

"Where to, Mother?" Hannah asked as she grabbed the handles on the bath chair.

On her mother's lap sat a small glass cube. The edges were sealed with copper and inside, it seemed, a tiny weather system swirled. Clouds formed and reformed, pushing against the panes of glass holding them captive. The mage rested her hands on the strange box. "The breakfast room, please, if that is where I will find Wycliff."

Hannah pushed her mother toward the breakfast room and through the door. Viscount Wycliff dropped the newspaper and rose from his seat. For the mage, he stood tall before offering a bow from the waist. Hannah had only warranted a slight rise from the chair.

"Lady Miles," he said.

"Good morning, Wycliff. I have something for you." She held out the cube.

He stared at the object as though he suspected it

would sprout teeth and tear out his throat. "Might I enquire as to what it is?"

"Since we have uprooted you from the bustle of London and transplanted you to the desolate countryside, I thought you might need a means of communicating with Sir Manly and the Ministry of Unnaturals," Seraphina said.

Wycliff took the cube in one hand, his long fingers stretched apart to hold it by the edges. He held it up and peered within. "How does it work?"

Lady Miles lowered her hands into her lap. "Sir Manly has a similar cube in his office, along with some tokens. If there is an urgent matter, he places the relevant token on the top of his cube. It will change the weather formation inside to a vivid red sunrise."

"A sunrise?" Both his brows drew together in a frown.

"Yes. Do you know the old saying, *Red sky in morning, shepherd's warning*? The red clouds will alert you that he has a matter of utmost importance requiring your urgent attention."

The eyebrows shot up as he stared at the captured clouds. "And if there are non-urgent matters?"

Hannah pushed the bath chair to the table while her mother spoke. "Sir Manly has a token that will make the clouds a vibrant yellow."

Wycliff held the cube in one palm. The clouds were pale grey lightening to cream and circled their enclosure on an invisible breeze. "How do we know if it works?"

Her mother fell silent. Not many people questioned her conjurings. "If it works and there is a matter requiring your attention, then the clouds will change colour. If it doesn't work, I imagine a rider will eventually appear on our doorstep to summon you in person."

He made what was becoming a familiar grunt in the back of his throat. "Thank you. I shall place it on my desk." With the barest incline of his head, he left.

Hannah let out a long sigh once his form had disappeared through the door.

"Have you been holding your breath the entire time, Hannah?" Humour lit Seraphina's words.

"He is like a wild dog in a confined space. I do not wish to make a sudden movement in case he lunges for me." Hannah glanced out into the hall to ensure the topic of their conversation had left and hadn't doubled back.

"You will simply have to become accustomed to him, Hannah. He would never harm you." Her mother poured a cup of tea and held its warmth in her cold hands.

"How can you be so sure?" There was something about the man that set her senses on fire with warnings.

"Because I see what others do not, and I know it is not in his nature." Seraphina lifted the cup to her lips, but did not drink.

Had she been able to see her mother's face, Hannah had no doubt it would bear an enigmatic smile.

# 2

After breakfast, Wycliff excused himself to work in his new study. He was an interloper in the lives of the Miles family and did all he could to minimise his impact on their daily activities.

*Beggars can't be choosers*, he reminded himself. Lady Miles' offer of accommodation had come just as his landlord had served the eviction notice. There were advantages to being under the same roof as the two people at the forefront of Unnatural research, and he found Sir Hugh an invaluable resource. Even if the man was somewhat blunt in his manners and speech.

He made a mental note to ask Sir Manly if he might attend the meeting of the Society of Unnatural Scientific Study. Miss Miles' rebuke had made him curious. The group's findings might have some relevance for the new Ministry, even if it only advanced his knowledge of the weaknesses of Unnatural creatures.

The one discordant note in his new living arrangements was the way Lady Miles set his nerves on edge. The mage watched him with unseen eyes and seemed to pluck his thoughts from his mind. He still held that the government wasted time and money in their attempts to find a cure for the Afflicted, but he grudgingly admitted that the unfortunate creatures could live quiet lives without endangering the whole of London.

He was forced to admit that the mage had a unique insight that might aid his future investigations. The immobilisation spell she had given her daughter last month had been useful in apprehending two murderous Afflicted. A tiny voice whispered that she could also help with his particular problem, if only he would ask for her assistance. He waved the idea away.

He was relieved to find a quiet companion in Hannah Miles. The young woman demonstrated an ability to hold her tongue at the table and saved him from inane chatter about bonnets and ribbons and whatever else young women talked of. At odd moments he caught himself wondering what it would be like to join her in the parlour in the evening. It would be pleasant to have intelligent discourse about politics or literature, but he didn't want to suffer disappointment if she failed to live up to his expectations.

Wycliff settled in the study with its view of the front garden and the road beyond. Not that there was any traffic to distract him from his work. In the week he had been sitting before the window, he had seen only one rider and the occasional lad herding sheep. He felt as though he hadn't moved a few miles from London, but had come to an entirely different world where contact with others was strictly limited.

There was another advantage to the isolation. One night he had crept out to take advantage of a moonless sky and no watching eyes. He loathed what lurked inside him, but if he didn't let the beast loose on rare occasions, he feared it would rip him apart in polite company.

Wycliff also found that no creditors ventured this far to wave past due invoices at him. He rearranged columns of numbers on the sheet of paper before him. With what he saved by boarding with the Miles family, he had more available to pay off his debts. He was cautiously optimistic that he would be debt free in another year or two, and able to revive his country estate.

A flash of light caught Wycliff's eye as he worked. Within the cube, the tiny trapped weather system swirled and changed colour. As though someone had poured dye in from above, the soft greys and white became yellows with a splash of orange.

He grunted in surprise. The thing actually worked.

Yellow meant a non-urgent matter, but this was tinged with a darker hue. What lay between urgent and non-urgent? Did it mean he was to present himself before the day was out? He needed a distraction, and this gave him the chance to verify the cube worked and this initial change was not merely random. He laid down his quill and rose from the desk. He grabbed his top hat and coat from the rack by the door and strode along the hall.

The maid emerged from the parlour and on seeing him, squawked like a chicken and shot back into the room. Silly woman had no sense at all. At least Miss Miles didn't cry out in horror every time she encountered him in the rambling house.

He pushed through the double glass doors that led to a flagged terrace, and then down the stairs to the lawn. Across from the house were large, roomy stables that had stalls for a dozen horses, but which housed only four.

"Can I help you, my lord?" the stable lad asked, looking up from where he sat oiling a leather harness.

Wycliff approached his horse. "Fetch my saddle, lad. I'm off to town."

He patted the mare's nose. His unusual situation allowed him to keep one thing hidden from his creditors' notice. The horse had been stabled in the cheapest mews he could find and every day he had expected to discover her sold to flesh out a stew. He had barely dared to check on the horse's welfare, not wanting to risk a debt collector's following him to the mews, and so had relied on hired hackneys to make his way about London.

Free of London, he was able to reclaim the valuable horse and move her to the Westbourne Green house. If anyone noticed, he would say she belonged to Sir Hugh.

He slipped on the bridle while the boy brought the

saddle, placed it on the horse's back, and then buckled up the girth. Out in the yard, he swung himself up into the saddle and put heel to the horse.

He was dimly aware of Hannah standing at the library window, watching him canter away.

As he rode down the main road toward London, he let his mind spiral over the surrounding fields. How he had fallen from his family's once vaunted position. When his father was a young man, their family had been respected by society. The previous Viscount Wycliff had his pick of pretty debutantes to find his bride. Then his father had spiralled into debauchery and taken the family's name and fortune with him.

Now Wycliff lived with a mad scientist, a dead mage, and a woman who wore a blood-spattered apron instead of a fashionable gown. At least none of them commented on why he had no valet and made do dressing and shaving himself.

If he minded his pennies, he had the opportunity before him to wrest his family estate back from the brink of ruin. The first job would be setting aside enough for new breeding stock. A prize bull could fetch an entire year's wages, but could father enough offspring over time to pay for a new roof on his country house.

As he cantered down Uxbridge Road with Hyde Park on his right, London loomed before him. A haze sat over the city, created by coal fires from thousands of chimneys. The smoke hung low today and softened the hard edges of the buildings. Traffic became thicker as he approached civilisation. Wycliff pulled the horse back to a trot. By the time he neared the building in Whitehall that housed the new Ministry of Unnaturals, he was forced to a brisk walk by the press of carriages, horses, and pedestrians.

He jumped to the ground and flung the reins over the horse's head.

"Need me to watch 'im?" a lad called from his pose on the front step.

"Yes." Wycliff tossed the boy a coin as he handed over the reins. "I'll not be long."

Wycliff pushed through the front doors and waved at the man sitting behind the large front desk. His boot heels rang on the wooden floor as he strode the short corridor to his superior's office, where he rapped sharply on General Sir Manly Powers' door.

"Enter," the deep voice said.

Wycliff pushed inside to find the general seated at his desk. Papers were neatly ordered in four piles before him.

He looked up from the missive in his hand. "Ah, Wycliff. The box works, then."

He stared at the cube on Sir Manly's desk, a twin to his own. Except this one had a square copper token on the top that appeared to seep yellow and a blush of orange into the clouds below.

"Indeed, Sir Manly, a most convenient contraption." He wondered if they could add more tokens for different messages. Green to notify him when his pay was to be collected or blue for mail.

"Something unusual washed up from the Thames that the Runners said is more our bailiwick. I believe a crowd has gathered and the fellow who discovered the thing was instructed to keep it contained until someone arrived to relieve him of it." Sir Manly held out a piece of paper with directions scrawled upon it.

Wycliff glanced at the paper. He was heading southwest to a stretch of the Thames between Westminster Bridge and Tothill Fields.

"Report back when you know what it is. While you are there, ask around about this so-called monster on the loose in Chelsea. Can't have Unnaturals terrorising honest folk. I need you to find whatever it is and tell it to behave or we'll lock it up." Sir Manly waved a large hand and he was dismissed.

Wycliff tucked the sheet into his coat pocket and reclaimed his mare from the street urchin. He turned southwest and fought the traffic swirling around Westminster Abbey. Pedestrians and vehicles thinned out as he approached the edge of buildings that turned into Neat House Gardens. The area was a bustling market garden, being both low-lying and with a high water table. The nearby pastures gave ample access to large quantities of manure to fertilise the ground. Among the many crops grown were cauliflower, asparagus, artichokes, spinach, and radishes.

Alehouses had sprung up to slake the thirst of the workers from the fields and the area had a reputation for revelry. Wycliff suspected pressure from the city would soon see the demise of the gardens and the land turned into housing. A great loss, in his mind. He preferred open country to the press of bodies around him.

A small group of people with nothing better to do had gathered on the bank of the Thames, giving away his destination. The water had receded at low tide, leaving a muddy stretch, and a few small boats used for fishing were drawn up to the grassy bank. A man sat upon an upturned wooden box and from beneath his buttocks came a regular tapping noise.

Wycliff sighed as he stared at the sticky mud. His boots would be coated with the stuff, as would the hem of his coat if he didn't hold it out of the way. He squelched his way to the seated man and hoped the beeswax on his boots would keep the worst of the moisture at bay.

"I am Viscount Wycliff, investigator for the Ministry of Unnaturals. What do we have here?" He pointed to the box.

The man let out an audible sigh. "We been taking turns to sit on it for hours, milord. If it's not weighted, it drags the box with it."

"Let's have a look, man." Wycliff gestured for the man to get up. He wasn't going to peer between his legs. From the noise, it sounded like an angry trapped rodent. A stench came up off the mud and assaulted his nostrils.

The man rose and the box shuddered along an inch in the mud like a hermit crab dragging its shell. The man jumped back a step. "Told you—only way I could stop it moving was to sit on it."

Chatter rose from the watchers. "Bet it's a cat," someone yelled.

Wycliff rested his palms on either side of the box and lifted one side out of the sticky ooze. It wasn't a cat, not unless it was a bald one, although the object did bear some resemblance to a cat. Long, narrow, and hairless, it was coated in muck but still recognisable.

It took him only a few seconds to identify the creature.

It was an arm with the hand still attached. But there was no sign of the rest of the body within the small container.

As he studied the arm, the fingers tapped on the side of the box like a man testing the limits of his prison. Then the fingers dropped to the ground and inched forward, dragging the severed limb behind them. When it butted up against the side of the container, it leaned into the obstruction in a fashion similar to a man who put his shoulder to a heavy load. The limb had been severed below the elbow. The wound didn't bleed and the arteries and tendons hung like dead worms. The flesh was a dull brownish red, probably from the swim in the Thames.

"It crawled up out of the water." The man gestured to a point by the water's edge. "We were bringing the boat up and thought it were a rat. But rats don't have fingers, do they?"

The box moved another inch. Where was it heading?

The man moved back a step as he waved at the upturned crate. "It ain't right, innit? Arms don't move on their own. Ought to 'ave a body attached. That's why the Runner sent for you and said it were none of 'is business."

Mutters rippled through the crowd. Dead bodies shouldn't move. Except they did, as people had learned with the appearance of the Afflicted and of vampyres in England. Wycliff leaned closer to the arm. There was something odd about it, quite apart from its being independently ambulatory.

"Has the rest of it washed up?" Wycliff asked.

A rough line of stitches encircled the wrist—two edges sewn together like a rip mended in a sail. Perhaps the owner worked around machinery, had lost the limb in an accident, and had it sewn back on?

"We ain't seen nothing, 'ave we?" the man called to his companions on the bank.

"No one's passed by and asked if we've seen 'is arm," one wit retorted.

"Do you have a bag?" Wycliff cast around. There was no point carrying the thing in the box when it could crawl out.

Someone on the bank tossed down a hessian sack. Wycliff shook it out and held the end open with one hand. He wrapped his free hand around the end of the stray arm and flipped the limb into the sack. He drew tight the string and knotted it. The arm thrashed around like a feral cat caught in a trap.

Somewhere out there was an Afflicted or vampyre missing an arm and a hand. If the limb was trying to return to its owner, would it work like a compass needle to find the rest of the body?

Wycliff reached into a pocket and extracted a card. “If you find any more of it, let me know. Have you heard of the monster prowling these parts?”

The man’s eyes widened. “Blimey. Do you think it’s part of ’im?”

Wycliff surveyed the gathered people. An assortment of fishermen, washerwomen, and the unemployed. They all looked prone to believing flights of fancy and scuttlebutt. He doubted he’d find any information of value from them.

“I would have to see this monster to ascertain if he is missing a limb. If you spot anything, contact me at the Ministry. There will be a reward in it for you.”

The man grinned and exposed the gaps of missing teeth. He touched the brim of his cap. “Will do, milord.”

Wycliff picked his way back through the mud to the bank. The horse snorted at the squirming sack. Wycliff couldn’t blame the mare; he didn’t like it, either. He was loath to tie it behind his saddle in case the hand could free itself. In the end, he decided to hold it to the side and ride with the reins in one hand.

Sir Manly wanted him to inquire about the Chelsea monster, but that would have to wait until he divested himself of the limb. He wouldn't put himself out on the strength of a drunken rumour and he had sown the seed of reward money with the man who had discovered the limb. That should do the work for him.

He had an awkward ride back to the Ministry headquarters, holding the sack out to one side while also ensuring he didn't knock any passers-by in the head with it. He crossed the floor, aware he tracked in mud with each step, and knocked once more upon Sir Manly's door.

"What was it? Some sort of rodent, I presume." His superior officer looked up from his paperwork.

Wycliff held out the sack. The movement was less pronounced now, as though the hand had worn itself out trying to escape. "A severed limb that wants to be reunited with the rest of its body."

Bushy grey eyebrows drew together. Sir Manly leaned back in his chair and the ornate swirls and curls in his moustache rose up and down as he ground his teeth. "Well. That's something new. Take it to Sir Hugh and then inquire at the hospitals as to whether they've seen the rest of it."

Wycliff bit back a retort that it wasn't his job to find bodies missing limbs, if someone had been so careless as to misplace their arm. Instead, he gave a stiff bow. "As you wish, sir."

# 3

After breakfast, Hannah and her mother adjourned to the library. More names had been inscribed overnight in the ensorcelled ledger that resided with Unwin and Alder. Each day the unseen staff wrote the names of any *donations* received for processing and sale to their elite clientele.

Hannah called out each name and Seraphina looked it up in the mage genealogies to see whether the deceased was an aftermage. Hannah hoped soon to have enough information to begin a trial, separating the Afflicted into two groups. A small group would be fed only aftermage brains, to see what effect the trace of magic had on their cursed bodies.

"Found her—fifth generation," Seraphina called.

Hannah wrote the notation *A5* next to the name. A wave of sadness washed over her as she gazed at it. The donor had only been twelve years old. A life cut short by either illness or injury. Were parents waiting for their child to be returned to them so she could be buried? Or had the girl died alone with no one to mourn her passing, her small body relieved of its most valuable asset and slipped into an unmarked pauper's grave?

"Hannah? Next name?" Her mother's voice cut through her maudlin thoughts.

"Sorry. I was just thinking of the lives lost and how they ended up in Unwin and Alder's ledger." Only three names had appeared overnight. Three individuals whose families, or those who had found their bodies, were compensated for donating a specific organ for wealthy Afflicted to dine upon. Not that the families knew the brain was removed. To explain the tidy row of stitches in the scalp, they were told it was a type of phrenology study and that measurements had been taken of the deceased's skull.

"Ah. Pondering the fragility of life?" One wheel on the bath chair squeaked as Seraphina rotated to face her daughter.

The dead mage was draped in cream silk today. A veil covered her face and long gloves were tucked into the cuffs of her sleeves. Embroidered cream flowers adorned the hem of her dress. A single orange rosebud was tucked behind her ear—plucked for her by Sir Hugh before he departed for the day. Apart from the flower, her mother appeared almost to be a marble bust.

Hannah traced the name on the page with a fingertip. "It doesn't seem fair. A young life gone to sustain that of a wealthy woman."

A soft chuckle blew out Seraphina's veil. "Now you are sounding like our newest resident. Are you adopting his views?"

Hannah shuddered and stuck out her tongue. "Banish the thought, Mother. Besides, I doubt Viscount Wycliff loses any sleep pondering the lives of the poor that are cut short. He seems rather preoccupied with finding fault in his superiors."

"Hannah, that is a particularly uncharitable remark. You have not walked his journey and should not presume to know his intentions." Her mother's tone bordered on sharp.

Hannah stared at the book and swallowed her words. Her mother was right. She had not lived the viscount's life to know the obstacles he faced. There was something about the man that rubbed her the wrong way and she could not help disliking him. Perhaps that was easier than the alternative—what if she *liked* him?

The horror. Imagine her mooning over his sharp visage across the table every morning.

"Sorry, Mother. There is something about him that makes me uncomfortable." What madness had made her mother extend to him the invitation to live with them? If her mother wanted more excitement in her life, they could have moved closer to London.

"Think of him like the porcupine. It may be covered in sharp spines, but if you are brave enough, you might find it quite soft to stroke." The wheel squeaked as Seraphina moved closer. She reached out and took Hannah's hand. "Do you know your greatest gift?"

Hannah blew out a sigh that made a wayward lock of hair dance away from her face. "Either Father's obstinacy or your curiosity."

Seraphina laughed. "You have both, that is obvious. But no. Your gift is your empathy. You have a concern for others that allows you to better understand them. Apply that gift to the viscount and you might be surprised at what you find."

"What if I don't like what I find?" The man already made her feel like a chicken left alone with the fox. What if on closer examination she found him to be a ravenous wolf? The shiver down her spine was tinged with something else.

Excitement.

"If you make a genuine effort for the rest of the month and still cannot tolerate him, then I will have no choice but to turn him into a goldfish. We will release him into the pond where he may live a happier life." Seraphina patted Hannah's hand.

"He would have a short life if the birds spotted him in the pond." Hannah would try. Perhaps in the attempt to understand him, she might learn more details of the campaign that had seen his regiment slaughtered. The idea of unravelling the tragic secret of his survival (she was quite convinced it would prove to be terribly tragic) perked her up. "Whatever motivates him, it doesn't make me feel any more comfortable about the young lives cut short who end up in this ledger."

Her mother wheeled herself back to the desk and the enormous genealogy book that recorded the seven generations of each mage family. "Bear in mind the Afflicted are not responsible for those who die in London. Illness, injury, and age are the three reapers who snatch people at all levels of society. We do not send forth invisible assassins to feed our hunger, Hannah. It was the enterprising Messrs. Unwin and Alder who were enlisted by your father to harvest what the deceased no longer needed, and present it in a form acceptable to the Afflicted among the *ton*."

The resurrectionists had been uniquely positioned when the French curse struck a small number of noblewomen. Hannah's father had sought their help to have sufficient brain matter on hand to feed the undead women. Once he had the support of the Prince Regent and the Prime Minister, that enterprise had grown into a legal business. Unwin and Alder supervised the gruesome task of supplying that which kept the wives, sisters, and daughters of peers from rotting. In return, they made a handsome profit on *pickled cauliflower*.

"I know, Mother. It is just so sad to see the names inscribed every morning and wonder about those they left behind." Hannah brushed a hand over the paper, as though she could gather up the memories of those written on the page.

Seraphina turned a page in the large tome as she searched for the last name. "Because you have empathy, my darling daughter. That is what makes you so extraordinary—your ability to place yourself in the shoes of another."

Hannah pushed the book away as though its pages were steeped in sorrow and she could touch it no longer. "Speaking of shoes, I shall need new ones for Lizzie's wedding. And a dress, I suppose, if finances will allow?"

"Of course you shall have a new dress for the wedding. We may live a modest life, but we are not impoverished. You shall have whatever you need."

"But we are poor, are we not?" Hannah frowned and tried to digest the meaning of her mother's words.

Seraphina laughed. "No, we are not poor. We are quite comfortable, due to the careful investments your father and I made over the years with my earnings."

Hannah's world spun on its axis and her mind was tipped upside down. "But we live out here away from London, and I am only ever allowed two or three new dresses each year."

"We live here because Hugh and I both value our privacy and prefer to live away from gossiping tongues. And the limit on your gowns was because we wanted to raise a daughter who valued books and learning, not ribbons and frocks." Seraphina spoke with her hands, and moving pictures appeared in the space between them. A room full of gowns and shoes turned into a library.

Hannah wanted to ball her hands into fists and throw herself to the ground, crying that it wasn't fair.

She had thought they were as poor as church mice and made do with her old dresses. But if they weren't poor at all, she could have had the latest fashions, and matching bonnets and ribbons and—

She leaned back against the window frame and blinked. Her rampant thoughts illustrated her mother's point. Was she really so vain and shallow a creature that she immediately thought of all the fripperies she could have possessed?

She banished the unworthy thoughts. "I never knew. I thought our modest life was due to insufficient funds."

"A child should never have to worry about being fed, sheltered, or clothed. I am sorry if you were under the impression we were poor." Her mother's head tilted, as though she were considering her.

Hannah pulled the ledger back toward herself and stared at the names. These were children who worried about empty bellies and who shivered in the cold. She had never lacked for clothing, comfort, or sustenance, thanks to her parents. She also had copious amounts of that most precious commodity—love.

"Perhaps it is just as well that I had no knowledge of our true situation. If you had told me we were quite wealthy, I fear I would have developed a terrible addiction to new bonnets and shoes." Hannah managed a smile.

"Now that you are older and have grown into a sensible young woman, I shall speak to your father. It is time you had a larger allowance, with more independence over your wardrobe. Or to purchase fripperies if you so desire."

Hannah rushed to her mother, flung her arms about her, and hugged her. "Thank you. I know it seems foolish to desire something beautiful, but I promise not to turn into a vainglorious creature." As she said the words, the image of Lady Gabriella Ridlington appeared in her mind. Hannah shuddered. No, she would never turn into such a shallow and callous creature just because she could afford a piece of ribbon or a brooch if one caught her eye.

A gloved hand soothed Hannah's back. "I am glad that is sorted and no longer weighing on your thoughts. Kitty has written, and advised that the modiste working on Lizzie's trousseau is only too happy to make your gown also."

Excitement trickled through Hannah as she contemplated her dear friend's wedding. The event was planned for the end of summer and was as oft discussed as the forthcoming royal wedding of Princess Charlotte. Then she remembered the gruesome murder on the night of Lizzie's engagement party. "Let us hope no unfortunate events mar the wedding."

"I shall concoct a spell to ensure everyone behaves." Hannah couldn't see her mother's face, but she could hear the humour sparkling in her voice.

With matters settled, they returned to work until the last name was notated as an O for *ordinary* in the ledger. Hannah put the book away on the shelf. "What's next for today, Mother?"

Seraphina waved a hand and the enormous and heavy mage genealogy book rose into the air and snuggled itself into a spot on a high shelf. "Next we have a stack of intelligence from Sir Ewan Shaw. His men are most diligent in trying to track Afflicted persons in France."

With the genealogy book moved, a map now appeared on Seraphina's desk. Mountains, trees, and tiny buildings grew from the surface as Hannah watched. Towers denoted the location of each French mage. Minuscule shadow people represented the Afflicted they had found. So far they were an equal distance from each mage. They had hoped they would cluster around the person who had created the French curse.

Hannah picked up the sheets of paper from Sir Ewan. "I'll read through and call out locations."

It was early afternoon when a sharp rap at the library door made both women look up. Mary had a soft and quiet knock. Only one man would bang on the panels like a debt collector.

Viscount Wycliff opened the door and took two steps into the library before halting. His black hair was more dishevelled than usual, the bottom of his coat and boots were coated in mud, and from him wafted a fetid odour.

"I'll not disturb you overlong, Lady Miles, as I am coated in muck from the Thames. But I wonder if Miss Hannah could be spared to assist me?" He held up a sack that squirmed and wriggled.

"Whatever do you have? It's not a kitten or a puppy, is it?" Had the horrid man scooped up some poor creature stuck in the mud? Although if he had brought it home, he was most likely rescuing it, not dining upon it.

He held the sack at arm's length. "No. It's a rather lively limb that needs to be contained until Sir Hugh can inspect it."

Hannah set aside the ledger and rose to her feet. "There are a number of suitable boxes in Father's work-room. Excuse me, Mother."

"You know where I will be, Hannah." Seraphina waved a hand in the air and the markers on the map began a slow dance around each other as she rotated the terrain.

"If you will follow me, my lord." Hannah led the way down the hall to the small staircase that linked her father's basement laboratory with the rest of the house.

In the large laboratory, Hannah surveyed the empty containers stacked on a shelf. "Does it require air holes?"

"No. Nor does it want anything with a lock it can reach from inside."

Hannah glanced at the sack, more curious than ever now to see what lay within. She selected a metal box that was rectangular in shape and possessed an external lock. "This should keep the item secure until Father has time tomorrow."

She placed it on the table and opened the lid. Wycliff put the entire sack, with the mouth still drawn, in the bottom. Then he closed the lid with a clang and held out his hand for the lock and key.

A curl of disappointment worked through Hannah as she passed him the heavy lock. She wanted to see what it was. "Father won't return until late tonight, but I'm sure he will be eager to see what you found first thing tomorrow."

Wycliff grunted as he locked the object inside and dropped the key into a pocket in his waistcoat. "Until tomorrow, then."

# 4

Hannah's father was in a fine mood when he descended the stairs the next morning. He wore a broad grin and hummed a song under his breath as he filled his plate from the hot dishes waiting on the sideboard. "Good morning," he said to the occupants of the room.

"How was the meeting, Papa?" Hannah asked as he took his seat.

"Brilliant! The discourse was wholly invigorating. Reverend Jones has an intriguing theory that the Afflicted continue to be animated because a residual piece of soul hides within them." Sir Hugh sliced his sausage into equal parts before loading up his fork with sausage, bacon, and potato.

"Still trying to prove that his God had a hand in our condition?" Seraphina held an empty teacup in a gloved hand.

Sir Hugh swallowed a large mouthful and gestured to his wife with the empty fork. "To give the man his due, his faith has been sorely tested these last few years and he is digging deeply to explain why the dead still walk. He believes that a religious ceremony to expunge the fragment of remaining soul and reunite it with the rest will result in permanent death."

Viscount Wycliff watched the exchange in silence, his eyes moving back and forth as though he observed a tennis match.

"By a *ceremony* do you mean some form of exorcism?" Hannah asked, trying to ignore the wraith in the room—who most certainly required an exorcism to remove him from her life.

"He avoids giving it such a label. Doesn't want to risk offending his wealthy patrons by implying their wives and daughters are possessed of demonic spirits." Hugh winked at his daughter.

Seraphina set down her cup. "And has he found any volunteers among my kind who wish to have these supposed fragments of their soul reunited?"

Sir Hugh loaded up his fork for its next journey to his mouth. "No. But I am going to call upon Lord Jessope and ask if we might attempt the ceremony on Lady Jessope. She is the most devout among the interred and prays constantly to be forgiven for her sins so that she might enter Heaven. Poor thing, I think she would be willing to undergo any trial to be united with her God."

Seraphina gave a most unladylike snort. “Well, if you don’t mind, Hugh, I might be absent when Reverend Jones waves the holy water. I don’t want to be inadvertently exorcised. I still have much to do here before I go quietly to my grave.”

“Never fear, my love. We will conduct the ceremony at his church in Chelsea,” Sir Hugh said.

“What of Doctor Husom and Lord Charles Dunkeith? How do their studies advance?” Hannah asked. Had her father asked if she might attend the meeting today? It would be more beneficial to see and hear first-hand rather than relying on his accounts.

Her father swallowed a mouthful before replying. “Husom is quite convinced the answer lies in the application of galvanism, whereas I think Lord Dunkeith has a more sound approach with his investigation of restorative potions.”

“Two very different approaches. Did you ask if I might attend today?” Hannah stared into her tea and pondered the advantages to being born male. No one told a man he couldn’t do something because it might be unseemly.

“I did indeed, and I said how beneficial it would be to have my very able assistant present. You will be pleased to know, Hannah, that the gentlemen agreed that you might accompany me.”

“Thank you, Papa!” Hannah leapt from her seat and kissed her father’s cheek. As she retook her chair, Viscount Wycliff cast her a withering glance that made her wish she might instead dissolve into the upholstery. "I'm sure listening to the lectures in person will prove most edifying and we will be able to discuss their findings later." She lowered her tone and concentrated on her boiled egg and toast.

"Husom and Dunkeith are two quite fascinating chaps, and I am sure, given that we all take such different approaches, one of us must surely stumble upon success. What do you think, Wycliff?" Sir Hugh directed his attention to their newest resident. "Do you think the movement of the Afflicted a mechanical process or a spiritual one?"

"I shall leave such contemplations to men more learned than I. I am only concerned with *what* the Afflicted do, not *how*." Having made his remarks as brief as possible, the viscount fell silent again and let conversation flow around him.

"A practical approach, my lord." Hannah decided not to let the interloper bother her, and braved a comment direct to the man. Her parents' presence at breakfast made her bolder. It did help that her mother could immolate him on the spot if necessary. "Papa, Lord Wycliff has something that requires your attention after breakfast."

Sir Hugh's eyes sparkled with interest. "Of course, my lord. Today's session doesn't start until mid-morning. What do you have for me?"

Wycliff laid down his cutlery. "An item currently in a locked box. It is a limb discovered on the bank of the Thames yesterday that is, for want of a better word, lively."

Sir Hugh's brows knitted more closely together. "Lively? That sounds most fascinating. Will you join us, Hannah?"

"If Mother does not mind a change to our usual plans. We go through the Unwin and Alder ledger after breakfast, but today we must not be tardy for the lectures."

Seraphina waved her hand. "Go with the men, Hannah, to look at this lively limb, and then to the boring old meeting with your father. I will hear your thoughts when you return."

After breakfast, Hannah followed her father down the stairs, with Wycliff at her heels and breathing down her neck in the confined stairwell. She reminded herself of her mother's words. She had not walked his path. What had he seen or done that made him bristle like an upset porcupine?

Beneath the ground in the usually quiet workroom came a steady *rap tap tap*.

Sir Hugh frowned. "Is that the limb tapping?"

"I said it was lively. At least we know it did not escape overnight." Lord Wycliff lifted the metal box from the shelf and carried it over to the stone autopsy table.

The gentle tapping from within reminded Hannah of a moth banging on glass, trying to reach the light.

Her father donned a canvas apron over his clothes.

"We will need some way to restrain it once it is removed from the box. It has a tendency to scuttle," Lord Wycliff said.

"Straps, Hannah, and I'll fetch the tongs." Focused on the box, Sir Hugh rubbed his hands together like a child expecting a marvellous present.

Hannah fetched two leather straps that could be fitted into slots in the table and used to secure the patient upon whom her father worked. She threaded the straps through holes in the stone and laid the ends out, ready to be buckled around whatever the box contained.

Her father selected a pair of tongs. His eyes were bright with interest as he nodded to the viscount. "Ready when you are, my good fellow."

Wycliff produced the key from his waistcoat pocket and fitted it to the brass lock. The tapping within fell silent when the lock clicked. He gestured Sir Hugh closer and then lifted the lid.

"It has managed to escape the sack," he muttered as he pulled the empty bag out and tossed it to one side.

Her father reached in with the tongs and extracted a wriggling, squirming...arm.

Hannah prodded herself into action. When her father placed the arm over the two positioned straps, she tightened one buckle at the end of the forearm, and the other over the wrist.

Secured on its back, or rather, with the inside of the forearm exposed, the fingers wriggled and curled into the palm, trying to reach the end of the leather that held it in place.

Hannah fetched a bowl of water and washed the remaining mud from the limb. It wriggled and twitched as she wiped it clean and then rubbed it with a towel to dry it off.

"How extraordinary." Sir Hugh put down the tongs and picked up his magnifying glasses. "Given the degree of animation, I assume this was severed from one of the Afflicted."

"That is what I am hoping you can deduce." Wycliff stood at one end of the table. "The rest of the individual has not yet been found, assuming he was also in the Thames. It is entirely possible only the arm was thrown into the water."

Hannah peered closer at the forearm and hand, taking in details with an artist's eye. It certainly hadn't belonged to a woman, having the larger and coarser appearance of a man's appendage. The forearm was covered in dark hair. The hand was broad, not unlike those of her father, and the palm bore several callouses from physical labour.

Male Afflicted were extraordinarily rare and she shuddered to think another with an uncontrollable appetite like that of Mr Rowley might be loose in London. Albeit this one was missing an arm. That at least would slow him down and make him instantly identifiable.

Sir Hugh examined the severed end and picked up a pair of long-nosed tweezers to pry among the tendons and nerves. "The wound is relatively fresh—there is no sign of decay. Interesting, Hannah, that the nerves appear inactive, in contrast to the activity exhibited by the hand and fingers."

"He has suffered a recent injury, judging by the stitching." Hannah pointed to the wrist and the large crosses of catgut. It was indelicate work, not at all like her father's neat stitches that any seamstress would be proud to call her own.

The limb reminded her somewhat of a large spider. The fingers tried to free the forearm that kept it trapped. It curled and spun and tried a different approach but couldn't bend far enough to grasp the buckle.

As she continued her own examination, Hannah noticed the tattoo on the inside of the wrist. It seemed to be a sailing ship, or rather half of one. One sail and what could have been a prow, stopped at the stitching line. Odd that the rear of the small vessel did not continue on the other side of the stitches. There did not seem to be any flesh missing that might have erased part of the tattoo.

Then she realised why not.

"They don't belong together," she whispered.

"What's that, my dear?" Her father looked up from his examination of the severed end of the forearm.

"This hand does not belong to that arm. That is why one is animated and the other is not. Look, Papa. The man has a tattoo of a sailing vessel on the inside of his wrist, but it is incomplete and doesn't extend beyond the sewn wound as it should. And the hand is rough and calloused, like a physical labourer, yet look at the forearm. The skin seems pale and there is no distinct muscular definition such as you might see in a person with perhaps a seafaring occupation."

Sir Hugh muttered under his breath something more befitting a rough soldier. "You're right, my clever girl. Someone has stitched the hand of one to the arm of the other."

"So we are looking for *two* injured people?" Lord Wycliff asked.

"It is a man, Papa. How many male Afflicted do we know of that might be missing a hand?" Hannah met her father's worried gaze.

Sir Hugh heaved a deep sigh. "None under my care."

Hannah called to mind her work with the ledgers. "Unwin and Alder have just two on their books. It will be easy to ascertain if either is missing a hand. And dare I venture to say, given their respective stations, that neither would be in possession of callouses."

"Then it is someone else." Wycliff glanced at Hannah. "Could it be another man infected by his lover, like Rowley?" The viscount had collided with their lives after a gruesome murder and had learned what happened when an Afflicted consumed the brain of a person they had killed.

"What of Rowley's first victim—was he not a dock worker?" Hannah asked her father quietly.

"We did not know of his death soon enough and he

was not dealt with appropriately. He had been buried by his family and that should suffice." Sir Hugh stared at the limb as though he expected it to contribute to the conversation.

"Should suffice? You mean you didn't confirm where his body was?" Wycliff's tone was sharp, each syllable a shot fired in the quiet room.

Sir Hugh laid his hands flat on the table as he studied the partial patient. "He is buried and I can assure you that he is not on the loose in London, either with or without an arm."

The temperature in the room dropped and goose-flesh sprang up along Hannah's arms.

"You cannot assure me, since you did not see the corpse. For all we know, there is a shuffling horror out there poised to prey on innocent Londoners." The viscount spoke quietly, but ice dripped from each word.

"It has been over a month now. We would have heard if he had dug himself out of his grave and gone looking for a brain to eat." Sir Hugh kept his eyes downcast.

"That is scant comfort. I struggle to comprehend how the government can allow the Afflicted to remain in society, when they have the capacity to spread their plague upon the general population." Lord Wycliff ground his teeth. "What of the other two that were murdered—the footman and cloakroom attendant. Have they reanimated?"

The hand ceased its attempts to escape.

Hugh poked at the hand with the tongs and the

fingers snapped at the tool. "The other two secondary infected were handled appropriately. I can attest to their being contained, as I oversaw it myself. Those in power allow the Afflicted to live out their lives just like any other subject of the Crown, as long as they obey the laws."

"If an ordinary man murders another he is hanged. He does not create an abomination that can propagate more abominations." Lord Wycliff gestured to the hand making a valiant effort to seize the tongs from the doctor.

"If you disagree, my lord, I suggest you take your objections to Parliament. Right now we need to concern ourselves with finding the rest of the man who belongs to this lively appendage." Hugh placed the tongs out of reach of the grasping fingers. "However this limb was removed from its body, this stitching is a crude type of surgery."

"Setting aside the possibility of an Afflicted epidemic should they go on murderous rampages, do you think this might be a practice surgery?" Wycliff asked. "It is possible he was dug up to supply the surgery schools and did not reanimate until after he was...disassembled."

Hannah tried to imagine what had happened to the hapless man. First he was murdered and his brain consumed. Then his body was buried by his family only to be, possibly, dug up and dissected in a surgery school. At what point might the French curse have reanimated his tissue? The entire course of events was horrible and better suited to a nightmare-inducing novel.

"Do the medical schools dispose of cadavers by throwing them in the Thames?" Wycliff asked.

"No. Of course not." Sir Hugh moved the tweezers farther from the hand as it made attempts to lunge at anything placed on the autopsy table.

"It might have escaped, though, which would not have been any fault of the school. It does seem rather determined." Hannah had a grudging admiration for the hand, still trying to battle impossible odds.

Her father tapped the forearm but it remained limp and dead in comparison. "There we go, Lord Wycliff. A simple explanation, is it not? The poor man was cut up at some point, probably before he reanimated, as no student would keep quiet if his bits were jumping about. I suspect the hand escaped when no one was looking."

Lord Wycliff crossed his arms and drew his brows together. "You are omitting one tiny detail, Sir Hugh."

"What's that?" Her father moved the discarded sack over to his workbench.

"Where is the rest of the Afflicted person?" the viscount asked.

Sir Hugh scratched his chin. "I'll make enquiries. Doctor Husom teaches when he has time and he will know what happens to cadavers after the school has finished with them. Usually remains are either buried in the potter's field or sent to the crematorium."

The hand fell still, as though it knew they talked

about it. But that was impossible. A hand had no ears to hear, or mind to process thoughts. So what drove it onward to escape when the rest of it might no longer exist?

*What drives any of us in the face of impossible odds?* Hannah wondered.

# 5

The second day of the SUSS gathering was again held in the Royal Hospital in Chelsea. It wasn't really a hospital, but a retirement home for soldiers known as the Chelsea Pensioners. Due to the needs of the residents, many of whom had been injured in battle, the building had a small infirmary, a surgery, and a lecture hall. Hannah's excitement at being allowed to attend was somewhat dampened by the black cloud that followed them.

Even worse, her father invited him to ride in their carriage. Since Sir Hugh took up a larger area, he had the front-facing seat to himself. Viscount Wycliff perched on the seat beside Hannah. He seemed as ill at ease as she. Both of them pretended to look out the window so each had an excuse to huddle closer to the side and farther from the other.

Her father chatted on, oblivious to the discomfort of the younger people in the carriage.

*At least I don't have to stare at him.* Hannah concentrated on the passing countryside. Yet the man emitted heat as though she had her back to the fire.

Was this what it would be like to have a sibling? One who rankled with their mere presence, but whom one had to tolerate under the same roof?

*He is no sibling*, a voice whispered from the depths of her mind. Hannah nearly choked out a snort at *that* idea. Ridiculous. She could barely tolerate being in the same room with him. Although there were many noble matches where the parties felt that way about one another.

"Are you all right, my dear?" her father asked as she caught her breath.

"Yes, Papa. I think I swallowed a bug." She glanced sideways, but the viscount continued to ignore her. "Did you hear Mary's tale this morning? She said Old Jim swears he saw Black Shuck in the meadow a few nights back."

Her father huffed a laugh. "He saw a black dog at night? There are many dogs that hunt at night."

Hannah remembered Mary's description quite clearly and it didn't sound like any local dog she recognised. "Old Jim said it was enormous, easily bigger than a mastiff."

Sir Hugh smiled at his daughter. "Perhaps the Highland Wolves are in town. The lycanthropes use the fields around London to shift forms and run."

"Wolves don't have fiery red eyes." Hannah glanced to Viscount Wycliff, on the verge of asking for his opinion, but changed her mind as he stiffened his shoulders.

"While the world contains many strange and unusual creatures, Hannah, some are still only found in fairy tales. I think the tale of Black Shuck is one such legend, spun after men have indulged in too much ale." Her father reached across and patted her hand.

The carriage stopped by the smaller western wing of the hospital known as College Court and they alighted. Hannah stared up at the grand building with its symmetrical layout. Men strolled the grounds in their distinctive red coats. The grounds included magnificent formal gardens constructed by Sir Christopher Wren. Canals, gazebos, and summer houses stretched down to the Thames and Hannah itched to explore.

"This way." Her father took her hand as he used to when she was a child who often ran off in search of adventure. He tucked her hand into the crook of his elbow, thus ensuring she couldn't wander off.

It would be rude anyway, she chided herself. She had petitioned both her parents to be included in the meeting. Perhaps at the end of the day there would be time to explore the grounds.

The members of the Society of Unnatural Scientific Study met in a small lecture hall that reminded Hannah of a Roman amphitheatre, or what she had seen of them in drawings. The room was rounded, with the lecture area the focus of all attention. The seats curved around the room and rose up steeply, ensuring everyone could see over the person in front.

A large blackboard covered the wall behind the lecture area. A table was draped with a sheet that did nothing to disguise the fact that underneath rested a body with its toes pointed toward the audience. An array of scientific equipment was scattered around the dais. Tall iron pillars were entwined with copper and a spiderweb of wires hung between them. To one side of a pillar was a large brass wheel with a dull black handle jutting out from a black cylinder the size of a horse's body. A wheeled table that might once have been a tea trolley held a collection of beakers with various coloured liquids.

Hannah followed her father to a row near the front and took a seat. Wycliff climbed to the back, no doubt to look down upon them in a disapproving manner.

"What is the topic for today?" Hannah asked, but her attention wandered to the cadaver. There was no visible rise and fall of the chest, but she couldn't tell if it was dead, Afflicted, or some other creature.

Sir Hugh rubbed his hands together before using them to flick out the tails of his coat to sit. "We call it the *resurrection challenge*. Some of the fellows have various theories about what animates the Afflicted. They will each have a chance to test their theory on the cadaver."

"You don't take part?" Hannah took a seat and pulled her notebook from her reticule.

Sir Hugh stared at his daughter with a sad look in

his eyes, then he patted her hand. “No. We know the cursed powder only works on the living and steals their lives. It does not raise those who are already dead. My study is focused on trying to find a way to reverse the curse, not replicate it. But it is informative to watch the fellows in their attempts.”

“Who is taking part today?” Hannah tried to figure out the contraptions and what purpose they might have. On the table of vials, the contents of one swirled and changed colour from cream to deep yellow and back again. Another that contained a black substance burped a dark brown cloud.

Sir Hugh waved to some of the older men who entered and shuffled along the rows to find seats. He gestured to the very front row, where three gentlemen sat. “Reverend Jones is first. Then Lord Dunkeith, who is convinced the answer lies in the apothecary arts. Last will be Doctor Husom, who is doing some fascinating work with electrical currents.”

More people trickled into the room. Some sat in twos or threes and others, like Viscount Wycliff, sought a spot well away from anyone else. The room never filled, but it contained more people than Hannah had thought were interested in curing the Afflicted. A group of young men sat near the back and chatted loudly.

“The meeting is well attended,” Hannah observed.

Sir Hugh glanced around. “Unfortunately, some are motivated by curiosity rather than genuine scholarly interest. The lads are medical students hoping to have an Afflicted paraded before them."

Hannah narrowed her eyes as she studied them, looking for two faces in particular. But none appeared to be either of the men she had discovered cutting Miss Emma Knightley for the novelty of watching her flesh heal.

An elderly gentleman walked to the middle of the lecture floor and the chatter fell away. "Gentlemen, and lady—" He bowed toward Hannah. "Let us begin the second day of the Society of Unnatural Scientific Study conference. This morning commences with what we refer to as the *resurrection challenge.* Three of our members will each attempt to bring this deceased person back to life."

"That's Doctor Finch. He runs all our meetings," her father whispered in Hannah's ear.

Doctor Finch gestured to the men seated at the very front. "Reverend Jones will be the first challenger."

Reverend Jones rose and stepped forward, clutching a Bible in one hand and a small glass vial in the other. A tall, lean man with a sombre expression, he appeared to be in his fifties, with white hair rapidly receding from his skull. Dark eyes darted back and forth as he approached the table. Once in position by its side, he nodded to Doctor Finch, who grabbed hold of the sheet and wound it toward himself.

The lads at the back chortled as the form of an overweight middle-aged man was revealed. He was naked except for underdrawers that stopped just above his knees. A large belly swelled over his sides. A thick swath of hair covered his chest and disappeared beneath the undergarment.

The laughter behind Hannah was cut short so abruptly she turned to discover the viscount glaring at the youths and burning away their humour. For once she appreciated his formidable stare. No one should be laughed at in death. The grim reaper would come for everyone, no matter their outward appearance.

The reverend stood at the dead man's side, presenting his profile to the audience. His whispered prayers filled the room as he fervently asked his God to return a piece of the man's soul to animate his flesh. Setting aside the Bible, he twisted the top from the vial and sprinkled the contents over the man.

"Holy water," Sir Hugh whispered to Hannah.

When the vial was empty, Reverend Jones dropped it into his coat pocket and took up the Bible. He rested one hand on the man's forehead and, lifting the Bible high, beseeched God to demonstrate His might by making the man sit up.

Hannah leaned forward, concentrating on the cadaver as she waited for the tiniest movement. Surely a plea from a churchman would elicit a quick response from their Creator.

After fifteen minutes of prayers, without even the faintest twitch from the deceased man's little finger, Doctor Finch coughed into his hand.

Reverend Jones smiled at the assembly. "It appears

our Lord has exceeded his allocated time to provide an answer to His supplicant."

He returned to his seat and Lord Dunkeith rose and strode forward. The noble cut a fine figure, clothed in the latest fashion, as though he were attending a soirée. While not particularly tall, he was what Hannah would call pleasant-looking, with a friendly face and a wide smile. He was in his early thirties, with ruffled light brown hair as though he frequently ran his hands through it, and his brown eyes sparkled with life.

Hannah wondered what drove his interest in the Afflicted. With a title, a more than sufficient fortune, and good looks, he should have been prowling the ballrooms, not the autopsy rooms. Perhaps he was the rare sort of man with little interest in gambling or other vices, and blessed with intellectual curiosity. An enquiring mind raised a man far higher in Hannah's esteem than the weight of his pocketbook ever could.

Lord Dunkeith approached the wheeled table and studied the selection of vials and beakers. He picked up an empty one and placed it before him. Then he began mixing. A drop from one vial extracted with a glass dropper. A larger portion from another measured with a silver funnel.

Hannah was mesmerised, as though she watched the finest musician playing a concerto. Lord Dunkeith moved with a relaxed grace as he narrated his activity in a dulcet tone. The ingredients ranged from the exotic and disturbing (excrement from a strix—a supernatural bird) to the everyday (rosemary for remembrance).

When he had used every liquid in varying proportions, he stirred until a faint green mist wafted from the top of the beaker and dispersed in the air. Some of the watchers covered their mouths and noses with fine linen handkerchiefs, but Hannah inhaled. The soft fragrance of rosemary carried a sharp edge that she couldn't recognise. She hoped it wasn't strix excrement.

Lord Dunkeith prised open the cadaver's teeth and inserted one end of a length of black rubber tubing. Inch by inch, the tube was slid over blue lips and down into the man's stomach. When he was satisfied that tube was in the correct position, Lord Dunkeith held the brass funnel attachment high in the air and slowly poured the smoking green liquid into the tubing. A wisp of green mist escaped from the dead man's lips as the potion disappeared down his gullet.

"Lord Dunkeith is a sixth-generation aftermage with a keen interest in the apothecary arts. He has a knack with potions and believes he is close to discovering the formula to rejuvenate the deceased," Hannah's father whispered.

"An unusual occupation of his time for a lord so blessed by the Fates. I wonder that he doesn't use his ability to produce potions for the ladies of the *ton*." Hannah watched the performance unfolding before her.

Lord Dunkeith removed the tubing and stood next

to his patient, waiting to see if his potion would have the desired effect.

"Apparently he was always a studious child. Not every rich peer lives a shallow and frivolous life. Some can be quite productive members of society." Hugh nudged her gently as he spoke.

Hannah couldn't help casting a glance to the back of the lecture theatre, where Viscount Wycliff watched the proceedings with a black stare. She wasn't sure which category he fit into. No one would ever mistake him for a shallow and frivolous creature, but Hannah couldn't quite label him as productive, either.

Although he had apprehended two Afflicted who were murdering servants.

Everyone waited as the grandfather clock ticked off the seconds. Soon the younger men in the audience began to fidget and chat among themselves. Hannah concentrated on the prone man. She studied the tips of his fingers and toes, hoping that the potion would restore him to life.

Seconds turned into minutes and after another quarter of an hour, even Hannah was squirming on the hard wooden seat.

The convenor of the event walked across the floor and raised his eyebrows at Lord Dunkeith.

"Thank you, gentlemen and lady, for your time and attention, but it appears my opportunity is at an end." With a bow and a smile flashed exclusively to Hannah, he walked back to his seat at the front.

Doctor Husom was last. The doctor was in his late

thirties, with dark brown hair clipped close to his head. While tall, he had the lean appearance of a scholar who often forgot to eat, and round gold-rimmed spectacles sat on his nose.

He walked to the metal pillars and the array of mechanical levers and gauges. He flicked a lever and then grabbed the black handle of the wheel. He turned vigorously and a gasp came from those assembled as electricity sparked from one pillar and ran through the wire mesh to the other.

Soon a steady blue arc connected the two pillars and a faint buzz filled the air. The hair on Hannah's arms rose as the room became charged.

"Doctor Peter Husom is exploring the effects of galvanism," Sir Hugh whispered as the man in the centre of the room spoke.

Hannah was aware of the scientific enquiry into the contractions of muscles. The process was named after Luigi Galvani, who had applied electrical charges to dissected creatures in the late 1700s.

Doctor Husom donned heavy rubber gloves and then picked up two long copper knitting needles. Wires connected them to the cylinder beside one pillar.

He thrust one copper needle into the dead man's forearm and the other higher up in the biceps. Then he returned to the wheel, turning it faster and faster and making the blue arc spit and crackle. The electricity climbed higher up the pillars until Hannah thought it would escape and ignite the ceiling.

As the electricity reached the top, Doctor Husom

pulled a lever and light flashed along the wires toward the dead man. A *bang* made Hannah jump.

A man behind her cried out, "Look!"

Gasps and cries erupted from behind her, but Hannah was focused on the dead man. His fingers twitched and convulsed, then his arm slowly contracted as though he intended to touch his fingers to his shoulder.

Applause burst out around the room. The doctor smiled and bowed. He flipped another switch on the machine and the electricity dissipated, along with the buzz that made Hannah's ears ring.

Everyone stared at the dead man as his arm slowly dropped back to the table.

"Muscular contraction," her father snorted. "Not resurrection."

"Would a larger electrical charge produce a more sustained physical response?" Hannah asked.

"Only your mother and God could produce enough electricity to find out. We have discussed attempting to restart her heart with an electrical charge, but Sera thought there might be other, more unwanted consequences." Her father clapped his hands as Doctor Husom bowed and questions exploded from the audience.

# 6

After the resurrection challenge, Doctor Finch led a spirited discussion on new ideas and theories about the Afflicted. Conversation swirled concerning how they remained animated and alert, despite the lack of a heartbeat.

Hannah kept to herself her idea of its being somehow linked to the condition of the actual heart. The concept was a newly hatched chick and she wasn't prepared to toss it from the nest and test its wings in public.

The gentlemen raised a number of theories. The simplest, that a beating heart was not required for life, failed to pass scrutiny of the role the heart played in the circulatory system. The most outlandish theory was that the Afflicted were inhabited by poltergeists who manoeuvred limbs like puppeteers. Reverend Jones keenly examined that idea, as he suggested it dovetailed with his remnant soul theory.

The meeting was called to a close in the early afternoon, just as Hannah's stomach began to object about the length of time it had been since breakfast.

Her father held out a hand to help her rise after the long time on the hard seats. "Shall we head home, Hannah, and see what Wycliff's limb is up to?"

In the excitement of being allowed to attend the meeting, she had quite forgotten the restless hand. "Oh, yes. I would like to study it more closely."

They waited for Wycliff to descend from the high back row to join them, and walked out to the waiting carriage.

"What did you think of the challenge, Lord Wycliff?" Sir Hugh asked as he helped Hannah into the carriage first.

"A shame nothing of any real practical application emerged from so much posturing and showmanship." He climbed in and positioned himself next to Hannah, turning his body slightly toward the window and away from her.

Sir Hugh frowned. "You call intelligent debate *posturing and showmanship*? We all strive for a cure, and that can only arise from sharing our theories."

Hannah glanced from one man to another. Both glared from under pulled brows and she had the distinct impression of two dogs with their hackles up, taking the measure of one another.

"What is to happen to the limb, Lord Wycliff?" Hannah grabbed at the first idea in her mind to divert the men.

His chest heaved in a short sigh and he turned to face her. "It will remain in custody. First I will verify whether or not it does belong to Joseph Barnes, who was the dock worker slain by Jonathon Rowley. If it is, I will try to find the rest of him."

"Would the hand work like a compass? Father has told me that a dismembered Afflicted will try to rejoin its pieces." On an intellectual level, Hannah found the hand a fascinating specimen. It was amazing that it did things independently of a mind to direct its actions.

Black eyes bored through her until she retreated further into her corner. Then he looked away and released her from his hold. "I am considering that possibility, although I'm not sure how one would restrain it so that it could not make its escape."

"Perhaps some sort of lead, such as is used for dogs? I doubt a hand moves very fast, however. It might be a slow search." How long would the hand take to inch down the road like a spider from their house to London? Hours at least, if not days.

Sir Hugh's eyebrows shot up at the change of topic. "If Lord Wycliff will allow, I thought this afternoon we might detach hand from forearm, Hannah. They will rot at different rates and there's no point distressing the hand by making it drag rotten flesh behind it."

"You make it sound sentient, Papa. Do you think it capable of independent thought? Given that Mr Barnes is a secondary Afflicted, the poor man is without any mind at all." If a person were robbed of their brain, how did they command their limbs?

Sir Hugh cleared his throat. "We have had no real opportunity to study the secondary Afflicted, since it was decided it is more humane to put them out of their misery. They still follow some directive, even without their brains."

Hannah concentrated on the pedestrians walking the road, laughing and talking, as she sought to remove the image of a secondary Afflicted from her mind. "I wonder if the hand will rot if the body is not taking the required sustenance?"

"Only time will reveal what course the rot takes in the hand. Another possibility is that without sustenance, it might enter a mummified state, such as the devout ladies in the Repository. This will be most interesting. We must write up our findings for the next SUSS meeting."

"I have no objection to your separating hand from forearm." Lord Wycliff spoke from his corner. "If Miss Miles would be so kind, she might turn her mind to some sort of harness that would allow us to see if the hand can lead us back to the body."

Hannah stared at her gloved hand and wriggled her fingers. Where could one attach a leash that those fingers couldn't find a way out of? "Something that goes between the thumb and index finger might work, so that it wouldn't be able to squirm out. I'm sure Mother could concoct an enchantment as an extra protection to ensure it didn't scamper off."

Lord Wycliff stared out the window while Hannah and her father discussed various aspects of the meeting.

In no time the carriage was stopping outside their Westbourne Green home. Sir Hugh helped his daughter down first. Then the viscount stepped to the ground and charged up the gravelled path ahead of them. Hannah was still shaking out her skirts and pelisse by the carriage when the front door banged shut behind the viscount's figure.

After a small luncheon, Hannah changed into a plain, dark brown gown and dropped her canvas apron over her head. She tied the apron behind her back as she took the stairs down to the laboratory.

"Will Lord Wycliff be joining us?" she asked as she laid out the instruments for the procedure.

"No. He has saddled his horse and gone back to London in pursuit of Joseph Barnes, or what is left of him. He mentioned going to the docks to ask if the man had a tattoo of a vessel on his inner wrist." Her father placed a magnifying lens over his head and angled it over his right eye.

Hannah fetched the locked box with its regular and muffled tapping. She unlocked it, then her father grabbed the occupant with the tongs and laid it on the table. Hannah worked quickly to secure the limb at both ends with the leather straps.

The forearm had the distinct mottling of rot now and a piercing odour wafted from it. She wrinkled her nose. How strange that while she had become accustomed to the sight of death, it was the smell that rapped at her brain for attention. "Do you think we should tell it what we are about to do?"

The fingers waved and fought and reminded her of a large pink hairless spider trapped on its back.

Hugh surveyed the supplies that Hannah had laid out on a trolley next to the table. "I suppose it would do no harm, but it has no ears or mind. How could it ever interrupt our words?"

"But the hand is still full of nerves that must be sending messages somewhere. What if Mr Barnes is trapped in a coffin, experiencing everything the hand does, and directing its movement?"

Sir Hugh picked up a scalpel and smiled at his daughter. "Remember, Mr Barnes is a secondary Afflicted and has no mind with which to think or feel. But I will not start until you inform Mr Barnes' hand of our intentions."

Hannah concentrated on the hand and considered how to commence. Plain and simple would be best. There was no need to use fancy terms. "Mr Barnes, I do not know if you can hear me, but my father and I wish to help you. We are going to remove the forearm that does not belong to you, before it rots away. That should make you somewhat more comfortable. Then, if you promise to behave, we shall attempt to find the rest of you."

It might have been mere coincidence, but the fingers stilled as Hannah spoke. Then the fingers closed and the thumb lifted in a gesture familiar to her, before spreading itself flat.

"Well, I never," Sir Hugh muttered. After a

moment, he began to slice the stitches holding the wound closed at the wrist.

When each was cut, Hannah took the scalpel and passed over a pair of tweezers. Her father tugged each stitch free of the flesh and dropped it into the bowl she held out.

With the clumsy stitches out of the way, Hugh worked with tweezers and scalpel to ease the two members apart. "This is most unusual. The tissue from the hand appears to have tried to connect to the fore-arm, but failed. Look here, Hannah, at the tendrils of nerves spanning the gap."

Hannah picked up a handheld magnifying glass and peered into the wound. It reminded her of a spider-web, with gossamer-thin filaments running from hand to forearm, but as her father opened the gap further, they slid down until they separated.

"Do you think it failed to heal because the forearm does not belong to the hand? Can you tell if this was attempted *post mortem*?" On impulse, she stroked a finger along the index finger of the hand and whispered, "You are being very brave. Thank you for holding still."

"A most excellent question. I think this was a *post mortem* surgery, rather than an attempt to stitch a hand to a living subject." Sir Hugh passed the scalpel blade down the wound and the forearm tipped back away from the hand. "The bones and tendons are severed, with no attempt to reattach arteries or tendons. It was a crude procedure. Whoever did this either didn't bother or didn't think that they needed to do any more than stitch together the skin of both ends."

Hannah unfastened the strap on the arm and pulled it away from the hand while the fingers shook themselves.

Free of the dead limb, the Afflicted one showed more animation. The tendons waved like tiny worms poking their heads out of the ground. Arteries closed and opened, like mouths seeking blood but finding none flowing from the heart.

"Incredible," she murmured as she watched this clear evidence of life after death in the hand's severed wrist.

"We will gather what information we can about the forearm, and then there is not much that can be done for it." Sir Hugh continued to work, teasing out skin from around the wrist to cover the exposed area.

"Why would someone do this *post mortem*?" Hannah asked. She passed her father a metal clip to secure two flaps of skin.

"Practice, most likely. Or perhaps the forearm belonged to someone who lost a hand in an accident and some doctor thought to replace it with another, but the chap died."

"I'm sure Lord Wycliff will get to the bottom of it." Hannah fetched a needle and a spool of catgut, from which she cut a length.

"Wycliff is a most thorough chap, which is exactly what Sir Manly wanted in an investigator. It was also what made him an excellent officer until— Well, that doesn't matter now." With the edges of skin folded over and clipped like the wrapped end of a present, Hugh took the threaded needle from Hannah and began to stitch.

Watching her father was like watching a skilled seamstress. People assumed that with such large hands, her father was only capable of butchery. Yet he used a needle with delicacy and made tiny, neat stitches that she swore were all exactly the same size and distance from one another.

When he finished the last stitch and cut the catgut, he gave a satisfied *hrumph*. The hand now sported a sealed wound with stitches so fine they could have been used to construct a ballgown.

Hannah glared at the plain metal box that had served as the limb's prison. "I know it sounds silly, but do you think we should find a container with holes in it, or possibly one of the cages with bars? It doesn't seem right to put this back in a sealed box when it is alive."

Sir Hugh wiped his hands and smiled at his daughter. "Not silly at all. I'm sure one of our many cages will be large enough, but the bars are sufficiently close that our friend here can't slip out."

Hannah surveyed the empty cages on the shelves. One had originally been used for ferrets, which were also slippery creatures with a knack for escaping. She pulled it down from the shelf and placed it on the table. Next she dampened a cloth and wiped out the faint trace of dust in the bottom. On a whim, she took a metal wheel that had been used to keep the ferrets entertained, and dropped it into the bottom of the cage.

"There, all ready," she said.

"You undo the strap, Hannah, and I will grab it with the tongs." Hugh picked up the metal tongs and pinched the end of the wrist that remained on the hand.

Hannah undid the buckle and the hand was deposited in its new home. It scuttled back and forth and spun the wheel on its way past. Watching it explore the limits of the cage brought a question to the forefront of Hannah's mind. "Why is this hand so active? The secondary Afflicted we saw were slow and shambling creatures. This limb is rather more alert than I would expect."

"An excellent question, Hannah, for which I don't have an answer. It is possible this is not Mr Barnes, in which case it could belong to a primary Afflicted or even a vampyre. Or perhaps there was something in the process of its amputation that has caused this reaction." Sir Hugh picked up the cage and placed it on the shelf next to the mice.

"If it is not Mr Barnes, I am sure the viscount will descend on the few male Afflicted we know of and demand to see their hands. I'm not entirely sure how one locates vampyres. I thought they all lived in Europe."

"Why don't you ask your mother about a hand harness so we can take this fellow out for a walk, and see if he can sniff out the rest of him?" Hugh winked and Hannah suppressed a laugh.

Whatever would the neighbours think when they took a human hand for a walk on a lead? Although they should be well accustomed to odd noises and sights at the mansion after the more than twenty years her parents had inhabited it.

What to use to construct a harness and lead? Hannah pondered several options as she took the stairs up to the library to seek her mother's advice.

# 7

Wycliff guided his mare through the busy London streets and toward the docks. He soon found the warehouse owned by Rowley and Sons, importers of fine champagne and brandy. However, the sons were down by one. After his murderous crimes, Jonathon Rowley now languished in the Repository of Forgotten Things—a situation that stuck in Wycliff's craw. Why should nobles escape a death sentence because they had money or lacked a pulse?

He intended to petition both Sir Manly and Parliament to ensure that when an Unnatural committed a crime that would result in a death sentence for a living man, it would be imposed upon the Unnatural, too. Technically the Afflicted were already dead, but he was sure there would be a way to deliver those individuals to the afterlife.

Wycliff hitched his horse and approached the warehouse with its wide open doors. Barrels, kegs, and crates were being carried down the gangplank of a vessel and into the dim interior.

"Can I help you, milord?" a man asked as he directed another individual carrying a crate off to a corner of the warehouse. The faint clink of glass came from within.

"Yes. I am conducting the investigation into the death of Joseph Barnes, and wish to speak to anyone who knew him." Wycliff peered into the dark, where men moved around placing crates one on top of another as they chatted and laughed.

The man screwed up one side of his face. "What do you need to know? I knew him. Argumentative bugger, begging your pardon, milord."

Wycliff arched an eyebrow. He didn't care about the man's disposition, only his physical description. "Did he have any tattoos or distinguishing features?"

The man screwed up the other side of his face in concentration. Then he yelled to the man carrying the crate, "Larry, can you remember if Barnesy had any *tattoos or distinguishing features*?" He mimicked Wycliff's accent.

"You mean apart from being ugly?" came the response.

"That's not helping his lordship here." The man had a strained smile on his face as he yelled over his shoulder.

Silence was the answer. Then another voice called, "'E 'ad a tattoo of a boat on 'is arm, down by 'is wrist. Think it was some vessel 'e sailed on as a lad."

"The left or right arm?" Wycliff asked as the speaker emerged from the shadows.

The young man looked constipated for a moment, then he pointed to the inside of his left wrist. "This one."

"Left. Thank you, that is all I need." Wycliff reclaimed his mare and vaulted into the saddle. That solved one mystery—the hand most likely belonged to Joseph Barnes, unless there was some other undead creature with a nautical tattoo. Now he just had to find the rest of the man to verify he lacked a left hand.

He had asked a Bow Street Runner to enquire where the man's family had buried him. He consulted the scribbled note and turned his mare in the direction of Bunhill Fields. His gut already told him the grave would be empty, but he wanted to confirm his suspicion.

The mare was left to graze under a tree. As Wycliff stepped onto hallowed ground, a vibration ran up through his legs and tugged at him. Like a fish on a hook, it pulled him closer to the rows of gravestones and markers. He closed his eyes while it seemed a thousand voices pressed into his skull as he neared. He shook his head until the sound settled down to a low murmur, then continued on his way.

The biggest hurdle turned out to be finding where Barnes had supposedly been laid to rest. The sexton scratched his head and fumbled in his tiny shed for a worn and dirty ledger.

As he waited for the sexton to find the entry,

Wycliff surveyed the cemetery. Bunhill Fields was fast becoming overcrowded. There were stories circulated of bodies dismembered so that more could be crammed into available space, and of coffins laid directly on top of each other. The ground bore fresh marks everywhere he looked. If he closed his eyes, those snatched from this earth too soon moaned, demanding he find their physical forms.

"How long ago?" the man called out as he flipped through pages.

"A month, approximately." Wycliff worked backward to when he remembered the Runner had said Barnes' body had been fished from the Thames. They thought fish had eaten his brains, but the culprit turned out to be Rowley, a wealthy heir who wanted canapés to go with his champagne.

The sexton made a triumphant sound and banged the ledger with his knuckles. "Found him. Joseph Barnes. Northeast corner, plot 132."

Wycliff pointed to the shovels leaning against the shed. "He must be dug up."

The man clenched his jaw. "We put them in the ground, not take them out again."

Wycliff bit back a laugh. The cemeteries of the lower classes were notorious for the comings and goings of their residents. Resurrectionists would dig anyone up if a body was worth a few coins. There was no one to guard their eternal slumber and there should be. He rubbed at his chest as an ache speared through him. "I only need to confirm he is in the grave. The family have concerns about body snatchers."

Certainly Unwin and Alder would have had no use for a man with his brain already removed, but the teaching schools still needed a steady supply of cadavers for their students. The man with the star turn in the SUSS resurrection challenge could have come from a graveyard such as this one.

The sexton tossed the ledger on a bench and picked up a dented and dirty hat to cover his balding head. "As you wish, milord. The lads are in that area. They'll have him up in no time."

They picked through freshly turned earth, tufts of grass, and weathered crosses. Most had a number scratched into the base of the wood, to identify who rested there. A few gravestones had flowers in varying degrees of decay placed at the base. The death of the flowers seemed to coincide with the growth of grass over the grave.

"One hundred and thirty two. Here we are." The sexton pointed to a patch of earth covered in sparse grass. The cross was newer, and black paint spelling out *Joseph Barnes* was still legible. A posy of long dead daisies sat at the base of the cross.

"You two, come here and start digging," the sexton yelled to two lads who were digging a grave farther along the row.

The lads exchanged looks, shrugged, and then shambled along dragging their shovels. Their lives were spent either digging holes, filling in holes, or digging up previous holes...the latter for extra coin at night, paid by doctors needing fresh samples.

"Why this one? He's been down for a while. Won't be pleasant." The lads exchanged looks and fidgeted with their shovels.

"Because the lord here wants to check on this one in particular, not a fresher one." The sexton rolled his eyes and muttered something about dealing with dimwits. A sentiment Wycliff shared.

"He'll be ripe. Perhaps his lordship could wait in the shed and we'll fetch him when we're done?" the taller lad suggested.

"I assure you I'm quite used to the sight and smell of death. You may begin." Wycliff crossed his arms. The reluctance of the lads confirmed his suspicions before they even turned a single sod.

As they scooped up shovelfuls of earth and piled it to one side, Wycliff contemplated how England had changed since the passing of the Unnaturals Act in 1812. That piece of legislation gave such creatures the same rights as every other English subject. It also made them beholden to the same laws. Monsters and demons who had once lived in the shadows, and who had been hunted for their hides, were allowed out into the light.

While he still believed that any creature capable of committing a horrendous murder shouldn't be allowed to roam the streets, perhaps he could grant them the same liberties as other men. Let them be presumed innocent until shown to be guilty. Then he would pursue them to the ends of the earth to ensure they were brought to justice.

Such a loosening in his views would please Miss Hannah Miles. Not that he cared at all what she thought. He couldn't imagine why he even considered her opinion. His gaze strayed to the brown and brittle daisies at the base of the cross. If he died, who would lay flowers at his grave? Certainly not the debt collectors—they'd be on the business end of a shovel to prise any gold from his teeth.

It didn't take long for one shovel to hit something solid. The men moved more carefully, scraping soil from the top to reveal Joseph Barnes' plain pine box.

"You sure you want to see this, milord?" the tall lad asked, his gaze darting sideways to his workmate. His Adam's apple bobbed up and down.

"Most definitely." He was quite enjoying making the two of them sweat from more than physical exertion. The shorter lad had perspiration running down his brow and they hadn't dug that deep. Barnes was in a shallow grave, either to make him easier to dig up again or because another coffin was underneath him.

"Getting filled up out here—we need to double stack them. In some graves they are laid right on top of each other," the sexton said as he glanced at his workers. Then he waved to the taller lad.

The youth handed off his shovel and hopped down into the hole, where they had cleared a small space for his feet. He curled his fingers around the edges of the lid and made a pantomime show of wrenching it up.

Wycliff nearly applauded his acting. With no nails to secure the top, it slid off without any real effort.

He flicked the lid to one side, where it rested against the dirt, while the others leaned in to see what the coffin held.

Nothing.

"Bugger," the sexton said.

"It would seem he has got away on you. It is so troublesome these days, with the dead refusing to stay put in their graves," Wycliff drawled.

"Do you think he's one of those dead people like some of them toffs and he wandered off?" The shorter lad's eyes lit up as he leapt on a possible excuse to explain Barnes' absence.

Wycliff knew how a cat felt at play with a mouse. There was something satisfying in tormenting a lesser creature. "Oh, I don't think that is the case here. Neither the Afflicted nor vampyres tend to bother with filling a grave back in. To whom did you sell him?"

The sexton went red in the face. "Now look here, milord, we're not body snatchers, you know—"

A wave of Wycliff's hand silenced the man. "Of course you are. Although given the fact that Barnes had been in the river, I'm not sure who would have wanted him. I don't care that you earn extra coin, I am merely trying to track what happened to him. Tell me where he went and we'll say no more about it."

The two lads stared at the dirt-encrusted toes of their boots.

"You can either tell me or I will be here every night

until I discover who it was. I expect my prowling the perimeter might cause a sudden drop in your nocturnal business." The idea settled something deep inside him. These dead deserved peace just as much as the nobles with their fancy mausoleums. But he couldn't be in multiple places at once. While they had no respect for the dead, these were human criminals, not Unnatural ones. The Runners could deal with them while he pursued his quarry.

"Newt Thackery," one of the lads burst out.

The other elbowed him so hard in the middle the lad doubled over and had to grab his shovel to stay upright.

Wycliff narrowed his eyes at the shorter lad. "Who is Thackery? A doctor?"

"No." He rubbed his stomach and glared at his comrade. "More like a delivery person. Told him we had a fellow pulled from the Thames with half his head missing and he was right interested, he was."

Most surgeons and students thought themselves too good to deal directly with the grave diggers. An intermediary was not unexpected, although it would draw out his chase. "Where would I find this Newt Thackery?"

The lad with the sharp elbow sighed. "Chicken's Run Inn. But we never told you nowt."

Wycliff stared at the lad, wondering how miserable he might make his day. If he were in a particularly foul mood, he could start pointing to recent graves to discover how many others were vacant. In London, death was a profitable business—from the sanctioned practices of Unwin and Alder, down to those on the fringes of the law demanding fresh bodies or cheaper brains.

Then he decided on expediency and turned back to his mare. The dank odour of death drifted from the damp soil and tickled his nostrils. He tried to hold his breath to stop inhaling the scent of decay and misery, but it permeated his body. A shudder ran over his skin as the voices whispered to him. Some angry, some taunting, others demanding.

"No. I do not have time. Leave me alone," he muttered as he took the reins in hand.

The Chicken's Run Inn was situated toward White Chapel in the sort of area where murder, theft, and rape were commonplace occurrences. Wycliff kept his wits about him. War had taught him that a blow never came from the direction from which you expected it.

Men missing limbs held out bowls and begged for coins. Some had crude signs saying they were war veterans. Too many men had given everything and come back to nothing. Others watched him ride past from darkened alleys, no doubt calculating the value of his horse, tack, and worn coat.

Let them try. They would find him prepared for any skirmish and in the mood to bloody his fists in a fight. He found a lad with cunning in his eyes and dropped a coin into his filthy hand to hold the mare's reins. Wycliff promised another coin if the horse was still upright when he emerged from the tavern. With his depleted finances, the way he was spending coin couldn't continue. He would submit an expense claim to the Ministry of Unnaturals and Sir Manly could either pay it or find himself another investigator.

He walked into the Chicken's Run, dropping his shoulders and lowering his eyes. At least he hadn't dressed like a toff today, and it was no stretch to say he was down on his luck. He lived with a dead mage and a mad scientist—if anyone needed a quiet drink to drown their woes, it was he.

"Help you?" the barkeep asked.

"Ale." He slid a coin across a gritty counter. He glanced at the scattering of patrons, most huddled in groups of two or three. Only two men sat alone in dim corners. "I'm looking for Newt Thackery. I'm told he can help me procure something I require."

The barkeep narrowed his eyes and stared at the man behind Wycliff's left shoulder. "You one of those medical types?"

Only if one employed a very expansive definition of the word *medical*, in that he was familiar with injuries and how to kill a man. "Yes. Can you point me in the right direction?"

The barkeep gestured to a table against the far wall. "The big chap playing cards by himself."

"Much obliged." He picked up his drink and crossed the floor, aware all eyes followed the stranger.

"Thackery?" Wycliff placed his beer on the table and dropped onto the hard seat. He tried not to think what stains might be attaching themselves to his breeches. Tomorrow would be spent compiling his expenses and scrubbing his clothes.

"Who wants to know?" The man didn't look up as he turned a card over and moved another to the discard pile.

"I am informed that you are an enterprising man. I wish to send some business in your direction." Wycliff glanced around him. He trod a delicate line to elicit information from the man without instigating an all-out brawl. Though he was confident he would emerge victorious if he had to employ his fists to learn what he needed.

"I don't conduct business with strangers." More cards were dealt from the pack.

"You took delivery of something from Bunhill Fields. A unique specimen with half his head bashed in. I want to know who paid you for him." The hairs on the back of Wycliff's neck lifted as shadows moved closer.

Thackery shook his head. "Don't know what you're talking about."

"I'm not leaving here until you tell me. Maybe I'll send a message to the Runners I know to come join me for a drink." They probably wouldn't come, since he didn't exactly have any friends among them, but Thackery didn't know that.

"You have no friends here." Thackery leaned back against the wall.

"I have no need of friends." There was something on his side, however, that no one else in the room had.

Wycliff reached deep inside himself and prodded his darkest secret. He had told Lady Miles he wanted the thing wrapped in chains and dropped in the deepest part of the ocean, but events had changed since that day. That which lurked within him might yet prove handy.

The beast simmered close to the surface today, roused by the visit to the graveyard. He let the dark flow through his veins and with it came heat and the faint whiff of sulphur. When he felt it surge up inside him he looked up and met Thackery's gaze.

The larger man sucked in a breath and pressed himself into the bench. "What are you?"

"A nightmare that neither of us wants unleashed. Tell me what I need to know and I'll leave as quietly as I arrived. Otherwise no one will walk away from here." The thing inside him set fire to his blood and the ale steamed in the mug in his hands.

Thackery dropped the handful of cards to the table. "I don't know his real name. He called himself Smith, but you could tell he was lying. I didn't care. His coins were real enough."

"Describe him." Wycliff gritted his teeth. Having woken his torment, he now had the difficult task of shoving it back into the locked part of him. The beast was growing belligerent and would no longer go quietly to the darkest corner. He had thought that letting it out to run on a moonless night would satisfy it, but letting it free had proved to be a mistake.

"Not much to tell. I never got a good look at him.

Said he was a doctor. Had a particular interest in any bodies I could procure that had head injuries and their brains missing."

A doctor trying to find secondary Afflicted? "What did you do with the body?"

"I took it to Chelsea, met Smith in a field where he had a cart. I loaded the corpse on, got my coin, and never saw him again." Thackery relaxed as he observed Wycliff's gaze return to normal. He picked up the cards and began to shuffle.

Wycliff slid a coin toward the man. "You've been most helpful."

A doctor in Chelsea? He recalled the SUSS meeting and those present. He had a good idea where he might start with his enquiries.

# 8

Hannah was quiet as she walked to the library, pondering the sight of the hand battling to escape so it could continue some unknown journey. How odd that she felt more sympathy for a small part of a limb than she did for all of Viscount Wycliff's ominous person. Why did she have such difficulty putting herself in his position? If she could answer that, truthfully, she might get to the bottom of why the man bothered her more than a burr under the saddle annoyed a horse.

"How went the surgery on your father's unusual patient, Hannah?" Her mother looked up from her study.

"It is fascinating. The hand displays an incredible determination to escape, whereas the forearm is inanimate and dead." Hannah took her usual spot on the window seat.

"Two different people?" Seraphina asked.

"Yes. One stitched to the other in a sort of forced marriage. We suspect the hand is from an Afflicted man —most probably the first victim of Jonathon Rowley. Lord Wycliff has gone to verify that today." A shiver ran over her skin at yet another thought of him.

"How odd for the hand to be active if it is from a secondary Afflicted. They are usually such slow, shambling creatures." Her mother waved her quill through the air and gentle strains of music filled the room.

Hannah closed her eyes as the soft music swirled around her. "There is a slim chance it could be from a primary Afflicted. There are not many, and I doubt it will take long to count their hands. It could even be from a vampyre."

Lady Miles chuckled. "The male Afflicted we know are rather dramatic by nature. I doubt they would have remained silent if some fiend had removed one of their hands. A vampyre might be more likely. But there is no evidence of any taking up residence in London."

The song seemed to melt away Hannah's worries and left her with a clearer focus. "The hand has a number of callouses, further, which makes it unlikely to be an Afflicted of our acquaintance. We shall have to wait for the viscount to return to know for certain. Until then, I require your assistance to create a harness for the hand. Lord Wycliff wishes to use the limb to find the rest of the body."

Seraphina clapped her hands and the music fell silent. "You will walk the hand on a lead? How marvellous. It has been some time since our family set society a-twitter."

"You did promise me a puppy, Mother. If I had a pet, I wouldn't be so looking forward to walking a hand that has lost its body." People would talk. Did she have the strength not to care?

"I have not forgotten your puppy, Hannah. I am merely waiting for the right one to show itself." Lady Miles wagged a finger at her daughter.

Joy ran through her veins. A puppy! She wondered what sort her mother had decided upon and whether it would be a female or a male. "I shall try to restrain my excitement. We do have Timmy's laughter to echo along the house's hallways now."

"And we have the viscount, for without him we would not be researching how to harness a hand." Seraphina pointed to a spot on the library shelf and two books wriggled their way free to float down to her desk.

"I am curious about Timmy, Mother. He is a strong third-generation aftermage. How is it his grandfather did not cultivate his talent and he was left alone in the world?" When she'd found the lad a few weeks ago, he was a lowly, orphaned stable boy.

Her mother wheeled her bath chair around the desk and patted Hannah's knee. "His grandfather is Mage Tomlin, a horrible old curmudgeon. His daughter, Timmy's mother, ran away with a groom and Lord Tomlin declared her and any offspring dead to him."

Hannah swung her feet to the floor. "How horrid! I cannot imagine anyone turning their back on their own blood. Yet the situation is to our advantage. The lad is bright and keen to learn, and I'm sure will be a marvellous doctor one day."

"The old goat will miss knowing the fine young man Timmy will become under Sir Hugh's tutelage. Now, let us find what we need for today's task."

Her mother consulted the old books and then sent Hannah on an errand to find the materials they required: old lengths of light chain and disused bridle pieces from the stables.

Using Hannah's own hand as a model, Seraphina wrapped leather straps and chain around her daughter's fingers as though she were a dressmaker draping silk on a form. They decided on a design that fitted around the middle finger, with another strap that went between thumb and index finger to encircle the palm. Those straps joined at the back of the hand, where the leash was attached.

Hannah wriggled her fingers and walked them across the desk. A faint tingle came from the leather.

Seraphina held the end of the long chain as Hannah tested the device. Her mother nodded, satisfied with their work. "There. The buckles can be tightened to ensure a good fit. I have written a spell upon the leather ensuring that whatever is contained by the straps cannot remove them itself. Only by another hand can they be undone."

"Then we are ready for our promenade. It would be marvellous if Mr Barnes' hand is able to find the rest of him." Hannah wondered how hand and body would be reunited. Would Papa need to stitch the two together?

"I hope the poor man is not suffering too much. You must be prepared, Hannah. You know secondary Afflicted cannot be helped and your father will have to enact the protocol." Seraphina laid her hand over the top of her daughter's and gripped her fingers.

Hannah stared at their connected hands, hers clad in leather and chain, her mother's in a linen glove. "The hand is so...alive. I find it hard to contemplate that the man had his brain removed by Mr Rowley. Perhaps we might find that he is an exception."

Seraphina squeezed Hannah's fingers and then released her to gesture for the books to return to their spot on the shelf. "Hope for the best, but prepare for the worst. Speaking of being prepared, you are expected at the Loburns' this afternoon. Kitty has the modiste coming to discuss Elizabeth's trousseau and you do not want to miss that."

"Oh! No." Hannah scrabbled at the buckles, but they kept sliding through her fingers. Then her mother's words penetrated her memory and she held out her hand. "Would you release me, please, Mother?"

Her mother chuckled as she undid the buckles. "Well done, Hannah. Now we know the spell works."

Hannah changed her plain and sturdy gown for her second best muslin in pale green. She layered a deep green velvet pelisse over the top and chose a shawl. The weather seemed disinclined to advance toward spring and it remained unseasonably cold.

People had begun to mutter that there was something unnatural about the cold that plagued England and Europe. England's mages were tasked with preventing crops from failing, due to lack of warmth and rain. People would starve if the earth couldn't sustain and nourish crops for harvest before next winter.

So many thoughts occupied Hannah's mind that she barely noticed the ride to the Loburn mansion. Always a dark shadow prowled the edges of her mind, and she heaved a sigh. What was to be done about the man? The situation couldn't be left to fester and the time approached when she would need to lance it with a needle. But what course of action did she want to pursue—demand that her mother evict the man, or make her peace with his presence?

The carriage rocked to a gentle halt and a footman clad in maroon and silver opened the door for her. The butler showed Hannah through to a bright parlour decorated in tones of cream and blush pink, and quietly announced her name. Not that anyone within noticed. Their attention was focused on something Hannah couldn't see.

Her dearest friend sat next to an older woman who wore a deep burgundy gown, her silver hair pulled up in a bun under a plain cap tastefully trimmed in lace. Lizzie wore a gown of pale rose and peered at a sketchbook on the older woman's lap.

Lady Loburn stood behind, looking down her avian nose at the visitor.

Before the two women seated on the chaise was a large leather trunk such as a lady might take on a grand tour. The lid was open and the contents strewn over the sides as green silk, pink muslin, lace, and ribbons in an array of colours tried to escape.

Whether her presence was noted or not, Hannah still performed the social courtesies. She bobbed a small curtsey. "Good afternoon, Lady Loburn, Lady Elizabeth."

Lizzie looked up at the sound of her name and smiled. She held out a hand to her friend. "Hannah! Do come and look at what Madame Fontaine is drawing. We are considering ideas for my wedding dress. Do you think it should have a train?"

"Of course it must! A long one, too. It will give your walk down the aisle more drama." Hannah took her friend's hand and then sat on the floor at her feet, beside the enticing trunk, so she could look at what the seamstress drew. The page was covered in designs, some with revealing décolleté, others more modest and with a variety of types of train.

"Perhaps we should settle on a colour first. How do we feel about pale blue, yellow, or pink?" Lady Loburn walked around the chaise and peered into the open chest of samples that sat before the ladies.

Madame Fontaine dove into the trunk and pulled out a length of silk. "For mademoiselle, ivory. It will complement your colouring and not overpower. We want your natural beauty to shine."

"What about some form of decoration? Plain ivory

silk sounds ever so boring." A faint line appeared on Lizzie's brow as she frowned at the sample.

Madame Fontaine tapped her chin with the pencil. "Perhaps around the hem we could embroider wildflowers, to make it appear as though you walk through a meadow in full flower?"

Hannah thought it was a charming idea and wished for such a gown for herself. Imagine having every step surrounded by wild poppies, cornflowers, and daisies. Then her dream expanded to include a good book in her hands as she sank into the bed of flowers to lose herself in prose.

Lady Loburn sucked in her lips. "Wildflowers? I think not. Elizabeth is to marry a duke, not a common lad."

"Roses," Hannah suggested, thinking of a more aristocratic flower and taking her cue from the decoration in the parlour. "In the palest pink to match her complexion. Perhaps a spray of them cascading over her shoulder?"

The modiste's face lit up. "Oh! *Oui.* As though angels had scattered roses over her from above. We could bead some of them so they appear to hold the dew of a new morning."

With quick movements, she sketched a new idea, showing roses tumbling from the right shoulder to scatter over the skirt and train.

"Oh, it's beautiful," Lizzie sighed. "Could my bonnet have matching silk roses?"

With the wedding gown decided upon, they moved

on to discuss the ensemble Lizzie would wear as she embarked on her honeymoon. That led to a discussion about possible locations and things to wear. A walking dress suitable for strolling the avenues of Paris was very different to that required if she were to sit under an olive tree in Italy.

Some hours later, the floor was littered with sketches, with pieces of fabric and trim pinned to the pages.

Lizzie leaned back on the chaise with a look both exhausted and fulfilled, as though she had consumed a wonderful banquet. "Now, what of Hannah? She is to be my bridesmaid and should also look becoming on my day."

"I don't need a new dress." A conflict arose inside Hannah, despite her mother's saying there were adequate funds for her to have a new outfit. She desperately wanted a pretty new frock, but such a desire seemed so shallow. It called to mind the porcelain facade of Lady Gabriella as she'd taunted Hannah for wearing a gown two seasons old. If she indulged in buying pretty things, would each such purchase make her a little more shallow and vain? She hoped not. She promised herself she would remain strong and committed to improving her mind, whatever she wore.

Lady Loburn smiled on her daughter's friend. "Need is irrelevant. This is a special occasion and you will have a new dress, Hannah. This will be the wedding of the season! You are to stand next to my darling Elizabeth while all of society looks on. What do you suggest, Madame Fontaine?"

The modiste turned a critical eye upon Hannah, who dropped her gaze to her hands. Was this how a specimen felt under her father's microscope? As though all its faults were laid bare?

The modiste clicked her tongue as she thought. "Mademoiselle has such strong colouring of hair and eyes, I think she needs a similarly bold fabric."

"Bold? Oh no, not for me. Perhaps a pale yellow?" If Hannah had a choice, she would opt for something the same grey colour as the stones of the church so that no one would notice her.

The modiste rummaged through the open chest. Then she made a triumphant noise and pulled out a piece of silk.

"This is from India and is what the women there wear. They call it the *sari*." She held the length up next to Hannah.

The silk had a rough slub and was spun in an orange so dark it bordered on deep red or brown. It changed hue as the fabric moved and reminded Hannah of embers flickering in a fire. The border was woven with an intricate pattern in a paler orange, red, and brown. Instead of wildflowers, Hannah would walk through fire. For some reason, that conjured Lord Wycliff's stern face in her mind and she wiped it away from her inner vision like a cobweb.

Lizzie clapped her hands together. "Oh, yes. It will look divine, Hannah. Don't you think, Mother?"

Lady Loburn nodded. "It does indeed suit you. Your mother would approve, I am sure."

"Thank you, Lady Loburn." Hannah would have to embolden herself to wear such an eye-catching gown. Surely a glass of fortifying champagne before the ceremony would be appropriate in such circumstances?

Lizzie picked up the final sketch of her wedding dress. "I wonder what present the duke will give me for our wedding? He says it will be quite a surprise for me."

"What if it is something scandalous, like having your name tattooed on his back?" Tattoos were much on Hannah's mind, with the half ship on the amputated hand. Such a thing was the most scandalous she could conjure.

Lizzie gasped. "He wouldn't dare! Besides, I wouldn't see it if it were on his back."

The modiste collected all the sketches into a pile. "My son had a tattoo, mademoiselle, because as he said, he loved his *maman*."

"What was it?" Hannah asked, curious how anyone decided to have an image permanently etched into their skin.

"A needle and a spool of thread. A loop of the thread made a heart and it said *Mère* inside. He had it placed here." She tapped her chest above her heart. "I scolded him when he showed it to me. Now I would give anything to see that tattoo again."

"Why can you not see it again?" Lizzie blurted.

Hannah wished she could recall her friend's hasty

words. Her heart tightened at the longing in the modiste's voice.

The older woman's eyes misted and her smile drooped. "We lost him last month. My poor boy. He looked like a lion but had the soul of a lamb. He had problems with his heart and the doctors did everything they could, but God had a higher plan and called him to his side."

"I'm so sorry for your loss." Hannah reached out and touched the modiste's sleeve.

The woman drew a lace handkerchief from a pocket and dabbed at her eyes. "None of us can control whom Death takes into his embrace. And I have ruined Lady Elizabeth's excitement with my maudlin tale. I am so sorry, my lady."

"No mother could bear to lose a child," Lady Loburn murmured as she walked to the tasselled pull hanging by the door. She gave a tug of the velvet rope. "Shall we have some tea and a change of topic?"

The footman appeared in the doorway and Lady Loburn sent him for tea and biscuits.

"How is your new houseguest behaving, Hannah?" Lady Loburn perched on a sofa opposite her daughter.

"La, Hannah! Is it really true that the horrid Viscount Wycliff is staying at your home? I could not believe it when I heard." Lizzie's blue eyes were wide with horror as she ventured the question.

Hannah clutched the dark orange silk a little tighter, then caught herself and smoothed the creases she had made. "Yes. Mother extended the invitation.

She thought it would assist the viscount in his investigations to be closer to her and Father if he had questions about Unnaturals."

Lizzie gasped and a hand went to her breast. "How terrible for you. Does he storm the corridors yelling at the servants and making unreasonable demands?"

Hannah frowned. "No. Rather the opposite. He is as quiet as a mouse."

Well, not like one of the Afflicted mice. They made quite a noise in their cages.

How to explain the effect of his dark presence as he swept along the corridors or the black gaze that drilled into her, searching out her deepest secrets? He did bring a certain something to the large mansion. Hannah just wasn't sure what that *something* was.

"Pythons are quiet. So they can sneak up on you and when you least expect it, devour you," Lizzie whispered. She nodded so vigorously her blonde curls bounced in front of her ears.

"Oh, Lizzie. He is no python waiting to strike." Hannah laughed and took her friend's hand. Then dark thoughts swarmed into her mind. He was more like a panther waiting to pounce.

Or Black Shuck roaming the moors with its death-inducing stare.

# 9

The next morning, Hannah scanned the newspaper headlines, and read them aloud as her father tucked into his breakfast. "More tales of the monster lurking in the area around Chelsea. It says the locals are banding together to patrol at night and that they are afraid the creature will snatch their wives and daughters."

Her father huffed. "That's all the area needs—a lot of drunken men waving pitchforks in the dark. We'll be lucky if no one is stabbed."

She flicked through the other articles but couldn't see any mention of a large black dog with fiery eyes terrorising Westbourne Green. Perhaps the scandal sheets could only cope with one monster at a time.

Wycliff entered the room and Hannah carefully folded the paper and slid it across the table for him to read. Then she took a large sip of her tea and held the fruity warmth in her mouth before swallowing. "The harness is ready, Lord Wycliff, if you wish to attempt to use the hand as a compass today."

The man in question served his breakfast from the buffet and took his seat diagonally across from her. He shook out his napkin and draped it across his knee before replying. "Yes. I did not find Mr Barnes in his grave, so let us see if the hand has better luck finding the rest of him."

"Us, my lord?" Hannah had hoped to be included when the hand was released, but she was also aware that their last attempt to work together had proved somewhat disastrous. The viscount had terminated her assistance with a terse letter.

He dragged the newspaper closer and spoke without looking up. "It would be useful if you had the time to accompany me. If Mr Barnes proves uncooperative, your mother's immobilisation spell might be handy."

"Oh." Her presence would be useful. Surely that was high praise from the viscount. Far better to be useful than decorative, she supposed. "I shall retrieve the spell before we depart."

"What spell, Hannah?" her mother said as she wheeled into the little dining room.

Hannah stood and helped her mother manoeuvre the bath chair close to the table. "Lord Wycliff suggested the immobilisation spell may be handy if we find the rest of Mr Barnes today."

Her mother picked up a porcelain teacup and ran a finger around its golden rim. "A brilliant suggestion.

Secondary Afflicted can be difficult, since they cannot be reasoned with. I will be most curious to hear whether the hand behaves itself."

Lord Wycliff snapped the newspaper shut and took up his knife and fork. "Can you ride, Miss Miles? The carriage is rather cumbersome."

Hannah stared at her plate. Lizzie was a lovely rider, but Hannah preferred to watch from under a tree. She seemed to lack the necessary grace to hold her position aside. "Not very well or with any skill, I'm afraid."

He grunted. Lack of sporting ability would no doubt be recorded as a strike against her name. She would be demoted from *useful* to *tolerable.*

"We have a small gig that might be suitable." Her mother poured coffee for her husband. "It is little used, as Sir Hugh prefers the comfort of the carriage."

The viscount stared at her from under drawn brows. "I have no objection to the gig, if Miss Miles does not."

"No, of course not, my lord." Except that it would be difficult to avoid him in the two-seater. Perhaps she could make Mr Barnes' hand play chaperone and sit between them. He could pinch the viscount if he slid too close.

"Don't forget to use your ring, Hannah, if you require my assistance," Seraphina said as she sipped from an empty cup.

"I won't forget, Mother." Hannah twisted the ring on the smallest finger of her right hand. It was shaped like a delicate peacock feather that wrapped around her digit. Made of mage silver, it enabled her to signal to her mother that she needed to talk. Likewise, her mother could make the ring tingle if she needed to contact Hannah. Her father had a similar token from the mage, but his was shaped like a bone that encircled his finger.

After breakfast, the viscount stalked off to see the horse harnessed to the gig while Sir Hugh helped Hannah fit a similar type of harness to the hand.

"Now, Mr Barnes' hand, we want to help you find the rest of your body, if you would be so kind as to cooperate." Hannah addressed the hand as her father carried its cage to the laboratory table.

The hand jumped from the ferret's wheel and then scuttled to the side of the cage closest to Hannah. Two fingers curled around the bars as it pressed closer.

Hannah held up the ensorcelled leather. "This is a magic harness, which means you cannot remove it. We want to help you, but we cannot have you running off."

The hand let go of the bars and dropped to the floor of the cage. He rolled over and exposed his palm.

"Does that mean you will cooperate?" Hannah asked. The reactions of the hand really were quite extraordinary, as though she spoke to an odd little creature rather than a dismembered piece of a larger whole.

The hand flipped back over, raised the index finger and waved it slowly up and down. The action appeared to be the equivalent of a nod of the head.

Hannah watched the movement. "Is that a yes?"

The finger rose up and down again.

"I say, Hannah, this is quite remarkable. I begin to wonder that some process has made the hand a separate entity, capable of independent thought." Her father peered into the cage to watch their latest specimen.

"I wonder the same thing, Papa. But we will not know until we discover the rest of Mr Barnes and learn what happened to him." She turned her attention back to the appendage, trying to establish a basis for their communication. "What is no?"

The finger moved from side to side in a gesture long familiar to Hannah. Her mother had used it often when Hannah was a child to tell her *no*—usually sneaking an extra biscuit from a plate.

"Thank you, that is most useful." Others would consider it odd to talk to a hand, but Hannah had been born into an unusual world where her mother made the impossible seem commonplace. What other child had hedges turn into puppetry or enjoyed lullabies sung by birds?

Her father opened the cage. Hannah lifted the hand out, set it on the table, and fitted the harness. He perched on her forearm, rather like an enormous spider.

Sir Hugh chuckled at the sight. "Have a good day, my girl. I look forward to hearing about your adventures on your return."

The index finger pointed toward the door and the rest flexed up and down, as though it bounced with anticipation.

Hannah carried the hand through the house and out the back. She kept the fingers of her right hand curled in the lead and her left forearm outstretched as though she carried a hunting bird.

Lord Wycliff stood next to the sturdy chestnut harnessed to the gig. The viscount narrowed his dark eyes at her. "Should it be out of the cage?"

He held out a gloved hand to help her into the gig while scowling at her new accessory. The hand scuttled up Hannah's arm and behind her neck to sit on the shoulder farthest from the viscount. He now impersonated a parrot.

The gig dipped to one side as Wycliff climbed in and took up the reins.

"The harness is ensorcelled and cannot be removed by the same hand as that wearing it. Besides, Mr Barnes' hand has promised to cooperate in finding the rest of him." It was a curious feeling to have a man's hand on her shoulder. If the rest of the body had been attached, it would have been wholly inappropriate and a shockingly familiar thing to do. Yet remove hand from body and the part was allowed liberties not available to the whole.

Or should Hannah scold him and make him sit on the seat?

Lord Wycliff clucked his tongue and the horse walked out. From the gate they turned toward London and he urged the equine to a trot.

Hannah moved the hand to her lap, but somehow that seemed even more inappropriate. In her mind she imagined he was a type of miniature dog, which made the familiarity more bearable.

"What direction, Mr Barnes' hand?" she asked.

The index finger pointed to the southeast.

"It is working, Lord Wycliff. The hand is leading us to something." The day was turning into an exciting excursion following the Unnatural compass. What treasure would they find at the end of the trail? If it were something unpleasant, Hannah had the immobilisation spell tucked into her stays.

Lord Wycliff guided the horse around the western end of Hyde Park and down through Kensington. "Might I ask you, Miss Miles, about the secondary Afflicted? Your father made mention of the footman and cloakroom attendant murdered by Rowley as having been handled appropriately, unlike Mr Barnes. What exactly is the appropriate method in such circumstances?"

Hannah tightened her grip on the metal lead and stared at the hand on her knee. The skin her father had stitched together over the wrist had healed and covered the tendons, nerves, and arteries. She didn't want to upset Mr Barnes' appendage with such a topic of conversation and risk it leaping from the gig.

"Their bodies were cremated and their ashes sealed before being interred in the Repository of Forgotten Things," she murmured.

Wycliff glanced at her, then returned his attention to the road ahead. "How odd that they were consigned to a funeral pyre but no other Afflicted were. Is it because those two were lowborn servants and the Afflicted whom you so vehemently protect are nobles?"

Heat flowed through Hannah and she fixed his profile with an unblinking stare. "You assume wrongly, my lord. Secondary Afflicted are in every sense mindless shambling creatures that cannot be reasoned with, for their minds have been stolen from them. They are driven by their hunger and are a danger to society."

Hannah dropped her gaze to the hand, wondering if she ought to apologise to him. He showed none of the customary characteristics of the secondary Afflicted. What if her father was wrong about them? But she had seen secondary Afflicted herself and the memory was a nightmare she wished she could erase.

At a crossroads, Wycliff steered the horse to the southeast. "Could they not be interred and fed a daily allotment, like the nobles in the Repository?"

Mr Barnes' hand sat still and unmoving, apart from a directional point at each crossroad. How much did he understand and why did he appear so alert? Questions swirled in Hannah's mind that relied on finding the rest of Mr Barnes before they could be answered.

She turned her thoughts back to the disagreement with the viscount and the nobles interred in the Repository. "Those Afflicted are held securely because we believe they can eventually be cured. What future awaits a person with no brain if we can restore their heartbeat but never their mind?"

Now the finger pointed straight out and Wycliff

guided them toward Chelsea. "Yet it remains that only servants are cremated."

"Unfortunately, that is not true. As you are aware, when the French curse first struck, two nobles who became Afflicted were driven to murder by their insatiable hunger. They killed relatives in their homes and were quickly seized and interred for the safety of Londoners. Their victims were monitored for any potential side effects and when they arose, my parents tried for some months to stabilise their conditions. But their appetites were monstrous and without relent. In the end my father had to issue the order for them to be taken to a funeral pyre. It was a horrible sight." Hannah swallowed and closed her eyes at the memory that swam before her.

She would never forget the cries of the wretched creatures as they were immolated, chained to pillars so they could not escape. Her mother had been unable to find a spell to ease their suffering; she could only increase the intensity of the fire to consume every part of the victims, killed twice over.

Lord Wycliff made that grunting noise and turned his attention to the passing fields. "You keep noble murderers sustained, but not their victims."

"Have you seen someone burned alive, my lord? Do I need to describe the process in detail to convince you that those present that day believe that even one person sent to such a death is one too many? After that horrendous day, the protocol was enacted that in the rare event of any secondary Afflicted being created, they were to be cremated before they arose, so that they did not suffer. But what do we do with the Afflicted who commit heinous crimes? As terrible as their crimes may be, we will not commit another heinous act by consigning them to the flames whilst they retain their minds."

He barked a short laugh and then turned to her. "Why, Miss Miles, unless I am mistaken, I believe you are advocating keeping them alive long enough to find a cure, so that they might be executed for their crimes. Since any Afflicted can make more of these cursed creatures, should they not all be locked away for the safety of society?"

Hannah stared at the hand in her lap. He didn't seem capable of creating more shambling, mindless creatures. But she should be on her guard, lest he try to remove her mind one day. "All men are capable of murder, my lord. Should we lock everyone of your sex away to keep women and children safe from murderous masculine impulses? Having the capacity and the inclination are two separate issues."

His black eyes were unreadable as he regarded her for a silent minute. "Fair point, Miss Miles. Most men can behave at least as though they are half civilised without giving way to their baser impulses. This raises another question—if secondary Afflicted are mindless, shambling monsters, why is this hand so active?"

"That I do not know." Even the colour of the flesh seemed healthy, which was remarkable given that the body had spent some time in the Thames after Mr

Barnes' murder. "I can only hypothesise that there is another factor at play here responsible for the hand's condition."

"More of the dark arts?" he asked.

Hannah couldn't stop the shudder that ran through her body. Dark arts created the Afflicted. Did more magic explain why the hand acted like an independent, thinking creature? "We will not know until we discover what happened to the rest of Mr Barnes."

She studied the homes they passed and wondered at the lives of the inhabitants. The jostling in her lap brought Hannah's attention back to the hand.

Lord Wycliff halted the horse. "It seems agitated here."

The finger pointed to a particular property across the road from where they had stopped. A tall clipped hedge encircled the perimeter. A narrow opening in the hedge allowed for an iron archway and gate. Beyond sat a windowless red brick building. At one end, a large chimney—disproportionately large compared to the rest of the structure—pointed to the sky.

"What is this place?" Lord Wycliff climbed down from the gig and offered his gloved hand to Hannah.

Hannah hopped to the ground and walked to the locked gate. "This is the crematorium. There are a few rare aftermages with the gift of pyromancy who can generate sufficient heat to burn remains. This place is used by some hospitals instead of mass graves for the unknown and unwanted."

Hannah stared at the red brick building and let out a sigh. She wanted to say *damn*, but that would be unladylike even though it summed up her frustration. If the rest of Mr Barnes had been consigned to such a fire, they would never know what happened.

"If we assume that Mr Barnes ended up here, how did his hand escape?" Lord Wycliff peered through the gate at the building and then at the dark green hedge.

"The hand is small and lively. It is not inconceivable that he escaped the same way as a rat might. There is another gate on the other side large enough to admit a cart, when remains are brought here under the cover of night. Perhaps the hand jumped free when the bodies were being moved." As Hannah spoke, the hand climbed her arm to settle on her shoulder once more. He uncurled a lock of her hair to latch a finger onto to anchor his position.

They left the gig and walked along the road, taking a corner down a narrower lane. Here the dense hedge parted to allow two larger locked gates, sufficient to let a cart through. The gravel drive led to double barn doors painted black in the rear of the building. The lawn on this side appeared to have a substantial mole problem. Mounds of earth made a random pattern across the grass.

The hand became agitated, bouncing up and down on Hannah's shoulder as he pointed to a grouping of mounds that were exposed earth. No grass had yet crept over these.

"I think we have found the rest of Mr Barnes." She reached up and patted the hand.

"It would appear his ashes are interred beneath one of those lumps." Wycliff took off his top hat and ran a hand through his hair. Then he turned back to the road.

Hannah followed. He seemed like a dog on a scent as his head swung from side to side. He stopped to stare at the Thames, visible on the other side of the road. "It is possible that the limb dragged itself through the hedge, across the road, and then made its way into the water and drifted to where it came ashore at Neat House Gardens."

As they stood by the road pondering past events, a curricle drawn by two smart matched bays came to a halt. The well-dressed driver peered at Hannah. "Miss Miles, I did not expect to find you lingering on the side of the road. Do you require assistance?"

Hannah walked closer to the sporting carriage with its glossy black paint. "Good day, Lord Dunkeith. I am assisting Lord Wycliff with a matter that has brought us here."

The hand scuttled around behind her neck, clinging to her nape like a limpet.

Lord Dunkeith turned his wide smile on Hannah. "You appear to have something on your neck, Miss Miles. Is it a new pet?"

As Hannah reached up, the hand pressed into her neck and tugged the edge of her bonnet over himself. For some reason he didn't want to show himself to anyone else. "It is a curiosity from my father's laboratory that is rather shy."

Before Lord Dunkeith could open his mouth to ask another question, Viscount Wycliff rested a hand on the curricle and asked one of his own. "It is most fortuitous to encounter you, Dunkeith. Do you obtain corpses to conduct your research in private?"

The smile disappeared from the handsome lord's face and his attention was dragged from the creature sheltering under Hannah's bonnet to the viscount. "That's a rather forward question, Wycliff."

The viscount pressed a finger against the paintwork of the curricle and left a tiny smudge. "I am seeking information about a body that was missing a goodly portion of its skull and brain. Has it passed through your laboratory in the last month or so?"

"I work in potions for ailments, sir. I am not aware of any potion that can restore a brain and head. Now, if you will excuse me, I have much to do in the Physic Garden." He touched the brim of his hat to Hannah and then cracked the reins. The horses trotted on down the road.

Wycliff untied their horse's reins from around the brake of the gig. "That was rather abrupt—almost as though he didn't want to answer my questions."

Hannah watched the curricle bowl down the road and disappear around a curve. Most people didn't want to answer the viscount's questions. "Perhaps he is truly otherwise engaged. And as he stated, his is the study of potions, not surgical procedures."

She settled on the hard seat and pried the hand's fingers off her nape to move him back to her shoulder. If they gave the limb a pencil, could he write his story and unveil how he had escaped the crematorium? Or tell them who had stitched him to a stranger's forearm?

"I have traced the corpse from Bunhill Fields. The body snatcher delivered him to a medical man waiting in the Chelsea fields, but he gave the false name of Smith and my informant could not describe him." Wycliff climbed into the gig and turned the horse and vehicle around.

"A medical man in Chelsea dealing with body snatchers? Surely not. This is a respectable area. What sort of doctor would perform such horrific procedures on the dead?" As soon as Hannah said the words, she realised how foolish they sounded, given that both he and she had witnessed three men attempt a resurrection challenge.

One such participant had just crossed their path while denying any knowledge of Mr Barnes. But could they believe him? And why had the hand hid under her bonnet with every evidence of fear?

# 10

They had a quiet journey back to Westbourne Green. Not that the trip to the Chelsea crematorium had been particularly chatty, but the silence carried a heavy air of unspoken questions. Who among her father's acquaintances, Hannah wondered, could have been responsible for the fate of Mr Barnes, and the change that had created the animated hand?

Then she considered the crude stitches made in the wrist. No doctor of good standing made such a terrible job of closing a wound. The body snatcher had said only a *medical* man. That broad description covered many occupations, from barbers who removed teeth, to grooms who saw to the ailments of horses.

Lord Wycliff offered her a hand down after he reined the horse to a halt outside the stable. "I will need to interview the men who participated in the resurrection challenge, to see if one of them took possession of Mr Barnes."

Old Jim, the family groom, took charge of the horse as Hannah moved the harnessed hand from her shoulder to her forearm. "Father and I would be fascinated to learn what process allows this appendage to function. But I do not believe it was one of his acquaintances. Members of SUSS share their research, and this is an exciting discovery unknown before today."

"You find this"—Lord Wycliff pointed to the hand that curled his fingers inward and squatted on her forearm—"exciting?"

"When Afflicted do not take the necessary sustenance, rot begins to consume them, starting in the extremities. This hand shows no sign of decay, despite the fact that the evidence indicates Mr Barnes was consigned to the crematorium. There is more at work here than the French curse." If anything, the hand seemed in far better condition now that he had been removed from the mismatched forearm. There was even a flush of pink to the skin, as though the severed veins were circulating blood.

They walked across the stable yard to the rear of the house. "Most women would reserve the word *exciting* to describe a new frock."

"I am not most women." While like most women, she would find a new dress exciting, surely a woman could be moved by more than fashion? It wasn't as if the fairer sex were limited to only one interest.

"As I am discovering." He held open the door and she entered with her unusual hawk. Another thing she found more interesting than clothing tapped on her mind. "What of the Chelsea monster, my lord? Is there a possibility that it might contain some part of Mr Barnes?"

He paused in the hallway. "If we rely on the hand as an indicator of where Barnes is, then his body is ash buried in the ground behind the crematorium. I suppose we cannot discount the possibility of some cobbled-together creature lurking nearby. I intend to patrol the area for the next few nights and see what I encounter."

"Do be careful of the militia with their pitchforks." She might not be fond of the man, but no one deserved to be skewered on a pitchfork because they were prowling in the dark.

He stared at her, then nodded before striding down the corridor to his study. But whether that nod meant a civil leave-taking or an assent to her request, she did not know.

"Come along, Mr Barnes' hand. I am sorry to say it is back to your cage for you. We also need to find something else to call you. *Mr Barnes' hand* doesn't exactly trip off the tongue." She carried the hand down the stairs to her father's laboratory.

The workroom was empty apart from the mice going about their lives in their cages. Hannah tried to place the hand in his cage, but he clung to her arm and refused to let go.

"Can I assume from the way you are attached to me like a limpet that you do not like the cage?" She shook her arm, but the hand refused to be dislodged.

He broke one finger free to wave it back and forth in the *no* gesture. Hannah considered her available options. She could attempt to scrape off the hand on the side of the cage, or use the immobilisation spell to make him let go. Both ideas seemed…underhanded.

"If I promise to speak to my parents about allowing you some liberty, will you let go?"

The finger moved in an up and down direction. Then the hand leapt off her arm into the cage. Hannah unbuckled his harness and closed the lid before he decided to escape.

The family, and their lodger, met over luncheon in the small dining room. Lord Wycliff apprised her father of their failure to locate the rest of Mr Barnes, and of how the hand had pointed to the burial mounds at the rear of the crematorium.

"The ash is cleared from the crematorium on a regular basis," her father said, "and boxed up and buried on the rear lawn. I doubt you will find much left of the poor man."

"I shall ask Sir Manly for permission to inspect the mounds more closely and to exhume the one that makes the hand most agitated, if Miss Miles does not mind acting as its *handler* once more." Lord Wycliff looked up and for once, didn't scowl as he asked for her assistance.

Hannah swallowed a laugh. Had the serious viscount actually made a joke? "I am only too happy to assist in determining what happened to the rest of Mr Barnes. Papa, we need to discuss what to do with his hand. He does not like being confined to the cage."

"If you wish to set him free, I can create a ward around the house so that he cannot wander the countryside," her mother suggested.

"Yes, please." Though given the size of the house, there were plenty of places for a hand to hide. "Perhaps you might add some way to locate him if we need to? We can't have him leaping from the curtains to terrify passers-by."

"I shall brew some mage silver to make a ring with which we may locate him." Seraphina sat with an empty plate. She took her sustenance in private each morning to spare the family the sight both of her consuming her pickled cauliflower, or her unveiled face with its signs of decay.

"Moving on to other business, Lord Jessope is agreeable to attempting the exorcism on his wife," her father said. "Do you wish to come to the Repository with me, Hannah?"

"Oh, yes. What an opportunity." Since her conversation with her parents, they had both made more of an effort to include her in their research. An effort she much appreciated. She finally felt as though she had a purpose. "It might also be an opportunity for Timmy, if he would not be too frightened by her appearance?"

Her father was delighted to have an apprentice with a trace of magic running through his veins and a particular talent for knowing what ailed people. Hugh was more like a child with a marvellous Christmas gift he didn't want anyone else playing with, but at the same time, he wanted Timothy to exercise his gift. The lad had much to learn academically before he would commence more rigorous medical studies. He needed to read and write proficiently first, then learn anatomy.

Hannah battled the envy that arose in her heart. If only she had been born a boy and with a magical gift such as Timothy possessed, then she might have assisted her father in a more encompassing way. She might even have risen to be his equal partner as the years progressed.

But she must not let those feelings impinge upon her work. The lad was not to blame for her deficiencies. And it had been her suggestion for the boy to reside with them and become her father's apprentice. It was her lot in life to arrange things so that others could succeed, while she found quiet contentment in their achievements.

"Timmy has lessons this afternoon and even if he didn't, the Repository is not an appropriate place for him," her father said with firmness. "Besides, Lady Jessope might indeed give the lad a fright with her appearance. The reverend is going to attempt his ritual at his church in Chelsea." Hugh finished his tea with one large slurp that made Lord Wycliff arch an eyebrow.

"I have heard of the Repository of Forgotten Things from Sir Manly," his lordship said. "Might I accompany you? I would like to verify for myself that none of the male Afflicted held there are missing their hands or other limbs."

Silently, Hannah pleaded with her father to say no. She wasn't ready to share a carriage with the man so soon after their outing that morning. Or after what she had endured during their investigation of the recent murders.

But her father was no clairvoyant, to hear her silent prayer. "Since you are Sir Manly's investigator, you may as well know the full of it. Although it will be a bit cramped, since we need to transport Lady Jessope. Would you mind accompanying us on horseback?"

"Not at all."

After the repast, Hannah fetched her bonnet, her green velvet pelisse to guard against the chill outside, and her notebook. Lady Gabriella Ridlington and her beau, Mr Jonathon Rowley, were now permanent residents of the Repository of Forgotten Things. While it was a deeply uncharitable thought, Hannah wanted to see how the two Afflicted had deteriorated without the means to satisfy their gluttonous (and murderous) hunger.

Hannah sat in the carriage across from her father while Lord Wycliff rode beside them on his fine mare.

"Quite a difference to have more bodies in the house, don't you think, Hannah?" Sir Hugh asked as he stared out the window.

"Young Timmy was a fortuitous find, and I am sure he will grow up to be an excellent surgeon under your tutelage." Hannah found herself staring at Lord

Wycliff's back as he sat easily in the saddle. He held the reins in one hand, the other resting on his thigh.

"And what do you think of our other new resident?" Her father followed her line of sight.

"I think Mother plays a game invisible to the rest of us." Seraphina had suggested Hannah might like a puppy and then thrust a hellhound upon her.

"Your mother would never play with people's lives, Hannah. Sera sees things that we cannot and her reasons will reveal themselves in the fullness of time. It is enough to know that the viscount has a part to play in whatever larger game is afoot." Hugh leaned back against the seat, seemingly content to go along with his wife's plans. Or perhaps a life spent together had given him a certain familiarity with how the mage manipulated events.

Hannah held in a sigh. At times she was no more than a puppet in life. When would she take control of her own destiny and step out of her mother's shadow?

Wycliff turned and met her gaze. Black eyes bored into her and forced Hannah to retreat into the shade of the carriage's interior. It seemed she wasn't quite ready to step from the shadows yet. But one day...

As they passed through the Repository's gates, the familiar tingle of magic ran over Hannah's skin. Wycliff's mare danced sideways as he rode her through the invisible shield that Seraphina had erected around the compound. A faint mist clung to the air within the high stone wall, as though it further obscured the house from curious eyes.

By the time Hannah and her father emerged from the carriage, Wycliff had dismounted and held his mare by the reins. The wraith stared at the solemn building. No movement came from within and it would have appeared deserted had it not been for the well-manicured lawn.

Might she suggest he move in here, instead of haunting their home? This was a far more fitting place for him to stride along corridors glaring at anyone he encountered.

He tied the mare to the hook at the back of the carriage and then joined them on the small porch.

Sir Hugh unlocked the door and pushed it open.

Hannah stepped inside and breathed in the calm silence. The stone building reminded her of a library, except here there were souls catalogued and stored, not books. As she let the solitude seep into her bones, it came with the realisation that it wasn't quiet at all. The grandfather clock ticked as it marked off the seconds sliding past. From other directions came the shuffle of feet, the rattle of a door handle, or a stray cough.

"Not what you were expecting, my lord?" her father said to the viscount.

Wycliff stared at a spot on the ceiling, the source of a muffled bump. "No. I thought it was a type of prison to detain those Unnaturals deemed dangerous to society."

"Not all prisons have visible bars and guards. But I assure you, the more dangerous inmates will not be leaving by any ordinary means." Her father tucked his hands behind his back and stood a little taller as he spoke of the prison crafted by his wife.

"So there is a possibility they could escape by non-ordinary means?" A black brow arched and his nostrils flared.

"Dark magic creates dark things, such as the Afflicted. We have done what is within our abilities to ensure they stay put, but I do not know what a determined enemy might be capable of. Do you?" Sir Hugh gestured for them to follow him.

"If these creatures are such a danger to society, perhaps there needs to be a more permanent solution?" Wycliff trod silently behind Sir Hugh.

Her father stopped with a hand on top of the newel post. "That is exactly what we are working on. You are welcome to join the next Society meeting if you have any pertinent ideas to propose."

"This is neither the time nor place for such a discussion, gentlemen." Hannah tugged on her father's sleeve as she joined him on the top step. "Let us not forget the purpose of our visit here."

Hugh patted her hand. "Quite right, Hannah. Let us ask Lady Jessope if she wishes to attempt a reunion with her Maker."

At the bottom of the stairs, her father called out a greeting to the guard who kept vigil over the inmates. "Lady Jessope, please, Fallon," he said.

"Certainly, Sir Hugh." The guard rose and drew forth the rattling ring of keys. He selected a slender iron one and walked to one of the metal doors. Once unlocked, he held it open for the party.

Wycliff glanced all around him before following them into the cell.

Lady Jessope resided within, laid out on the wooden cot with her hands crossed over her chest. Her lips moved continuously as she prayed. Words whispered over dried lips. Her skin was stretched tight over her mummified form. The plain linen shift added to her eerie appearance.

Her father approached and knelt at the Afflicted woman's bedside.

Wycliff leaned closer to Hannah. "Do they all become like this?"

"No. Lady Jessope is one of a handful of particularly devout sufferers who refuse to take the necessary sustenance. Their denial of their craving has mummified, and therefore preserved, their bodies. It is fascinating and quite the opposite of what occurs in those who succumb to their gluttonous appetites." She wanted to step away from him, but the little cell gave nowhere else to go. At the same time, she couldn't help but inhale him—he smelt of sun-warmed earth that reminded her of sunny days by the river spent in quiet companionship. She rather fancied he should have smelt of sulphur, not a comforting aroma that made her want to close her eyes.

"Is this not, then, a solution, rather than feeding their monstrous appetites?" His tone was low, as though they conversed in a church.

"How many of us are so devout we could deny a craving that allowed us to continue to...*live*, for want of a better word? Not every person is suited to a monastic life of prayer and solitude. And suffering." Hannah couldn't do it, as horrible as it was to contemplate. She would rather have her mother at the table pretending to drink tea than a holy relic whispering prayers and locked in a cell.

He made that rough bark in the back of his throat and stepped into the corner, as though ceding the floor.

Sir Hugh rose. "Lady Jessope agrees to attempt the ritual. We will use a bath chair to convey her to the carriage."

The more Hannah studied Lady Jessope, the more similarities Hannah saw to pictures in books of unwrapped Egyptian mummies. Egypt kept bubbling to the top of her thoughts. She needed to know how her mother progressed with her research in that direction.

"May I see the others while she is conveyed above?" Wycliff asked.

Sir Hugh waved to the guard. "Show the viscount where the others are kept. Make sure you stick to the wall on the right, Lord Wycliff, and do not venture near the bars. They are most determined to reach one of us."

## 11

"I will visit the other Afflicted with Lord Wycliff, Papa, while you make Lady Jessope comfortable." Hannah waited out in the corridor while the guard collected his flintlock and found the key for the next locked door. Her father disappeared into another room to find the bath chair needed to move Lady Jessope.

The cries and moans seeped into the hall as they waited, and escalated when the door was pushed open. This was a different room from the one where the original five mad Afflicted were held. That branch of the underground labyrinth was full, and now a new area took in residents. Hannah wondered how many such cells were available in the Repository. Would there be enough if Wycliff got his way and all the Afflicted in London were rounded up and incarcerated?

Hannah couldn't remember seeing this room on any of her previous visits to the Repository. It seemed to have sprouted a new wing specifically for

Lady Gabriella and Jonathon Rowley. She was sure the door was entirely new and yet the masonry appeared decades old. When she laid a hand on the cool surface as she passed, the faint tingle of magic ran up her hand. Of course. Her mother's handiwork.

"I demand to be set free immediately!" a familiar feminine voice called out.

Mr Rowley was in the first cell, closest to the door. He paced back and forth with his arms clasped around his middle. When he spun to face Hannah, she gasped. His skin showed the blue-green mottling of rot. His lower eyelids pulled downward under their own weight. Tufts of his thick brown hair had fallen out and exposed the skull underneath.

"Feed me," he rasped.

When she didn't answer, he lunged at the bars and Hannah jumped back. Wycliff moved in front of her and reached behind him to steady her.

"You've killed enough innocent people to satisfy your lust," the viscount said.

"Wycliff? Is that you? I knew you would come to rescue me," Lady Gabriella called.

"Stay here and do not approach him, Miss Miles," he said before walking down to the next cell.

Hannah rolled her eyes. She knew the rules and had no intention of letting Mr Rowley crack her skull open. She found his rate of deterioration fascinating. While he received the sliver a day that was enough to sustain any other Afflicted, he had the appearance of one who had gone weeks without nourishment, not mere hours.

Since his plaintive plea had gone unanswered, Mr Rowley curled one hand around the bars and thrust the other one through. He growled and snarled as he attempted to reach her. A foul odour came from him, as his internal organs liquefied and seeped through tears in his flesh to stain his clothing.

As much as it shamed her to admit it, Hannah experienced a small surge of glee as she kept to the wall to peer at Lady Gabriella. Then the glee turned to pity. The lady was rotten inside and out and now anyone who looked upon her saw the true embodiment of her character. For that, she deserved compassion.

Lady Gabriella still wore the latest fashion, but it was stained with the fluids that leaked from her body. Her once renowned porcelain beauty was now a thing of horror and disgust. Like her beau, her hair had fallen out in clumps. The flesh sloughed from her bones and sagged as she moved.

"Wycliff! You will release me, won't you?" Lady Gabriella smiled, but it exposed gaps in her gums where her teeth had fallen out.

He crossed his arms and remained unmoved by her pleas. "No, madam, I will not. You are a murderess and if you had a beating heart, you would have been hanged until it stopped. You will continue your sorry existence within these four walls until the Ministry of Unnaturals finds another way to punish you for your crimes."

Lady Gabriella screamed and lunged at the

viscount through the bars. He held his ground as her rotten fingertips swiped the air mere inches from his body.

"It is she! She has poisoned your mind against us," she screeched.

"I find Miss Miles to be eminently sensible. Unlike you." He held out an arm to Hannah. "Time to leave these criminals to seek atonement from their Creator, Miss Miles."

Hannah blinked at him. When he behaved in a civilised manner toward her, she lost her grip on how to act sensibly. "You wanted to ascertain the number of hands on the other Afflicted, my lord."

Hannah was relieved when the guard swung the thick door closed and locked it behind them. The noblewoman's screamed curses became muffled whispers. They ventured into the other block of cells next and Lord Wycliff satisfied himself that the Afflicted men within were all in possession of their left hands.

By the time they returned upstairs, her father had wheeled Lady Jessope up a hidden ramp and lifted her into the carriage. Another black-clad guard had materialised from somewhere in the building and assisted Sir Hugh in loading the bath chair onto the tiger's platform on the back of the carriage. After they lashed the chair on with a rope, they were ready to depart.

Hannah sat next to her father with Lady Jessope stretched out on the opposite seat. Sir Hugh's eyes shone with excitement as he knocked on the ceiling in the signal to move off. Hannah kept watch over Lady

Jessope as they travelled, anxious in case the woman should roll off the seat.

Reverend Jones had a living with a modest church in Chelsea, an area that had long been a desirable location for the wealthy who wanted to be outside of London. It was also home to the Royal Hospital and the Physic Garden, founded in 1673 by the Worshipful Company of Apothecaries. Aftermages whose talent lay in potions often visited the garden to source rare and unusual plants needed in their work.

"Lord Dunkeith has a house in Sloane Square and often frequents the Physic Garden," Sir Hugh said as the carriage rumbled along the road.

"Lord Wycliff said the man who took Mr Barnes' body was a medical man who met him in a field near Chelsea." Hannah peered out the window, her mind on other things. Where did the monster hide during the day? If it wasn't Mr Barnes, then who was it?

"Anyone can say they are a medical person, Hannah. That doesn't mean it was one of the fine chaps we know," her father said.

The carriage halted on the gravel drive outside the church, which was tucked into the corner of a grand estate. The reverend's two-storey grey stone manse sat across a narrow stretch of lawn from the church. The graveyard was picturesque, its lush grass scattered with wildflowers. Even the gravestones were of a better class than those found in the cemeteries crammed with common Londoners, with the stone here scrubbed free of moss or lichen.

Reverend Jones, clad in black, was waiting on the gravel and rushed to open the carriage door.

Hannah and her father stepped down as Wycliff dismounted from his horse and handed the reins to Old Jim.

"Help me with the chair, would you, Lord Wycliff?" The two men untied the chair and wheeled it to the carriage door.

Then Sir Hugh lifted out Lady Jessope and placed her on the seat as Wycliff held it still.

The reverend recoiled and looked away from the once grand lady. "I will meet you at the altar when you are ready."

Hannah glared at his back as he retreated inside the church. Then with great care, she arranged the mummified woman's limbs so that her hands lay modestly in her lap. She wrapped a light shawl around Lady Jessope's upper body and tucked it in. Next, she draped a square of gauze over Lady Jessope's head, turning her into an odd bride of Christ.

"Let us take you to meet Reverend Jones, Lady Jessope." Her father took hold of the chair and wheeled the silent Afflicted up the aisle.

Reverend Jones had donned his vestments and waited for them in the chancel before the altar. He clutched his Bible and only glanced at the gauze-covered Afflicted before fixing his attention on Hannah's father. "Thank you, Sir Hugh, for this opportunity to reunite this poor soul with our Creator."

"Lady Jessope believes she should no longer walk

this earth, since the French curse stopped her heart. She is most desirous of an attempt to send her to death's embrace." Sir Hugh kept a hold on the bath chair.

"I shall ask God to gather your soul to him, Lady Jessope." Reverend Jones spoke loudly, as though he thought the lady not only dead, but deaf as well.

Rasping sounds came from under the veil, and her father bent forward to catch her whispered words. Sir Hugh straightened his large frame. "She asks whether she might join in your prayers, or if it is best for her to remain silent during the ceremony."

"Oh. I had not considered that." The reverend usually attempted his ceremony on the properly dead, who didn't move or speak. A frown appeared on his forehead. "Perhaps she could remain silent, but we could all recite the Lord's Prayer when I get to that part?"

He directed his questions to Hannah's father, disregarding the unfortunate woman in front of him. Hannah wanted to ask him why he bothered, if he couldn't even face Lady Jessope or converse with her. The woman was broken and lonely, and deserved to be treated with kindness and dignity.

The way the reverend overlooked the woman was at odds with his voiced concern to help the Afflicted. Or was he really helping them? What if he strove to help himself in some way? If his religious ceremony worked, he could bring about exactly the outcome Lord Wycliff desired—seeing all the Afflicted cold and still in their graves.

Society would be cleared of their presence and normal life could resume. Or as normal as possible, since that still left vampyres, lycanthropes, gorgons, and any number of other Unnatural creatures to fit into a seating plan for a dinner party.

Hannah chided herself for being uncharitable. The reverend had probably never seen an Afflicted in such a condition as Lady Jessope before. His reticence might be entirely because he had yet to become accustomed to her desiccated appearance. His servant at the door had bolted when they removed her from the carriage. At least the reverend held his ground.

Still, Hannah tucked her questions away for later consideration.

"Shall we begin?" The reverend cleared his throat and looked to her father for approval.

"Are we to do anything?" Hannah asked.

"If you could recite the Lord's Prayer with us. Otherwise I would only ask that you direct your silent prayers to our Lord, and ask him to reunite this poor creature with the rest of her soul in Heaven." He smiled at Hannah, but it was a bland thing, as though done by rote, without any warmth behind it.

Hannah touched Lady Jessope's shoulder. Kindness took so little effort, but had great rewards. "I shall pray for you, my lady."

A mummified hand lifted and brushed against Hannah's as Lady Jessope rasped, "Thank you."

The reverend began in the same manner as he had during the resurrection challenge. He anointed Lady

Jessope with holy water. Then he rested a hand on her veiled head and began to pray in Latin.

Hannah bowed her head and listened. Out of the corner of her eye, she could see Wycliff prowling around the ends of the pews, never staying still. *Perhaps he needs to keep moving to avoid a lightning strike.*

"Our Father, who art in Heaven..."

Hannah recited the long-familiar words when that portion of the ceremony was reached. As time ticked by, her attention wandered. She alternated between watching Wycliff pace, and reviewing the notes she needed to make about the conditions of Lady Gabriella and Mr Rowley. Rot had set into their limbs on what they considered a starvation diet. Lady Gabriella's famed beauty sloughed from her face and dripped to the stone floors.

The reverend's voice rose in tone and Hannah refocused her attention on the altar. Reverend Jones now clutched his Bible in both hands as he shook it over Lady Jessope and commanded her remaining sliver of soul to join the rest of it.

A shiver raced up Hannah's arm and over her torso. For a moment she wondered if the reverend's exorcism was working and Lady Jessop's soul was leaving her wizened husk. Then she realised it was the peacock-feather ring curled around her smallest finger.

Her mother was summoning them.

Her father rubbed the bone that encircled his own finger and looked around.

Her mother would need a conduit to talk to them.

"Hugh? Is Lord Wycliff still with you?" Seraphina's voice whispered from the back of the church.

Hannah glanced upward and found what her mother manipulated to reach them. Above the entrance of the church was a stained glass window of a maid with animals at her feet. The ears on the rabbits and lambs twitched as the woman bent down and peered out at them.

What Hannah's body had responded to with a shiver was her mother's use of magic, not the reverend's passionate pleas eliciting a response from God. How sad for Lady Jessope that the incoming communication was not the one she so fervently desired.

"Yes. Wycliff is here," Sir Hugh replied.

The glass woman waved a hand and spoke again. "He is needed urgently by Sir Manly."

"Dear God!" Reverend Jones exclaimed, staring at the stained glass window that moved. "What is this sorcery?"

"Lady Miles' mage silver allows her to locate us, then she only needs to find a nearby conduit with which to get a message to us. It's rather handy." Her father smiled up at the young maid clothed in shades of yellow and red cut glass.

Wycliff gazed up at the stained glass window to address Lady Miles. "I will be on my way. I have my horse here." He hurried down the aisle.

"There is no point continuing the ceremony now. It is possible that our Lord's work will take some time to achieve, and may even require several attempts before the poor unfortunate's soul departs her earthly form." The reverend set the Bible down on the altar and removed the stole from around his neck.

"If Lady Jessope is agreeable, we can try again another day." Hugh took hold of the bath chair.

A sob came from beneath the veil and Hannah's heart broke a little for the woman. To have vested such hope in the ceremony, only for it to fail.

She knelt and took her hand. "We must try to be patient, Lady Jessope. The reverend says he might need to repeat the ceremony, but we will find a way to end your terrible affliction. Many men have devoted themselves to discovering a solution."

Her father nodded to the reverend and then wheeled the Afflicted woman from the church. Outside, the viscount had collected his horse and departed. Without his chilly presence the sun seemed a little warmer, although the season struggled to progress past winter.

"It is unseasonably cold, is it not?" her father said as they lifted Lady Jessope into the carriage.

"There is talk that we might not see a summer, which would be a terrible thing for Lizzie's wedding." Once seated inside, Hannah stared out the window. Her friend's wedding was to be the crowning moment for the end of summer, which would be rather difficult if winter refused to budge.

Her father rapped on the roof of the carriage and it moved off. "Even your mother has no explanation for the cold that has descended upon us. The mages of

England and Europe are convening to find a solution. We can only hope it is not more of the French dark arts. If crops fail, untold people will starve to death come winter."

Hannah's heart was heavy. How much more death and misery could dark magic bring to the world, and how could it ever be stopped?

## 12

Wycliff cantered back along Chelsea Road and then cut over to The Strand toward the Ministry of Unnaturals in Whitehall. He let the horse navigate the growing traffic while he considered his situation. There were advantages to residing with the Miles family. Day by day he increased his knowledge of Unnaturals, their distinct abilities and weaknesses. But he trod their floors feeling like an unwelcome interloper.

The maid Mary squawked and ran whenever she saw him. Sir Hugh appeared to exist in a state of perpetual distraction, and Wycliff wondered whether someday the doctor might walk right through him, presuming him to be an apparition. Lady Miles was unfathomable even though she had extended the original invitation. And Miss Hannah Miles...

Wycliff nearly trotted into the back of a stationary carriage as he tried to think how to categorise Miss

Miles. With her intelligence, determination, and her active role in assisting her father, he had never encountered anyone the likes of her. She evaded any simple labels. Something about the young woman was under his skin and no matter how much he tried to scrub at the spot, he couldn't remove her.

He recalled an earlier conversation with Lady Miles in the overgrown garden, when she had said he was adrift on an unfamiliar ocean and needed an anchor. If he were honest with himself, he had accepted the invitation to board with the family because of the dead mage. A voice whispered that she could help with his situation and that Miss Miles would be pivotal if he was to find a tether.

He set those thoughts aside to consider later, when he was alone. He dismounted from the horse and threw the reins to a waiting urchin with the promise of a coin when he returned. Then he jogged up the wide stairs, burst through the doors, and rapped sharply at Sir Manly's inner sanctum.

"Ah, Wycliff. There's been a bit of a fuss reported down by the Physic Garden in Chelsea." Sir Manly's moustache sported extra curls today and would have required an inordinate amount of wax to hold its extreme shape.

Wycliff bit back a sigh. He had just come from near there. If Lady Miles had imparted *that* bit of information, he could have saved himself a fair amount of time spent riding back and forth. He held in his frustration and asked a more pertinent question. "What sort of fuss, sir?"

"A body has been discovered that bears similarities to the limb that washed up. A Runner was sent at first, and he sent back word it was more our department. He is waiting for you there." Sir Manly waved a dispatch at him.

Had more parts of Mr Barnes escaped the crematorium after all? "I shall investigate immediately, sir."

Sir Manly handed off the dispatch and picked up another from his desk to wave it at Wycliff's head. "Good man. Report back when you're done."

Wycliff reclaimed his horse and retraced his steps. This time he bypassed the estate that held the small church, and continued on until he found a crowd gathered at the edge of a field adjacent to the Physic Garden.

*Not too far upriver from where the arm came ashore.* He hitched his horse to a nearby tree.

He found the Bow Street Runner scribbling in a notebook. The man looked up as he approached. He squinted and then tucked away his notebook. "You Wycliff from the Ministry of Unnaturals?"

"Lord Wycliff, and yes, I am an investigator for the Ministry." He surveyed the crowd. Men stood with arms crossed or clutching various farm implements. Women huddled close to the men, as though afraid of being snatched if they wandered too far.

"This was reported this morning. One of the locals said he saw a monstrous man out here last night, but the creature ran off when he hollered and fired a shot. He didn't get a chance to see what the monster had been about until first light, when he found...her." The Runner gestured to the sheet-covered form at his feet.

Wycliff knelt to lift one edge of the sheet. A woman lay underneath. She wore a torn shift that had slipped from one shoulder...where a stitched line bisected shoulder and upper arm.

"She appears to be all woman," he muttered. From a cursory glance, none of her limbs looked masculine. This was no remnant of Barnes, but another cobbled-together piece of flesh.

"It's the monster! Killing good people and doing that," a woman yelled from the safety of the large and gloomy-looking man beside her.

The crowd murmured agreement. "Ain't right, what he done to her. What sort o' monster chops up women?"

"Sort that lives with a dead mage," another voice called.

Wycliff narrowed his gaze at the assembled people. Was someone trying to implicate Sir Hugh Miles? They spoke out of fear and ignorance. The physician had his own laboratory and didn't dump bodies in open fields. Not that Wycliff had observed in his time under the doctor's roof, in any event.

"She was alive when I found her, poor mite." A scrawny man stepped forward, his cloth cap held in his hands and his vest hanging from too-thin shoulders.

"Are you sure?" Wycliff found the man's words

hard to believe. The woman looked as though she had been dead for a period of days, given the mottling under her skin. Or she might be one of the few Afflicted who were ambulatory for a period of time and then inexplicably fell permanently dead.

The man nodded and swallowed. "She were muttering, but I couldn't catch what she said. Then she pointed over that way, toward the Physic Garden."

Wycliff glanced in the direction the man indicated, but nothing struck him as noteworthy. The field ran up to the hedge that encircled the apothecary garden.

"She might have lived if I had found her last night, but I'm a little fellow and I wasn't going to search out here with that monster lurking in the dark." He twisted the cap in his hands, making the cloth do penance for his shortcomings.

"From the state of her wounds, I doubt she would have survived." Wycliff now had two bodies that had been stitched together. What was going on out here?

"What do you want done with her, sir?" the Bow Street Runner asked.

Wycliff dropped the sheet back over the woman. "Move her to the Royal Hospital—that's the closest place. Sir Hugh is otherwise engaged today, but there is another doctor who may be able to examine her."

At least the Runner was of some use—he had commandeered a cart to transport the woman. The body was lifted in, and with nothing more to see, the crowd dispersed. Wycliff mounted his horse and followed the cart on its short journey to the Royal Hospital.

The driver pointed the horse toward the wing that held the small infirmary and lecture room used for the SUSS meeting. As luck would have it, Wycliff spotted Doctor Husom as he dismounted. The doctor crossed the courtyard with two more men at his side.

Wycliff hailed him. "Doctor Husom, I require your expertise if you have a moment to spare."

The doctor looked up and handed the papers in his hand to a younger man at his side. "Of course. How can I help, Lord Wycliff?"

"A woman was found this morning not far from here. I need her to be examined, as there are *peculiarities* about her condition. Sir Hugh is unavailable at present and I believe it requires a surgeon somewhat familiar with Unnaturals." Wycliff kept silent on the rest. Better the doctor saw for himself.

"Peculiarities and Unnaturals? I am intrigued." A faint smile flicked over his lips. "My man will bring her to my examining room."

The much brawnier of the two assistants picked up the sheet-covered bundle from the cart and then trod behind the doctor. Wycliff followed them into the building and along a corridor. Doctor Husom opened the door to a room with a long, narrow window placed high on one wall. The sunlight illuminated the grey walls but didn't allow a view in or out.

A bench ran the length of one wall and another wall was taken up by white painted shelving. A large table dominated the middle of the room. The top appeared similar to marble in shades of grey and green.

"Marble?" Wycliff asked as he ran a finger along the cool surface.

"Slate. Unusual, I know, but it is waterproof and as such is much easier to clean. Neither does it stain. Not to mention its durability. Slate will last a lifetime." Doctor Husom collected an apron from a hook behind the door and slipped it over his head, before tying the ends behind his back.

The assistant laid out the woman and adjusted the sheet to fully cover her body. "Do you require my assistance, Doctor Husom?"

The doctor glanced at Wycliff. "No, thank you. I'm sure Lord Wycliff can assist if necessary. I assume you're not squeamish, sir, since you observed the meeting this week."

Wycliff nodded and waited until the young man was dismissed with a wave and had pulled the door shut behind him.

"Let us see what you have discovered." Husom removed the sheet and tossed it to the bench.

The woman's shift was dirty and torn, as though she had run through brambles and fallen to the ground. Perhaps she had fled from somewhere, which would account for the state of her hair and dress. Her long hair was tangled and matted and could have been dark brown or a paler shade under the filth.

The doctor cut the fabric away from her form with

large scissors, then tugged the ends free of her body. The ruined garment joined the sheet in a pile.

Once naked, her sad state was more evident. The woman's age was difficult to determine, even exposed as she was with all her faults and blessings laid bare. She could have been anywhere from her early twenties to late thirties. Her limbs appeared straight and well nourished, if one ignored the raised stitches made with large crosses.

Her skin was mottled much like the slate upon which she lay. She bore several wounds, all crudely stitched and none symmetrical. Her right arm was stitched at the shoulder, the left below the elbow. A red line of stitches encircled her left ankle and another the knee, but her right leg had only the one line of stitches at mid-thigh.

Wycliff stood at the end of the table by the woman's feet, the light coming in to the side. She resembled a painting or perhaps a sculpture—one depicting the horrors that awaited sinners in Hell. He drew shallow breaths as the sharp odour of death caressed his nostrils and demanded admittance.

Doctor Husom began his examination, working from head to toe. "Hmm...she appears to have been used for surgical practice."

"Is that common?" Wycliff wondered who would let student surgeons practice such deep cuts and sloppy stitching. What level of desperation drove a person to such extremes, or what amount of money?

The doctor shook his head as he ran his hands

down the woman's arm and splayed her hand to inspect her fingers. "No, but that doesn't mean it doesn't happen."

"Is the patient or her family compensated for volunteering for such practice?" He stared bankruptcy in the face, but no matter the amount of coin offered, he would choose life under a bridge to being strapped to a table while men sliced into his body.

Doctor Husom said, "That would be pointless, since it is conducted on the poor dead with no relatives to care what happens to their bodies."

Wycliff thought such deceased usually went through the doors of Unwin and Alder, but this woman's hairline was intact, with no evidence that her skull had been cracked open and her brain removed. There was also another niggling fact. "This woman was alive when she was found this morning."

Doctor Husom peered over the tops of his spectacles and three deep frown lines dug trenches from hairline to brows. "Impossible. Quite apart from the fact that no one could survive this, her skin shows the distinctive mottling of decay. She has been dead for some days."

War had proved one thing to Wycliff, and that was that men often survived impossible injuries while others succumbed to what appeared to be minor complaints. A person's determination to remain alive often played a bigger part than the extent of the injury. "The man with her said she was alive and whispering when he found her."

The doctor huffed. "He probably mistook air escaping her lungs from decomposition for whispered words."

Wycliff hoped the answer was that simple. London was becoming overrun with deceased individuals who refused to go quietly to their graves. "He was most adamant that she had spoken, and also raised her arm to point to the Physic Garden."

The doctor rested both hands on the slate and stared at the woman's abused body. "I say again, impossible. You have observed my work in making a corpse raise and lower a limb, but that did not mean the man was alive."

The doctor raised a valid point. Except the woman hadn't been attached to some galvanism device that used electricity to force a muscle contraction. She had been lying in a field. "Why are you so sure she couldn't have survived the surgery?" This was a doctor who pursued the study of the Afflicted and other Unnaturals. Why did he dismiss with such certainty the possibility of the dead talking?

The doctor picked up the corpse's left arm and held it on either side of the stitches that encircled the flesh just below the elbow. "These aren't just practice incisions and stitches. These are full amputations with a subsequent attempt to reattach the limb. Watch when I wiggle the arm." He twisted, and the bones on either side of the incision moved in different directions. "The bone is severed. Even if she survived one amputation, do you know many people who survive all four limbs being sawn off and reattached?"

Wycliff thought of the Afflicted hand that tried to escape its cage and the forearm someone had stitched to it. "Do all the limbs belong to her?"

The doctor's eyes narrowed. "What are you suggesting? That someone took pieces from several women and stitched them into one being?"

An exasperated sigh tried to worm up Wycliff's chest, but he held it in. For a doctor, Husom seemed distinctly lacking in imagination. "Yes. I believe that might be exactly the case. Is there any way to tell?"

Husom walked around the woman's body and lifted her arm, resting his other hand on her shoulder as he tested the limb. "I will need to conduct a thorough examination, including detaching the stitched limbs and measuring the bones to see if they match. I find your hypothesis most implausible, though."

What bothered Wycliff more was the smell of death rising from the woman. It was obvious she had died a few days ago, yet it was clear she had been running through fields and whispering to the living. "And yet I saw you use electricity to make a dead man raise his arm."

The doctor was silent for several long seconds with his head bowed, as though he prayed over the woman, or women, on his table. "It is one thing to bring an intact man back from death so he might return to his family. It is quite another to play God and butcher people to create a new whole from several pieces."

"An odd distinction to draw, is it not?" Wycliff studied the doctor and the play of emotion across the man's face.

He seemed to wrestle with some internal beast before whispering, "We all have lines we will not cross."

At least that was something both men could agree upon. Whoever had created such an abomination had crossed a line, and Wycliff would find him and bring him to justice.

"There is a possibility she was not the first. In the last month, have you seen a man pass through the medical school who was missing a substantial part of his head?" There was a chance the medical man who had taken possession of Barnes was standing in this room. Yet his reaction to cobbling together a human made Wycliff doubt he had had any part in it.

Doctor Husom walked to his bench and selected a blade and pair of tweezers. "We don't see many fatal injuries here."

The woman before them didn't appear to have any accidental injuries. What had been done to her had the look of cold deliberation. "Where do you procure your corpses for lectures?"

The doctor waved the scalpel toward the door. "The Chelsea pensioners. Those without families often bequeath their mortal remains to us, so that we might advance man's understanding of himself."

Wycliff needed a direction for his enquiry. He would start with trying to identify the woman. Then at least he could trace her last few days and see if anything matched what he knew of Barnes. "Is there someone here who can draw? I would like a sketch made of her face."

"There are a handful of artists among the retired soldiers here. Peters, the man who brought her in, will be able to find one up to the task."

"Have someone draw her face before you...disassemble her." The hospital was full of retired soldiers who would gossip like washerwomen if they knew what would occur in this room. Rumour already reached for Sir Hugh, and Wycliff would rather deal in facts than fear-mongering.

"I will cover her with the sheet while the man works. Let us do that first." The doctor put down his implements and fetched the discarded sheet.

Wycliff helped drape it over her form and up to her chin, to cover the scar around her neck. "Good. Once I have a drawing, I can leave her in your care while I attempt to discover who she was."

# 13

S*ir Hugh Miles the Chelsea Monster?*

*Woman Mutilated by Surgeon Found in Field.*

Hannah read the headlines aloud and then tossed the paper far away from her in disgust. "What a load of tripe! Can you not do something about such outrageous lies, Mother? Surely it is libel to say Papa could commit such a terrible act."

Seraphina waved a hand and the newspaper scuttled along the carpet to jump up into her lap. "Perhaps a spell that would stitch each wagging tongue to the roof of the owner's mouth?"

Hannah screwed up her nose. That sounded painful, to say nothing of the fact that a person would starve, or die of thirst, if their tongue were sewn to the roof of their mouth. She certainly wouldn't wish death on those ill-informed people pointing the finger at her father. "It doesn't have to be that extreme. You diverted attention when that horrid murder nearly ruined Lizzie's engagement ball."

Her mother waved her hands. The newspaper rose into the air and then burst into a ball of flames. The falling ash vanished before it could stain the white tablecloth. "Some rumours are strong, unfortunately, especially those fuelled by fear. But I will set something free to distract attention. Perhaps concerning the upcoming royal marriage of Princess Charlotte."

All through breakfast, thoughts swirled in Hannah's mind like hot desert sand caught by the wind. *Egypt* whispered through her head and became the buzz of locusts that would not be ignored. She excused herself from the dining room and let the noise be her guide. Hannah stood in the middle of the library and revolved slowly until a tug that was half physical, half mental pulled her toward a shelf.

"Aha!" Her hand rested on a heavy tome. *The Sacred Rites of Mummification in Egypt*. Perfect.

Hannah eased the book from the shelf and carried it to her favourite plush rug close to her mother's desk. Gathering her skirts under her, she sat cross-legged in front of the book.

Expectation built in her stomach as she opened the cover and leafed through the first few pages. Then disappointment doused the excitement in cold water. She couldn't read a word of the text, it being written in some cursive form of hieroglyphics. At least she could look at the pictures.

"Oh, I say," she whispered as another turn of the

page revealed a mummy in the process of being wrapped in linen.

The dry, tight skin over bones echoed the image of Lady Jessope and her devout fellow Afflicted. They were so like the image, only separated by thousands of years.

"What are you studying, Hannah?" her mother asked as she entered the library.

"Egyptian mummification. There is a startling resemblance between mummies and the most devout Afflicted who have denied themselves sustenance." Hannah turned another page where the priests placed herbs between the folds of linen as the body was wrapped.

Her mother stopped by her side and stroked Hannah's hair. "I believe your intuition has pointed our efforts in the right direction at last. I have been studying Egyptian beliefs. Did you know that during mummification the organs were removed and the stomach, intestines, lungs, and liver were all placed in canopic urns?"

"What of the heart?" Hannah recognised the organ missing from her mother's list.

"Ah. The heart of the matter." Seraphina waggled a finger at her. "The Egyptians believed the heart was the seat of the soul, and as such, it was always returned to the body."

Seraphina wheeled past her daughter to the large desk. She waved her hand and the scattered papers rearranged themselves. One drifted to her outstretched hand.

"The heart is the seat of the soul," Hannah repeated to herself. As she traced the detail on the drawing with a finger, she imagined a ceremony long ago to preserve a pharaoh. "Mummification was the process of preserving the body for life after death, which describes the Afflicted, for they live on after death. Oh, Mother. Does it not all seem too similar to be mere coincidence?"

Laughter drifted from her mother. "I keep telling you that you possess your own kind of magic. Your enquiring mind has put the answer within our reach at last. I can feel it. I will study what herbs were used in mummification. It is possible that the foundation of the spell used to create this dreaded curse will be found in that ceremony."

"I cannot even fathom why the French would create such an evil curse. It has spread death, misery, and suffering to many innocents." In the drawing under Hannah's fingers, the person being wrapped wore a serene expression, eerily similar to that of Lady Jessope.

"War drives people to do horrid things. Do not forget its first purpose was to assassinate me and remove me from the battlefield. Who knows—perhaps that in itself was retaliation for the French mage killed by our navy. In the months that followed my death, the French mage changed how the curse functioned. I and my two companions were poisoned via our tea and it worked quickly, for we all fell ill within two hours. The face powder took a few weeks before it claimed its victims."

Hannah considered the difference in how quickly the two poisonous potions worked. "Why do you think they changed it to have a delayed effect?"

"To give them more time to infect as many people as possible. A fast-acting epidemic would have seen us react quickly, and people would have been warned how it was spreading."

Hannah abandoned the book and drew her knees up to her chest. Her mother recounted a nightmare that, thankfully, had never fully been unleashed upon the population of England. "We are fortunate it was limited to two or three hundred of the *ton*."

Seraphina wrote with a quill as she spoke, the peacock feather swaying back and forth with each word formed on paper. "Indeed. It was not our enemy's original plan to target only the wealthy ladies of London. When Sir Ewan found the caves used by the smugglers to bring the barrels to English soil, they contained thousands of containers of face powder and snuff. If that cache had not been destroyed, they could have poisoned thousands of men and women at all levels of society."

Hannah's mind extrapolated what might have happened, and a shudder ran down her spine and raised gooseflesh along her arms. "With so many men and women killed to arise as the Afflicted, there would never have been enough *pickled cauliflower* to keep them all sustained. Desperation might have meant thousands unable to control their hunger, who would have murdered more innocents and created a legion of the shambling secondary Afflicted."

The horror played out in Hannah's mind with scenes of murder and chaos. Screams seemed to echo around the room as imaginary soldiers sought to drive back the ravenous Afflicted. Massive funeral pyres would have sprung up around the countryside as those cursed were driven into the flames. Thick black smoke would have blanketed the fields and spread despair.

Seraphina clapped her hands and Hannah's nightmare dispersed, to be replaced by soothing music. "Let us be thankful only two barrels of infected powder were mixed up by the smugglers. Sir Ewan prevented a most terrible fate for England, and the French ultimately failed to defeat us."

Hannah managed a smile as she thought of the handsome officer and lycanthrope. Would having a wolf shifter in the house be as disconcerting as living with a wraith? "We are indebted to the Highland Wolves. But now that we have our own mission, what can I do?"

Seraphina finished her task and dropped the peacock feather quill into its elegant silver holder. "Let us divide tasks. I will continue with my study on mummification if you would run an errand to the Physic Garden. I need a number of herbs that we do not grow here."

An idea flowed through Hannah, one that warmed

her cheeks with a slight blush. "I could call on Lord Dunkeith and ask if he could assist."

"An admirable idea. The garden is closed to the public and jealously guarded by the Worshipful Society of Apothecaries. But you cannot call upon his lordship on your own. It wouldn't be proper." Her mother picked up a shaker and dusted the page with sand.

Hannah's daydream of wandering arm in arm through the fragrant garden with a handsome lord vanished, the image torn apart by an interloper. "I could take Timmy for an outing."

Seraphina laughed. "Certainly not. We are still teaching him to mind his manners around us. He is in no way fit company to call upon a lord. Take Wycliff."

At that moment, as though summoned by Seraphina's call, the library door opened and the dark mood personified appeared. "Might I intrude, Lady Miles?"

Seraphina laced her hands on her desk as though she had been expecting him. "Of course. In fact, your presence is most timely."

"Oh?" Viscount Wycliff stepped further into the library.

"Hannah needs to run an errand for me to the Physic Garden and I suggested you might be persuaded to accompany her. She cannot call upon Charles Dunkeith on her own." Her mother gestured to her, sitting on the rug like a young child.

Wycliff turned to regard Hannah from under his dark brows. They weren't drawn close in a frown today;

instead, he wore a more open expression. "This is indeed fortuitous. I came to ask if I might use the carriage to do that very thing. My mare had quite a run yesterday and I'd like to rest her today, but I need to see the Physic Garden. A body was found close by there yesterday."

Hannah's attention perked up. "A body that requires your attention? Was it the one mentioned in the newspaper that had been most horribly mutilated? That those ghastly scandal sheets are trying to link to Papa?"

He inclined his head in her direction. "Indeed. The woman has been constructed in a manner similar to the hand and forearm I retrieved from the Thames. Doctor Husom is ascertaining for me whether the limbs belong to her or to others."

"Why don't you run along, Hannah, and have Old Jim harness the horses? That will give me time to ensure I have everything on the list." Her mother pushed herself away from the desk.

"Of course, Mother." Hannah closed the book on mummification.

A hand appeared before her face, as Lord Wycliff offered to help her rise from the floor. Not wishing to offend by refusing, she placed her fingers in his and he closed them in a hot grip.

Once she gained her feet, he bent to retrieve the book. "Shall I return this to its shelf?"

Hannah gestured to a low table. "No, if you could

leave it on the side table, please, I'd like to continue reading it later."

After Hannah found Old Jim and asked him to hitch the carriage and bring it around, she headed upstairs to her bedroom. She stared at her wardrobe and contemplated her limited choices. She chose a spencer in dark grey with ornate frogging that would match her sombre grey gown. Next she donned a bonnet with the same grey grosgrain ribbon before trotting down the stairs.

Wycliff waited for her in the yard and took her hand to help her into the carriage. Suspicion wormed its way through Hannah. Why was he being so...gentlemanly? She had grown accustomed to his rude and blunt manner. When he behaved in a civilised fashion, it was enough to make her think it must be an elaborate prank.

Then she chastised herself for such thoughts. Perhaps this was his normal behaviour when not set upon by the world. Her parents found quiet refuge in their home. Was it at all possible that the calm environment was rubbing off on their houseguest?

It was a quiet drive from Westbourne Green and down through Kensington to Chelsea. Hannah kept to herself and stared out the window, not wanting to bother Lord Wycliff with inane chatter.

Though she did want to bombard him with questions about the recently discovered body. Eventually curiosity got the better of her and she simply had to voice the most pressing of them. "Might I enquire, Lord

Wycliff, about the woman found yesterday? Did she possess any Afflicted limbs?"

"None appeared ambulatory or lively like the hand. I have had a portrait drawn to aid in my search to identify her." He spoke without looking at her, his attention fixed on the passing scenery.

In her mind, Hannah drew a line through *Afflicted limbs* and moved on to her next idea. "Do you think there is a connection between the limb that crawled from the Thames and this woman?"

Now he did turn to regard her. An odd feeling coursed through Hannah at being his sole focus. "They were both discovered not far from each other, and both bear similar surgical wounds. Beyond that, I cannot speculate until I know the results of Doctor Husom's examination."

Lord Dunkeith maintained a smart town house a mere stone's throw from the Physic Garden on the north side of Paradise Row. The carriage turned into the sweeping drive and came to a halt in front of the portico. There was no fence around the property and the lawns were scattered with large, spreading trees.

Hannah smiled to herself as Wycliff forgot his attempts at civility and jumped down from the carriage to bang on the house's front door. She might have known it was too good to last as she waited for the driver to drop the steps and help her down.

The house's glossy blue front door swung open and Wycliff disappeared inside, still without so much as a backward glance at Hannah. She waited in the tiled foyer as voices rose and fell beyond an open doorway.

Lord Dunkeith burst out of the room. He took her hand and kissed her knuckles with such enthusiasm that heat raced over her cheeks. "Miss Miles! What an honour to have you visit my humble home."

Hannah bobbed at her knees. "Lord Dunkeith, thank you so much for agreeing to see us when we have arrived uninvited."

"Nonsense." He beamed at her, a smile that conveyed warmth like brandy. "You and your father are the trailblazers in trying to find a cure for the Afflicted and I am most humbled to be of service."

"If it is not too much trouble, my lord, my mother requires a number of herbs that might be found in the Physic Garden." Hannah pulled the list from her reticule.

Lord Dunkeith scanned the list. "Feverfew, goldenseal, tansy, *cannabis sativa*...this is quite an eclectic mix."

Bother. If they did not grow in the Physic Garden, could they be found anywhere in England? "Do you think we can find them all? Mother wishes to prepare an ancient spell that may be the elusive key to the cure."

"Oh, yes. Most definitely. The Physic Garden is only across the road...if you would stroll with me?" He held out his arm and Hannah placed her hand on his forearm.

She glanced back to the viscount, who stood in the foyer with a familiar scowl on his face.

"Oh, be a good sport, would you, Wycliff? There is a basket and secateurs by the door. We'll be needing those." Lord Dunkeith waved at the basket before leading Hannah through the front door.

She bit back a laugh at the murderous look on the viscount's face, before she turned her thoughts to more pleasant topics—like the exceptionally good company of Lord Dunkeith.

"Have you always had an interest in potions, my lord?" They walked along the driveway to the road.

"Ever since I was a wee boy. Apparently I made the best pot of tea as a whippersnapper. It wasn't until a few years later that my gift for apothecary became evident and my parents realised that was how my after-mage gift manifested itself." Lord Dunkeith pulled her to a halt before checking for traffic upon the road. Then he escorted her across to the Physic Garden.

An eight-foot brick wall surrounded the garden and they stopped before the ornate wrought-iron gates. High above their heads, the ironwork met and held up the emblem of the Worshipful Society of Apothecaries. A golden Apollo held a bow in one hand and an arrow in the other as he overcame Pestilence, represented by a wyvern.

"A bit fanciful, isn't it?" Lord Dunkeith said as Hannah gazed up at the emblem. "Our motto is *Opiferque Per Orbem Dicor*, or *Throughout the world I am called the bringer of help.*"

"I cannot imagine any greater calling than relieving the suffering of others." She glanced back to Wycliff. Could any potion allay his suffering, or was it his soul that sickened, not his body?

Lord Dunkeith had extracted a key from his pocket and unlocked the gate. "Ladies first."

Hannah stepped into the garden and didn't know which direction to take first. Lime chip paths ran between beds. Some beds held neatly contained plants; in others, shrubs attempted to escape as they climbed over the hedging. She was glad to have a guide with whom to navigate the lush growth.

"This way first." Lord Dunkeith gestured down one path. "I am curious as to how the Physic Garden is relevant to your investigation, Wycliff?"

The gravel crunched behind Hannah as the viscount followed them closely. "A woman was found not far from here. She pointed in this direction before she died."

Lord Dunkeith stopped before a low shrub and took the secateurs from the basket in Lord Wycliff's hands. "A coincidence, surely? If the poor soul had been on the brink of death she could have been pointing at anything. Perhaps an angel come to reap her soul. Or it might have been a mere contraction as she died and of no import at all."

"Or it might have been a clue," Wycliff said as he held out the basket to receive the herbal offering.

# 14

"Who has access to this garden?" Wycliff asked. A heady aroma of both foliage and flowers drifted from the multitude of plants crammed into the gardens. A sneeze tickled at the back of his nose and he tried to shake it away.

"Only members of the Society and, as you can see, they do not often visit." Dunkeith gestured around them. The paths were empty and they saw only one other person, a gardener on hands and knees weeding between the bushes.

"Is there any record of who comes here? In particular, who was here yesterday?" The sneeze was back and this time Wycliff had to avert his face as the pollen tickled his nose and had to be expelled.

Dunkeith laughed and steered Miss Miles down another pathway. A willow hung over the path like a green veil.

"We all hold a key. But our secretary, Mr Mossman,

is an aftermage and he knows when each key is used." He stopped at a plant that looked much like all the others and snipped off a section.

"If you could provide his address, that would be most useful." Wycliff held out the basket and took the next smelly offering.

"Of course. I have his card at home and will fetch it when we return." Dunkeith waited as Miss Miles stopped and knelt.

She smelled a purple flower, and turned to ask Dunkeith a question about its properties with such an open smile that Wycliff frowned at the man. Why was she looking at him like that? Perhaps he was making her inhale a scent with some sort of hallucinogenic effect.

"Are there many more herbs to collect?" he asked, to move the interview along.

"In a hurry to be somewhere else, Wycliff?" Dunkeith helped Miss Miles to rise and they disappeared under a weeping branch of lacy foliage.

"Yes, actually—somewhere that doesn't smell like a cheap brothel," he muttered under his breath as he followed.

At last they were done, and Wycliff handed Miss Miles and her pungent basket of foliage into the carriage. "I'll not be returning with you," he said. "I am going to show the drawing around Chelsea."

"Very well." She clutched the basket on her lap as he closed the door and signalled Old Jim to drive on.

Wycliff had spent the previous day stopping pedestrians and showing them the sketch of the woman's face. Today he walked the streets once more, stopping everyone in his path to show the drawing in the hope that someone would recognise her. Many of the people took the opportunity to harangue him about the monster roaming the fields at night, as though he were personally responsible for it.

Every time he showed the sketch and someone shook their head, it reinforced his dread that he pursued a false trail. The woman might not even be from London. Since she had supposedly been pointing at the Physic Garden, he had begun with the assumption she might be local.

The day had lengthened into afternoon when he pressed the drawing under the nose of a man selling vegetables in the market.

"She looks familiar."

Wycliff was so used to hearing *no* and *sorry* that the words failed to register for a moment. "You know her?"

The man scratched his head and screwed up his face. "Think so. Looks like Charlie Warren's girl, Beth."

It was the advancement that made the miles he'd walked, wearing away the soles of his boots, worthwhile. "Where would I find this Charlie Warren?"

The street vendor waved back along the road. "Chelsea Bun Shop. He's one of the bakers."

Wycliff nodded his thanks and hurried along the road. At least Easter had passed and the winding queues for the spiced buns had gone. Even so, the Chelsea Bun Shop still drew a large crowd eager to sample the baked goods that bore the shop's name. The shop was still busy with many patrons. The interior was an odd homage to events over the last hundred years since the shop opened in 1711. A toy man wedged inside a bottle sat under a portrait of the Duke William. Models of soldiers in old-fashioned uniforms guarded the corners.

Patrons sat at small, round tables and nibbled their buns, accompanied by hot chocolate. Chatter filled the room and the noise pushed against Wycliff as he made his way to the counter and glared at the shop girl in her white apron. "Where would I find Charlie?"

Her eyes widened and her mouth opened and closed. Then she swallowed and gestured over her shoulder. "In back, milord."

He walked around the counter while the lass called fruitlessly, "You can't go through there, sir!"

The temperature in the working part of the bakery would have suited one of the levels of hell. Ovens lined one wall, fed by fuel underneath their scorched brick interiors. Gaping mouths had offerings given or taken by long-handled paddles.

"I must speak with Charlie," Wycliff announced. "Is he here?"

"Who wants to know?" A man in an apron covered in brown stains looked over as he slid a steaming loaf from a paddle to a tray to cool.

Wycliff held aloft the drawing. "I'm trying to identify this woman, who was found in the fields the other day."

"That's my Beth." A broad gent wiped his hands on his apron and approached, his gaze fixed on the drawing. "Is she all right? Where is she? She's been missing for over a week now and no one has seen hide nor hair of her."

Sweat trickled down between Wycliff's shoulder blades, partly due to heat and partly due to the news he now had to deliver. "I am sorry to say she is dead, sir. I am trying to determine what fate befell her."

The man went as white as though he had fallen into the flour. He whispered, *"No,"* before keeling over backward. A faint flour cloud rose from the impact as his colleagues rushed to help.

War had taught Wycliff not to assume how a man would react to news of this kind based on his physical appearance. The largest man could fall like a tree while insubstantial saplings held their ground. While he waited for the man to revive, he reviewed what little he knew. The woman had gone missing, therefore it was safe to assume she had not died of injury or sickness. She had a family who missed her, making it unlikely that her cadaver had been sold to a medical school.

The question he most wanted answered was, how had she ended up looking like a surgery practice doll?

Two men helped Charlie over to a stool by a window, where he leaned on the sill. Wycliff gave him the sketch and he clutched the paper in his hands. Tears meandered over his cheeks and one fell onto the page. "What happened to her?"

Wycliff rested his shoulder on the wall and let the

fresh breeze cool the sweat on his brow. "I was hoping you could help me determine that. She was found in a field not far from the Physic Garden two mornings ago. No one knew her identity, and I have spent yesterday and today showing that drawing in the neighbourhood. When did you see her last?"

Charlie traced the lines of the woman's face with a fingertip. "Just over a week ago. She had a cough and was going to see the doctor about it. She never came back. When I asked after her, no one knew where she had gone."

"How bad was this cough?" Perhaps the woman had taken a turn for the worse and expired on her way to the doctor. An opportunistic person might have sold her still warm corpse to the unknown surgeon.

The baker shrugged. "I didn't think it was that serious, but she said it kept her awake at night. Lemon and brandy didn't shift it, so she insisted on seeing one of them doctors about it." He screwed up his eyes and the tears trickling down his floury face turned into a rivulet.

"Do you remember the name of the doctor she saw?" How convenient if the physician she had visited turned out to be the one who had murdered her to possess her form.

Charlie shook his head. "Don't know. They hold a charitable surgery at the Royal Hospital twice a week and anyone from around here can go. It depends who was there that day. I can't believe she's gone. Are you sure it's her?"

Wycliff bit back a sarcastic retort about one dismembered corpse looking much like another. Miss Miles would probably frown and remind him of the father's grief. He chose a different tack instead. "Your daughter is the first person I have found who matches the sketch and who is missing. Did she have any distinguishing characteristics that could confirm her identity?"

Sad brown eyes lifted and fixed on him. "She only had one leg."

"One leg?" Unless Beth had grown a new one, this confirmed that at least one limb was not her own.

Charlie wiped both hands up over his face and spread flour into his greying hair. "Lost it as a youngster when she got run over by a carriage."

"Which one?" Had Beth's torso received one donor leg or two?

"You expect me to remember what carriage did it after all these years?" The baker eased out a crease in the paper where he had clutched it too tightly.

Wycliff squeezed the bridge of his nose. Lord save him from idiots and the bereaved. "Which *leg*?"

"Oh—her left. The wheel took it off just above the knee." He patted his own leg at mid-thigh.

That fitted with the scar Wycliff remembered on the body. Had someone tried to make Beth Warren whole again? But that didn't explain the amputation and reattachment of the other leg and both arms.

Charlie held the sketch closer to his chest and his voice dropped to a quavering whisper. "Can I see her?"

"That might not be wise, given it has been some time since her death." Doctor Husom had dismembered the woman to ascertain which limbs were hers and which might have belonged to other women. Given the father had fainted on the news of her death, finding his daughter a limbless torso might be too much for his constitution to bear. Wycliff would rather not have the man fainting away twice in one day.

The baker's bottom lip quivered. "Can I at least have her back, to bury?"

"Of course." He was sure that could be arranged. If Husom reattached most of the limbs and she were dressed in a high-necked gown, the man might never know what had happened to his daughter. Wycliff, on the other hand, did need to know.

"Did anyone go with your daughter to see the doctor, or is there anyone who might have seen her that day?" Answers led to more questions. At least now he knew the woman had gone to the Royal Hospital, but what had transpired from there?

The quiver of the lip became a full-on shake and Wycliff suspected a hysterical outburst was not far away. "Nancy—she's our neighbour. She went with Beth that day. She said Beth stayed to talk to the doctor and she came home alone."

Wycliff extracted directions on how to find Nancy, and a description of her. Then he told the bereft father he would ensure his daughter's remains were returned to him, omitting that she would need to be pieced back together first.

As Wycliff left the bakery, his feet began to protest the miles he had walked. He chided himself for growing soft and focused instead on finding the next clue in his puzzle. The baker had given remarkably good directions and soon he stood on the footpath and stared at a row of brick terraces. A woman he assumed to be Nancy, from the description given, sat on a step with a swollen belly as she knitted and watched a child at play.

He approached, but stopped out of reach of the child, who had grubby hands. "Are you Nancy? I am Viscount Wycliff, with news of Beth Warren."

"Turned up at last, did she? Where did she get herself to? Bet it involved a handsome face." The woman rolled a ball of red wool toward the child with her toe.

Interesting that she assumed her friend had disappeared because she was with a man. "She is dead, but I am investigating what might have happened to her."

"Dead?" Nancy dropped her knitting onto her belly and tears welled up in her eyes. "But it were only a cough, it weren't serious."

"That is why I need to know what happened before you left her. Her father says you accompanied her to the charitable surgery at the Royal Hospital?" Wycliff watched the child ignore the ball of wool and instead fix on a beetle crawling along the footpath.

"Yes. Once or twice a week they put up a tent in the grounds and you can go talk to a doctor for free. We both went. Beth had a cough and Fred here had one, too." She gestured to the child, who had the bright eyes and pink cheeks of rude good health.

Wycliff lifted his boot as the beetle made to crawl over his toe. "Did Beth have any plans for afterward? Perhaps a beau she planned to meet?" That would explain the handsome face comment. A jealous man seemed the most likely place to start. Perhaps she had stepped out with one and consequently enraged another. Was it too much to hope that she had been seeing a student doctor?

"No, she wasn't seeing anyone. I was only joking. She would have told me if she were. We didn't keep secrets between us. I had to leave 'cause Fred was restless and I left her talking to that big doctor." Nancy brushed aside her knitting and grabbed the back of the child's shirt to haul him back to the step.

A cold finger stroked down Wycliff's spine. "Which big doctor?"

She raised a finger to the child in a *stay* motion and then handed the boy a ball from her basket. "The one married to the dead mage."

"Sir Hugh Miles," Wycliff blew out the name on an exhale.

Nancy looked up and nodded. "That's the one. Last I saw Beth, she was chatting right happily with Sir Hugh."

Fuel would certainly be added to the rumours about Sir Hugh's being the Chelsea monster if *that* snippet got out.

"You know she's not the only woman gone missing lately." Nancy pulled her child even closer.

Cold dread seeped into Wycliff's bones. "There are more?"

She nodded and looked up and down the street. "People talk. Apparently there's some other women who haven't been seen for weeks, either."

Wycliff pulled out his notebook and extracted the scant rumours and scuttlebutt the woman knew. Then, with theories taking form in his mind, Wycliff hailed a hackney and headed for the Royal Hospital.

He found the doctor in his study, the door open. Wycliff rapped on the door. "Doctor Husom, have you further examined the woman?"

The doctor looked up from his papers and swivelled in his chair. "Yes. And I have some most interesting findings to share."

"As do I. The girl has been identified as Beth Warren. I found her father and learned she only had one leg." Wycliff gestured to his left leg and the approximate place her father had indicated.

The doctor pushed his spectacles up his nose. "Ah. That fits with my findings. Come, let us go to my examination room."

The two men spoke as they walked, their conversation limited to snatches when no one else passed by.

Doctor Husom waited until two red-clad pensioners passed, both leaning on their canes. "Her flesh deteriorates quickly. She will have to be buried or assigned to the crematorium very soon."

Why did she deteriorate and yet what remained of Mr Barnes showed no sign of rot at all? Even given the hand's Afflicted state, with no sustenance it should have begun to decay. "Her father wishes her body returned to him, although I would recommend a closed casket and removing the leg she is missing from her form."

The doctor coughed and drew a handkerchief from his pocket for the next cough. "It will be a case of replacing, not removing. I have removed all the limbs from the torso to facilitate my examination."

They reached the examination room at the far end of the building. The doctor pulled a key from his pocket and unlocked the door. "To ensure privacy," he said.

A sheet covered the form on the table, but the fabric sagged between the end of each limb and the torso. The doctor removed the sheet with a flourish. Around the woman was a series of dismembered pieces. "I have examined the bones and main tendons and arteries at the end of each limb. I have ascertained that *none* appear to belong to this woman."

"All four limbs are someone else's?" What sort of madman was he dealing with? Barnes had been taken after death, but what Wycliff had learned pointed to the probability that Beth had been murdered. And what of the other missing women? Had they provided the limbs that were stitched to Beth's torso?

Wycliff ran a hand through his hair. He had too many questions and too few answers.

"Yes." Doctor Husom stood to one side of his patient.

"So even the right leg, which was whole, has been removed and replaced?" Wycliff pointed to the limb in question. What drove a man to violate a dead woman in such a way?

"Correct. I also made a discovery in her throat. I have a drawing to show you." The doctor picked up a sheet of paper from his workbench.

"Oh?" Four limbs and none were hers. Had they come from two other women, or more?

"Her hyoid bone is fractured, which is an indicator of strangulation." The doctor pointed to the drawing that looked vaguely like a chicken's wishbone.

"Could this be proof of murder?" The crimes committed against the woman continued to mount. "She saw a doctor for a cough. Would that produce such an injury?"

The doctor pushed his spectacles further up his nose with one finger. "I've not seen a cough that results in this particular fracture. I am confident she met her end by the hand of another."

Wycliff held in a sigh. Whoever their surgeon was, apparently grave digging didn't satisfy their needs and they were killing the living for the limbs they desired. "Thank you, Doctor Husom, you have been most helpful. I have no further use for the remains, if you could ensure she is returned to her father for burial. Charlie Warren, a baker at the Chelsea Bun Company."

Doctor Husom picked up the leg that would not be

required. "Tell me, Lord Wycliff, did Sir Hugh make any discovery from the remains he took away?"

"What remains?" Wycliff searched his memory for other incidents. The only other parts found had been the arm and hand, and he wouldn't classify that as a body.

"It was two weeks ago. Sir Hugh had a torso with only one leg. All the other limbs and the head were missing. He asked me if I knew anything about it. The conversation became quite heated at one point, almost as though he didn't believe my denials." The doctor fetched a small silver basin with implements rattling inside.

"He never mentioned it to me." A leg and torso? Facts began to piece themselves together in his mind.

Doctor Husom looked up and narrowed his eyes. "How odd. It sounded similar to this case, as I believe the leg was kicking out at anyone who came too close."

A kicking leg? Most curious. What was the likelihood it had belonged to the supposedly cremated Mr Barnes?

It was time for Wycliff to return to Westbourne Green, and a conversation with Sir Hugh. Perhaps that surgeon required a *kick* as an *aide-mémoire*.

# 15

The next morning, the newspaper headline declared, *Monster Continues to Terrorise Chelsea Fields.*

Hannah held in a sigh at such a grammatical error. The fields themselves were probably ambivalent about the existence of a monster. It would be those out at night who feared encountering it. The subtitle posed the question, *Is Sir Hugh Miles experimenting on more than mice?* She tried to read the lines upside down as she buttered her toast, but had to resort to pulling the paper closer.

"What has caught your interest?" her father asked as he entered the room.

Hannah pushed the newspaper along the table. "Another ridiculous and fallacious article about the possibility of your being the creature that roams the fields around Chelsea. Now the scandalmongers speculate on what you do in your laboratory. It says young women are being snatched off the streets."

Sir Hugh carried his plate from the buffet and took his seat at the head of the table. "It will pass. These things always do. I suspect some people like scaring themselves with the idea of a monster stalking the dark, looking for a vulnerable victim. Usually these supposedly vanished young women have taken employment elsewhere or run away with a beau."

"But how can they make such horrible accusations about you? They are simply not true!" Her father was a good man and it riled Hannah to think people could believe such nonsense. If the stories continued, what would be next—a torch-carrying mob marching along their road?

Did women truly disappear without telling their friends or family? She could not imagine being so enamoured of someone that she ran away with him on impulse, without at least telling her mother first. No passion could be so all-consuming that a person forgot common decency and omitted to notify their worried family of their whereabouts.

"With Lord Wycliff investigating the matter, I am sure he will unmask the true monster in due course." Sir Hugh tucked a napkin into the top of his waistcoat and then picked up his cutlery.

Hannah poured coffee for her father and stirred in two lumps of sugar. "The article dwells on the wounds seen on the woman found near the Physic Garden.

Lord Wycliff said she bore many similarities to Mr Barnes' hand."

"Is that so?" Hugh looked up from his breakfast, his eyes narrowed with interest. "Ah, here is the man himself."

Hannah tried not to jump in her chair as the viscount appeared in the breakfast room. He had a way of walking without making a sound, even though he had hard soles on his boots.

"Tell me, Lord Wycliff, about this woman found in the fields. Was she Afflicted like Mr Barnes?"

The viscount nodded to Hannah and then collected a plate from the end of the buffet. "That I do not know, Sir Hugh. But the woman bears the same surgical scars as the hand and forearm we examined. Except in this case, all four limbs have been stitched to her torso."

Her father paused and his eyes rolled to one side in thought. "All four? That is remarkable. Are they all hers?"

Lord Wycliff took a seat across from Hannah, not the usual one diagonally opposite. "Doctor Husom is investigating that hypothesis. Are you aware of any medical school that amputates and reattaches the limbs of cadavers?"

Sir Hugh swallowed his mouthful before answering. "It would be a decidedly odd thing to practice. We normally just saw off damaged limbs and close over the wound. I've not heard of anyone having success in reattaching a limb. There are so many veins and tendons that must be joined. Even a third-generation aftermage with healing magic would struggle to complete such a surgery before the patient died."

Hannah recalled what she had witnessed during the SUSS meeting. "Could it be an extension of the resurrection challenge, Papa? Perhaps there is a scholar trying to determine the nature of life and how it can be infused into dead flesh?"

Her father chewed his mouthful and took his time to swallow and answer. "None of the others have mentioned it to me, but then, some keep their research closely guarded. I could not entirely dismiss the idea. What of Lord Dunkeith, Hannah? Did he strike you as the sort to be stitching together corpses in the parlour of his Chelsea mansion?"

Hannah laughed. Lord Dunkeith seemed far too civilised for such a monstrous undertaking. He had a disposition suited to mixing potions, not plunging his hands into the flesh of another. "After we gathered the plants for Mother, he showed me his work area. He uses the conservatory attached to the house. It is a place surrounded by plants and sunlight. Quite apart from not being the sort of place for such a gruesome undertaking, the walls are made of glass. Anyone could glance inside and see what he did."

"Perhaps he has a secret underground autopsy room elsewhere? I understand flesh lasts better in the chilled air below ground," Lord Wycliff said.

Hugh pointed at Wycliff with his knife. "Quite so, Lord Wycliff. No one can tell from a cursory glance what a man might be concealing far beneath the surface."

Wycliff narrowed his eyes and huffed. Then he made a show of flicking the newspaper open.

Hannah stared at her toast, but her throat seemed particularly dry. Society had cast her father as a mad scientist performing awful experiments in the underground laboratory. They didn't need such prejudices fuelled by false newspaper articles, or an investigator casting aspersions in the wrong direction.

"What of Doctor Husom, Papa? Have you seen his laboratory where he studies galvanism?" To master electricity seemed both terrifying and exhilarating.

"No, I have not. Although I am given to understand that he only possesses the equipment that he demonstrated at the meeting. I wonder if that would generate sufficient charge to animate an entire body, as opposed to making an arm rise?" Sir Hugh drained his coffee and set the cup to one side.

"Animating the body still does not return the mind. Even if he were successful, would he not create something akin to your secondary Afflicted?" Wycliff asked.

Sir Hugh screwed up his face at the idea. "An excellent point, although I would assume he tests it on cadavers who still possess their brains, whereas the secondary Afflicted have been robbed of theirs."

"Perhaps that is a question best addressed to Reverend Jones? It seems a philosophical debate as to the distinction between the matter of the brain and the content of a man's mind." Hannah thought the viscount raised an interesting question, but she refused to acknowledge its validity after his pointed remark concerning her father.

Sir Hugh tapped his blunt fingernails on the table. "I have made a decision, Hannah. I shall see if I can extract an invitation to visit Doctor Husom's laboratory. Leave it to me."

"Thank you, Papa." Hannah beamed. What a marvellous opportunity. How would she concentrate on her studies today?

Breakfast passed in animated conversation. Hannah would have lingered to listen to her father and Lord Wycliff discuss theories, except her mother summoned her to the library to begin their day. The morning passed in their usual task of notating the Unwin and Alder ledgers.

Hannah studied her list of aftermage donors they found among the names. "We could start our research now. I believe we have sufficient aftermage brains for a small control group. I will confirm with Papa."

Their next task would be placing the Afflicted into three groups to monitor their progress. Hannah sighed as she glanced at her mother's linen-covered form. If only they could find a cure or a way to reverse the curse. The ledgers were put aside as she turned her attention to Egypt and the mummification process.

It was midday when her father burst into the library waving a letter. "Excellent news, Hannah. Doctor Husom has agreed to see us this very afternoon."

"Oh! Marvellous." What an incredible opportunity to see the doctor's equipment up close.

Somehow, Hannah managed to complete her daily chores, listen to Timmy practise his reading, and take Mr Barnes' hand for a walk in the garden. All the while she checked every clock she passed, waiting for the hours to be whittled away.

At last Hannah waited at the bottom of the stairs for her father. She clutched the larger of her two reticules—a deep green one that swallowed her notebook and pencil. She would have much to reflect upon later, when she had quiet time to herself.

Lord Wycliff trod the hallway on silent feet and glared at her. "Might I enquire where you are going, Miss Miles?"

Even his dark expression could not ruin the tingle of anticipation building in Hannah's stomach. "Papa is taking me to see Doctor Husom's personal laboratory."

One black eyebrow shot upward. "Indeed? I thought you might have been about to embark on a shopping expedition, from the smile on your face. But then, I forgot for a moment that you are no ordinary young woman, to indulge in an activity as shallow as shopping."

She refused to let his grim presence douse her excitement. "I am looking forward to the pursuit of scientific knowledge, my lord, not the acquisition of a new shawl."

He grunted and with a brief nod, continued along the hall.

Dour man. Did he find no enjoyment in life? It was no business of his if she were waiting to peruse the shops. Venturing out with Lizzie was a type of anthropological expedition, as she watched how women behaved in the presence of small, expensive items. But sometimes regarding something beautiful was good for the soul. Not everything had to be deep and worthy in order to be enjoyable.

At last the stairs rattled with her father's weight as he descended to join her. "Ready, my girl?"

"Indeed." She practically bounced on her toes.

He held out his arm and escorted her to the carriage as though they made a society call. Their journey took a now familiar direction toward Chelsea and an area not far from Sloane Square. The carriage came to a halt outside a house that stood at the end of a long row of respectable pale stone terraces.

Hannah stood on the walk and looked up. "Oh." A tinge of disappointment crept into the single word.

Her father joined her. "Did you expect something else? A brooding gothic mansion like the one we live in, perhaps?"

How to sum up the disappointment that washed through her? "It just doesn't seem the sort of place for a laboratory and it's rather...plain. Do you think the doctor's neighbours know he experiments with cadavers and electricity within?"

"I suspect not. Most people keep their curtains closed at night and don't peer into their neighbours' windows." Her father rapped on the shiny black door and they waited on the patterned tiles that led from door to walk.

The house looked much like its neighbours, with the polished black railing out front. There were a few slight differences, however. Being on the end, it had large trees sheltering one side, their limbs reaching out to brush the masonry. Part of the roof line had glass, unlike the slate tiles on the rest of the roof, and a tall metal spire reached up to the cloudy sky.

Her father knocked again and they continued to wait. Time passed with her father rapping on the door ever more loudly and Hannah staring at windows.

"It appears some of Doctor Husom's neighbours do peer out the windows, Papa," she whispered as the people in the next house twitched their curtains aside to spy on their neighbour's visitors.

At length, the door was swung open by a dishevelled Doctor Husom. His brown hair stuck out at angles and something was smeared over one lens of his spectacles. A stained apron covered his clothes, and underneath he wore a shirt with the sleeves rolled up to the elbows. He stared at them for a long moment as if he couldn't think who they were. Then a smile broke over his face.

"Sir Hugh. I quite forgot you were coming. And Miss Miles, how excellent." He gestured for them to come in, peering around them to look into the street before closing and locking the door.

They stood in the small foyer in awkward silence.

The doctor took off his spectacles and cleaned them on his apron.

"How does your research progress, Doctor Husom? You have the look of being interrupted while deep in thought," Sir Hugh said.

"Quite. I apologise, I was in the middle of something and at first thought you were a tree knocking on the stone." He curled the arms of the spectacles around his ears and cocked his head at Hannah. "I trust, Miss Miles, that you are of a sensible disposition? Many would be disturbed by the nature of my research."

"I am no stranger to death, Doctor Husom, but I thank you for your consideration. I assist my father during autopsies and can assure you I am no delicate flower who will faint at the sight of blood." She straightened her back and met his gaze squarely.

He grinned and exposed even white teeth. "How blessed you are, Sir Hugh, to have a daughter with such a mind and temperament to assist you."

Her father laughed. "Our Hannah is extraordinary, just like her mother."

"Please follow me." Doctor Husom led the way up the stairs.

Hannah took in her surroundings as they climbed through the house. It seemed in many ways to be untouched by his occupancy. There were no personal effects such as pictures on the wall, no ornaments on end tables, no scattered belongings. Even the floors were bereft of carpets to offer colour or comfort.

The next staircase was narrower as they made their

way to the very top of the three-storey house. The laboratory took up the entirety of what would once have been the attics and servants' quarters. Walls had been removed to make one expansive space. Given the house seemed empty apart from the doctor, he presumably had no need for beds for his phantom staff.

Small windows at either end had been thinly whitewashed so they allowed light but not prying eyes. The skylight above their heads flooded the room with watery light and drew a grid on the floor from the metal dividing the panes. Three large tables were lined up underneath the skylight. One contained an odd assortment of shapes covered by a sheet. The other two were empty.

A large brass and copper tube the size of a horse's torso dominated the centre of the room. Cables sprang out from either end of the metal and ran upward, where they twisted together like snakes climbing vines in the jungle. They merged at a metal rod that hung down from the ceiling. More wires escaped from its hook and scattered over the ceiling to attach to other hooks holding aloft frames of varying sizes. Some frames were bizarre paintings, displaying body parts.

In one, a hand and arm eerily like that of Mr Barnes dangled by a hook through the top of the arm. Another held a cat, its four paws stretched to each corner.

Hannah clapped a hand over her mouth and she steadied her breathing.

"Are you all right, Miss Miles?" Doctor Husom

asked as he approached what were not paintings at all, but framed specimens.

"Yes. Silly that the sight of dismembered people does not bother me, but a cat makes my heart stutter." She stopped herself before she reached out and stroked the feline. The grey fur was tinged with silver and the long white whiskers drooped downward. Had some child lovingly patted the creature and now cried at night over its loss?

Doctor Husom gestured to the spread-eagled animal. "If it alleviates your distress, these creatures were all deceased when they came to my laboratory. The cat was trod on by a horse and killed instantly. Now that their time on this earth is over, these specimens are vital in advancing our knowledge of mortality."

"I did not mean to offend. I am merely surprised at the range of subjects you have. Sir Hugh mainly utilises mice. We have on occasion used rats, ferrets, and other small mammals, but mice have proven to be the most responsive specimens." When the opportunity arose, they also delved into the secrets kept by the Afflicted or other Unnatural creatures who ended up on her father's autopsy table. Still, a human cadaver didn't rouse her emotions as much as a once loved pet stretched out for examination.

Her father was walking around the room, stopping at each instrument or specimen and staring as though he stood in an art gallery enjoying the works on display.

What struck Hannah about the laboratory was its

order, at odds with the doctor's appearance. Everything was clean, the floors were swept, notes made neat stacks, and even the equipment seemed aligned with invisible marks on the floor.

"Have you had any success in animating anything larger than a limb, Doctor Husom?" she asked as she peered at the array of copper wires and tubing used to conduct electricity.

He ran a hand through his tousled hair and made another piece stand on end. "Not yet, although I believe the key lies in generating sufficient electricity for the task."

Sir Hugh stared upward at the cables clinging to the lightning rod. "Like a lightning strike?"

"Yes. But the problem is being at home when nature strikes. I missed the last storm, as I was working at the hospital." He cast his eyes downward, as though embarrassed at the lost opportunity.

Her father laughed. "That is easily remedied—I'm sure Sera would be happy to oblige. Tell me a day and time you will be at home and I'll have her send a storm to your lightning rod."

"Truly?" The doctor's eyes widened and he gestured toward the idle equipment. "That would be marvellous. Shall we say Sunday night at seven o'clock?"

"Make sure you're here to throw the switch on that machine and my dear wife will deliver as much electricity as you need." Sir Hugh winked at Hannah.

Hannah glanced from her father to the doctor.

"Perhaps Doctor Husom would grant me the great honour of assisting? I can also relay to Mother whether the lightning was enough, or if more were needed." It was presumptuous of her to insert herself into his research, but the opportunity was too amazing to let slip past.

The doctor rocked back on his heels and frowned. "I usually work alone."

"Of course. I understand." That would teach her to be so forward. A lady should wait to be invited to an experiment. Hannah buried her disappointment and turned to examine the shape under the sheet.

"But I would be most grateful for Lady Miles' assistance, and yours, Miss Miles, if you could spare the time." He recovered his composure and his eyes shone behind his spectacles.

"It would be wonderful. Thank you for the opportunity." She was as giddy as though a handsome noble had asked her to dance. But if she were to be of use, she would need a better understanding of his work. "Would you mind explaining why you use such a variety of subjects?"

He beamed and gestured to the frame holding aloft the arm. "Of course. I am investigating the flow of electricity through different creatures with varying muscle and tendon compositions..."

Time passed in a marvellous afternoon of scientific discovery. Hannah left the doctor's home feeling as though she had consumed a bottle of champagne and danced all night.

"Doctor Husom is on the brink of an incredible discovery, don't you think, Papa?" Hannah asked as she took her seat in the carriage.

Sir Hugh chuckled at her as he signalled for Old Jim to take them home. "There is certainly an interesting application in galvanism. If he succeeds in restarting a dead heart, we will see whether any Afflicted wish to attempt the procedure."

Hannah leaned back against the blue silk lining of the carriage. If it took a lightning strike to restart a heart, would any of the Afflicted want to be the one standing in place when her mother called down Nature upon their heads?

# 16

Hannah went to bed that night and dreamt of lightning strikes and watching body parts reanimate. Then a puppy wandered through the dream and she had to grab it before the doctor strung it to a metal frame.

She awoke the next morning and scrubbed her hands over her scalp. "I need to spend more time with Lizzie and less with dismembered bodies."

What Hannah needed was a lighter activity. Today, she and Seraphina moved outside to enjoy the sunshine. Hannah sat on the rear steps and laughed so continuously that her sides ached and tears rolled down her cheeks. Even her mother, the terrifying undead mage, laughed hard enough to blow the veil away from her face.

The source of their mirth were the family chickens, and one determined lad.

Timmy rubbed his hands together, crouched low,

and then leapt upon his target. As he landed in the dirt with an *oomph*, the chicken squawked and flapped her wings as she ran to evade him. "This is useless!" He rolled onto his back in the dirt and stared at the sky. "Why am I trying to catch chickens anyway?"

"Because chickens, like people, can get sick. This is a way for you to exercise your gift," Seraphina said.

"The only thing I am exercising is my legs, my lady." The lad crossed his arms in what appeared to be an act of passive resistance to the idea of diagnosing chickens.

Hannah bit back her humour. Timmy needed a hand; he couldn't practice his gift if he couldn't catch anything. "He has a point, Mother. Chickens are rather difficult to catch when they are in a capricious mood."

Her mother's head turned as she tracked the chickens running around the yard. "I shall even the odds in your favour, my lad. I shall slow them down."

Percy the peacock sat to one side, partially obscured by the foliage of the forest. His all-seeing eyes were draped in the grass under the trees.

"Come, my friend, and lend the chickens some of your dignity." Hannah's mother reached out a hand and the peacock strutted over and rubbed his head against her palm. There was a special relationship between a mage and a peacock. Their feathers were a necessary ingredient in many spells, and their touch could augment a mage's power.

"Thank you." Seraphina curled her fingers as though she had caught some essence from the peacock.

She brought the closed fist to her face and whispered before flinging the unseen contents at the chickens.

All at once the chickens squawked and flapped into the air. Then they returned to the ground, but their actions were now more tortoise-like. Time had been slowed down for them and each chicken took slow, measured steps as though she waded through pudding.

The lad glared at the fowl from his spot on the ground. Hannah jumped to her feet and walked behind a chicken that laboured to take one step. She picked up the bird and tucked her wings against her sides as she carried her. Timmy sat up. Now that Hannah had caught a feathered patient, he appeared more interested than sullen.

She lowered herself to the ground next to him, holding the chicken under one arm as she put the other out for balance. "Do you want to hold her now?"

"She won't peck?" The youth glared at the chicken as though he expected it to grow teeth and take a piece out of him.

"No. Stay calm and she won't panic and struggle to get free. Although my mother's spell has slowed them down quite considerably." Hannah placed the chicken in the boy's lap and placed his hands over her wings to hold her still.

"However you use your gift on a person, do the same with the chicken," Hannah instructed quietly from beside him.

He nodded, his shoulders heaved in a deep sigh, and then he closed his eyes. His head nodded forward and brown hair brushed his face and covered the silver scar at his hairline. After some time he opened his eyes. "I don't feel anything."

"That's fine. Let her go and we'll catch another one." Hannah gestured to the others taking exaggerated movements, as though their feathers were covered in honey.

Timmy placed the chicken on the ground and she moved at a glacial rate toward a shrub to peck at insects.

Hannah caught another chicken and they did the same thing. Timmy laid his hands on the bird for a few minutes and then shook his head. Hannah tried not to be discouraged as she caught number three.

After stroking this one's feathers for a quiet moment, he opened his eyes and grinned at Hannah. "This one has a sore tummy and it feels like something is stuck."

Hannah nudged him with her shoulder. "Well done. It sounds like she might be egg bound. We are lucky you caught it early—a chicken can die if she doesn't pass the egg."

"Oh. What do we do now?" The lad held the chicken closer to his chest as she slowly closed her eyes.

"Run inside and ask Cook to boil a pot of water," Seraphina said.

"You can't eat her just because she's sick!" Timmy's eyes widened and he curled his slender body around the chicken.

Hannah laughed and petted the chicken's head. "No one is going to eat her. Steam will help her pass the egg and so will a warm bath, if she will cooperate."

At that moment Lord Wycliff pushed through the back door and trotted down the steps. He stopped at the bottom to frown at the chicken, before glancing to Hannah and her mother. "Lady Miles, Miss Miles."

Hannah looked up at him and a spike of mischief burst into life inside her. "Timmy is practicing his gift on the chickens, my lord. Would you like him to take your hand and see what ails you?"

His dark eyes narrowed. "No. If you will excuse me, I have business in London." He walked around the chickens and strode across the yard to the stables.

"Now, now, Hannah. It is my job to tease the viscount. You are supposed to be the gentle one," her mother whispered under her breath.

They finished wrangling the chickens, all of whom showed no signs of illness. The egg bound hen was treated to a steam bath over a pot and then tucked up in a warm box to help her pass the obstacle. Seraphina took Timmy to the library to work on his reading and writing, leaving Hannah free for the afternoon. Not that she actually had free time, but another task to put her mind to—finalising Lizzie's wedding arrangements.

Hannah washed and changed and was conveyed to Mayfair. But somewhere during the ride, the gaiety of the morning was washed away by more sombre thoughts.

At the Loburn house, she stared at her tea and wished the steam would form the answers she required.

Hannah was supposed to be studying the floor plan for the ball. Instead, she fumed over the way the newspapers had latched onto the idea of her father's being a murderous monster and wouldn't let go. Her mother crafted rumours about the forthcoming wedding of Princess Charlotte to the impoverished Prince Leopold, but even that couldn't distract the people from their gossip.

What Hannah needed to do was identify the person who was truly responsible. But who sought to create a new whole from disparate pieces? Her mind turned to three men, each with his own methods and each with his own reasons for wanting to create immortality.

Reverend Jones turned to prayer; Doctor Husom used galvanism; and Lord Dunkeith, with his aftermage gift, brewed potions. Could one of them be responsible for the monstrous crimes laid at her father's door? Two of the three had no medical training. Could that explain the crude stitches that had bound Mr Barnes's hand to the forearm of another? To Hannah, the irregular size and shape of the stitches was a clear indicator that her father could not possibly be culpable.

The three men she considered all frequented Chelsea and they all pursued the same dream. But none of them struck her as a deranged murderer. Not that her judgement was to be relied upon in such matters. While she had taken an instant dislike to Lady Gabriella Ridlington, she had never imagined the woman was helping her lover murder servants so they could scoop their still warm brains from their shattered skulls and consume them.

"Have you heard a word I just said, Hannah?" Lizzie tapped her on the arm.

Hannah shook her head. "I am sorry, my mind was elsewhere."

"What on earth could occupy you more than arranging my wedding?" The tiniest frown marred the bride's forehead.

Hannah had been called upon to help arrange the wedding, timed for the month after the royal wedding. Her task was to mark on a drawing of the ballroom where her mother would set enchantments for the wedding celebrations. But instead of true love, cake, and magical butterflies, Hannah's mind was full of severed limbs and a creature hiding in the shadows waiting to snatch a victim. "Murder, dismemberment, and the Afflicted," she confessed at last.

"How horrid! We shall institute a new rule that you are to leave such dreadful thoughts on the doorstep." The table before them was piled high with short lengths of ribbon in varying hues of pink, cream, and green. Lizzie dropped a pink ribbon and picked up a lighter shade. She was determined to find the perfect colours to feature in all the decorations.

Hannah thought it somewhat like a general trying to decide on the exact shade of red for uniforms before sending out the infantry to be shot. Not that marriage was anything horrid. Lizzie would marry her duke and live out the fairy tale. Rather, it seemed such a trivial detail when everyone's attention would be focused on the bride and groom themselves.

"Another investigation for Viscount Wycliff?" Lady Loburn asked. She examined the pages of a large illustrated volume of flowers.

The wedding would have enormous floral arrangements, if they could settle on which flowers to include. Then Lady Miles would make the seeds flourish and bloom in special containers, once they picked seeds upon which she might cast her spells.

"Yes. His investigation is tied to the Chelsea monster and the types of surgical procedures conducted on the discovered bodies. The viscount is trying to ascertain who is responsible." The man's image flitted through her mind. Even her most private moments were not spared his presence.

Lizzie dropped the ribbons, but due to their insubstantial weight, they fluttered to the table. "Mother, say something to Hannah. This talk is most disturbing."

"Real life often is, my treasure. Surely there is a simple explanation? Do not student surgeons undertake such work?" Lady Loburn made a note on the sheet of paper next to the book.

"They do, but there are certain...peculiarities to this case that have prompted Lord Wycliff to investigate. It is possible someone trying to find a way to reverse the Afflicted's condition might be responsible, but the newspapers seemed determined to see my father held accountable." Hannah put down her tea and picked up a selection of ribbons to sort.

"Whatever your father is about, I am sure his motives are honest and well intentioned." Lady Loburn put a green ribbon marker in the large volume.

Hannah glanced up. "You sound as though you believe the rumours."

Lady Loburn pushed the book to one side and cleared a space for the ribbons Lizzie had selected. "I have known your mother all my life, and your father for over twenty-five years. I was by your mother's side when she had to fight for her position at court—something that should rightly have been bestowed on her as a mage. There is only one thing I know for certain. Sir Hugh would do *anything* for your mother, such is his all-consuming love for her."

"Father loves me, too," Hannah whispered. A heavy lump settled in her stomach. Lady Loburn was right. Her father would do anything for his family. *Oh, Papa, could it be true?*

"Do you really think Sir Hugh would cut people up?" Lizzie's eyes were wide and her delicate complexion even paler as she considered such an idea.

"Of course he does," Lady Loburn scoffed. She rose and walked around the table to survey Hannah's drawing. "That is what battlefield surgeons do, my child. Many men required amputations after a skirmish."

Hannah picked up a pencil and drew an X at the base of the stairs on the plan. The first enchantment should envelop people as they descended to the ballroom. "Whatever surgeries Father might have performed, they do not make him capable of the monstrous things the newspapers claim. There are rumours of women abducted off the streets and most horribly murdered for their body parts. Men now patrol the night, intent on discovering the monster."

She glanced at the floor plan and her mind split in two directions. Part of her calculated how far people should walk across the floor before enchantment number two was released. The rest of her mind worried at the allegations against her father like a terrier with a bone. "Father is not the only scientist in London with an interest in finding a cure for the Afflicted. Doctor Husom experiments with galvanism, which is a way of using electricity to animate limbs. Reverend Jones believes in the power of prayer, and Lord Dunkeith seeks an answer among potions and herbology." Of the short list of suspects, Doctor Husom seemed the most likely. Hannah kept seeing the arm rise on a corpse, and the pieces framed by copper and hanging in his laboratory.

Lady Loburn tapped a spot on the drawing halfway out onto the floor, and Hannah drew another X for the second enchantment. "Ah! Charles and Diana, there is a sad tale. Such a tragedy for Lord Dunkeith," Lizzie's mother said.

"What tragedy?" Hannah thought the man a vision of happiness. Certainly he had everything laid at his feet—good looks, charm, wealth, and a title.

"Well, more accurately, the tragedy befell his fiancée." The marchioness rummaged through the ribbons and selected a dark green that reminded Hannah of moss under a shady tree.

"I did not know he was engaged." A creamy pink leapt out at Hannah, the perfect shade to complement the moss green in Lady Loburn's hand.

Lady Loburn took the ribbon that Hannah offered and laid it next to the green. "He is not any longer. He and Lady Diana Morgan were quite the whirlwind courtship of their season. The two were in love as much as are Lizzie and her darling duke, and we all anticipated their wedding."

"Lady Diana Morgan? I know that name." Lizzie handed her mother a pin to secure the two pieces of ribbon together.

"She was one of the first to die in London from using the face powder." Lady Loburn's voice dropped in tone.

Now Hannah placed the name—one of the many Afflicted who existed in private, protected by their families. Her needs were met by Unwin and Alder and their monthly delivery of *pickled cauliflower*. "Oh. How sad. As one of the Afflicted, she could not marry. Did Lord Dunkeith set her aside?"

Lady Loburn dropped her hands to the table and a sigh came from her hawk-like frame. A wistful light appeared in her eyes. "Far from it. He was most determined to stand by her side. His family threatened to cut him off if he did not distance himself from her. Not only is she prohibited from marrying, but even if she did, she cannot fulfil her wifely duty of providing an heir. He was devastated. Apparently he still sends her flowers every week, made to resemble her wedding bouquet."

The tragic image speared Hannah's heart. Such devotion beyond even death. Imagine sending your beloved a wedding bouquet every week. "I now understand his determination to find a cure. If her heart can be restarted, they can resume their lives together."

She had been to his home where he worked in the light and airy conservatory. Plants had draped the walls and hung from the ceiling. That had not been the workshop of a madman who dismembered bodies. How could a man who loved so completely even contemplate taking the life of another? No. She discarded the very idea.

More and more she wondered about the mysterious Doctor Husom. And who knew, perhaps there was a skeleton rattling in the depths of Reverend Jones' closet.

"Now let us return to another fairy-tale love—Lizzie's wedding. How many layers should the cake have?" Lady Loburn asked.

Lizzie erupted in joyful suggestions and while Hannah commented with her favourite colour of icing and decorations, her mind returned to the monster who laboured at night to dismember a woman and reattach limbs. Who was he? If only the figure would step from the shadows, she would know whom to accuse.

She prayed it wasn't her father.

# 17

Wycliff had wanted to question Sir Hugh in private, without his daughter or wife present. Yet the large man proved slippery to catch. He evaded Wycliff's questions by being called away suddenly to the Repository of Forgotten Things and did not return that night or the next day.

While he lay in wait for an opportune moment, Wycliff organised his notes about his investigation. On the sheet of paper bearing things to follow up, he noted Doctor Husom's information about the kicking leg Sir Hugh had taken away. It had to be another part of Mr Barnes, but why had Sir Hugh not mentioned it?

Another matter of concern was the reports of missing women. Now that he had asked the Runners to keep their ears open, his pigeonhole at the Ministry was stuffed with slips of paper bearing names, descriptions, and last known whereabouts. Most might simply have moved to another area without a forwarding address. If even a few were possible donors of the limbs attached to Beth's torso, the monster had a large appetite and had to be stopped.

With no other direction in his investigation to suggest who might have strangled and dismembered Beth Warren, Wycliff knew what he had to do to advance the case. He waited until full dark and the household had settled into sleep. Even the servants slumbered in their rooms tucked up under the roof. He crept from the Miles house on silent feet and headed across the road to the open fields.

He walked until he found a stand of trees that offered protection from any other nocturnal eyes in the area. He drew a deep breath and steadied his nerves, then let what lurked inside him...out.

The world around him changed and he stayed still among the trees while his vision adjusted. Night was now like day to him. Things unseen by human eyes were now revealed. Trees emitted a fine green mist as they exhaled. The edges of buildings were blurred, as though the lines of a drawing had been rubbed with a finger.

On silent feet, he loped across the field. Up ahead, a man wandered through the grass. He shook his head and wrung his hands as he muttered. As the man passed a hedge, the hawthorn branches brushed through his insubstantial form. Wycliff gave the figure a wide berth, so he didn't attract the ghost's attention.

In the few times he had let this form loose, he had learned one startling thing. The dead wandered the earth, unseen by the eyes of the living. Ghosts were made substantial—or at least of thicker stuff, like their equivalent of a pea-soup fog. What would he see if he encountered one of the Afflicted in the dark? Would they appear as a ghost or as one of the living?

He ran toward Chelsea and only slowed as the flickering lights behind windows stabbed through the haze. Wycliff kept to trees and hedges and let the shadows roll over him to hide him from sight.

The vigilante group was easy to avoid. The men were noisy and the lit torches they held aloft shone like small suns. He padded close enough to catch their words, in case they had discovered anything in their rounds.

"Ain't right, cutting up Beth like that and then dumping her body in the field," one said.

"We'll catch him, then he'll be the one gettin' cut up," another man replied.

"Strung up first, then cut up!" another jeered.

*Idiots.* Mob mentality very rarely resulted in justice. Evidence needed to be appraised with a calm, rational mind, not one soaked in alcohol and fear.

Wycliff left the men expounding upon what they would do if they caught the Chelsea monster and headed northeast, toward the crematorium. He paced the hedges and sniffed the air. The smell coming from the very brick wormed up his nostrils and burrowed into his mind. He shook his head, but the odour refused to budge.

He followed the hedge around the side of the

building and peered through the wider gate for carts. Puffs erupted from the mounds that dotted the lawn. A grey rounded cloud escaped from one and drifted away. Were these the cremated dead? He wondered if he dared ask Lady Miles.

Not finding any clues, he let the smell drive him away and back across the fields. The pleasant aroma of damp earth drifted up with each foot he placed, and removed the acrid smell from inside his head.

For hours, he wandered around Chelsea and found nothing. A different kind of heat prickled along his back and warned of approaching dawn. He must head back to Westbourne Green. He veered northwest to cross through Brompton. The whimper caught his attention first and as he neared, it turned into ragged sobs.

Wycliff ducked behind a large copse of trees with shrubs and ferns growing around their feet. He dropped low to the ground and peered at the figure.

A woman with long, dark tangled hair held out her hands in front of her, stumbling blindly across the meadow as she wept. Her shape shimmered like moonlit water. She wore a dirty, torn shift that tugged at Wycliff's memory. When she turned her face to the sky, the memory took sharp form.

*Beth Warren.*

Gossamer threads tore from her gown and ran behind her, where they attached to the shifts of two other forms. Both had long, dark hair, like Beth. One scratched at her arms incessantly. The other clutched her belly and moaned.

Three women, bound together. A shiver ran over his form. Stitched together in death as their bodies had been in life. Here was the chance he needed, if he could elicit anything sensible from any of them. He emerged from his hiding place and approached the women slowly.

"Help me. I cannot find my way home," Beth rasped on seeing him. When she turned, the other two women turned with her.

Another thing he had discovered was that the dead had no fear of him, as though on some instinctual level, they turned to him for help. Wycliff wondered what to tell her. She could no longer go home, but he wasn't entirely certain what the alternative was for her or how to send her there.

"What happened to you, Beth?" he asked, projecting the question directly into her phantom mind.

"The doctor...the doctor said he would heal my cough, but my throat is ever so sore now." She clawed at her neck.

Doctor Husom had said the woman had been strangled. Little wonder her throat was sore.

"He gave me some medicine for my cough, but it made me ever so sleepy." She held out her arms and stared at her hands. "I don't feel right. My arms and legs are numb and tingly."

When her shift slipped down, a silvery line of

stitching showed around her shoulder. If a body were dismembered and put back together, did the ghost retain its phantom limbs or the ones belonging to others that were sewn to their torso? Beth's ghost possessed two legs and walked without the aid of a stick. The women behind her were likewise intact.

Perhaps death remedied what life had taken away.

"Who are the others, Beth?" He gestured with his head toward her companions in death.

"Nell and Tabitha are my sisters. We three are one," she said.

He tucked the names away. He was certain that both were on his list of missing women, but he would need to consult his notes. "Did they see the doctor, too?"

"Nell itches and Tabitha is sick. We all need medicine," Beth spoke for the other two.

Wycliff assumed Nell was the one scratching herself like a dog with fleas. Tabitha must be the one clutching her middle.

"Which doctor gave you the medicine?" Had there been more in the medicine than something for a sore throat or an itch? A woman who had fallen asleep would be easier to move to another location and, he hypothesised, strangle while unable to fight back.

She shook her head and placed her hands against her ears. "It hurts. My throat hurts."

"Who, Beth? Who was it?" He wanted to grab her and shake the information loose. But he couldn't.

"The doctor at the surgery." She waved one arm in

the general direction of the Royal Hospital. Then she fell to the ground and curled up in a ball. The other two women lay on either side of her and covered Beth with their arms, as sobs racked their bodies.

It had to be Sir Hugh Miles. The last man to be seen with Beth. Would he find that Sir Hugh was likewise the last to be seen with the other two? Not that Wycliff could present the word of a dead woman as testimony. Nor would he be getting any more information from her tonight.

The sobs rose in pitch and became wails, each one a slither of sound that hammered into his ears. The dead women resembled one of the mounds puffing smoke behind the crematorium as all three keened and their cries became visible in the chill air.

With no more he could do, Wycliff hurried back to the Miles house, regained his human form and senses, and reached his bed just as the birds roused from the hedgerows to greet the dawn. He fell into a deep sleep and only arose close to midday.

While he slept, someone seemed to have crept into his room and stuffed wool into his ears and rubbed him all over with embers. His head felt worse than a hangover from cheap gin and his skin ached as though abraded with fire. He poured cold water into the basin on his dresser and immersed his whole head. Only when his lungs protested did he emerge from the chilly water and towel his hair. After a shave and a change of clothes, he once more felt normal.

What he needed were books concerning the dead

and ghosts to determine if he could elicit more information from Beth's spectre or the other two attached to her. Ignoring the growl of his empty stomach, he headed for the library.

He pushed open the door without thinking and found Lady Miles deep in conversation with a gentleman, who leaned over the desk and gestured to markers on the map. The man's mere presence made a ripple flow down Wycliff's back, as though all the hairs stood on end. That was all it took for him to recognise the lycanthrope, Sir Ewan Shaw.

Sir Ewan looked up with a piercing blue predator's gaze as Wycliff advanced across the carpet.

"Ah, Wycliff, we missed you at breakfast. Are you acquainted with Sir Ewan Shaw?" Lady Miles gestured from one man to the other.

"By reputation." Wycliff inclined his torso. "Sir Ewan."

"Lord Wycliff. Lady Miles said there was a personal matter upon which I might be able to advise you." The man's handsome face remained impassive as he regarded Wycliff.

"You are misinformed. I am not in need of advice." The mage needed to stay out of his business. His residence under her roof didn't give her an invitation to meddle.

"Forgive me, sir, but I beg to differ." Sir Ewan took a step forward and then halted. He narrowed his eyes and his fine nostrils flared. "What are you?" He enunciated each syllable clearly.

"An abomination. Or that is what most of society declares me to be. That, and they say I am incurably rude, with no redeeming features apart from my title." Wycliff clasped his hands behind his back and sucked in a short breath to stand his ground under the inspection. What had the wolf perceived that had escaped the notice of everyone save the mage?

Sir Ewan remained still, but focused, with tense shoulders, as though he coiled his muscles before pouncing. He cocked his head and seemed to peer through Wycliff to what he hid inside. "I am not sure I can assist in this matter. It may be outside my expertise. But Lady Miles knows where to find me should you wish to discuss your particular...case."

"I can assure you there is nothing to discuss." He dug his nails into his palms as the lycanthrope continued to hold his gaze. A small voice whispered that he ought to lower his eyes and expose his throat—for only in society's eyes did Wycliff outrank him—but he ignored it.

"As you wish. Lady Miles, a pleasure as always." Sir Ewan bowed to the dead mage. As he turned to leave the room, he passed close to Wycliff, his gaze flitting sideways. "I have one piece of advice to share," he murmured. "If you don't make peace with it, it will destroy you." Then he continued on his way.

Wycliff waited until the library door had closed behind him. Only then did he let out the breath he had held while the lycanthrope appraised him.

"Sir Ewan is collecting intelligence on the French

Afflicted. He brought me news of five more." Lady Miles gestured to the forms made of ash that wandered the map of France.

"Have you told him what you know of me?" Anger flared hot inside him. The mage had no right to reveal his secret.

"No. As I told you before, your secret is yours alone to reveal. But I did suggest to Sir Ewan that you might have something in common. Apparently I was mistaken. Is there anything else I can help you with?" Her tone was light, and try as he might, he didn't think she mocked him for not taking the offered assistance.

"I wish to read any books you might have about the dead. Ghosts in particular, and those aftermages who can commune with them." Séances and talking to the dead were popular amusements. Perhaps someone with the gift of clairvoyance could obtain more than he from Beth and the women who had been dismembered.

"An interesting topic. I have several books on the subject." She wheeled herself away from the desk and to the middle of the room, where she faced the wall that held her books on magic, myths, and legends.

Lady Miles held out one arm and her finger ran through the air, as though she perused the shelves. Periodically she would stop and tap the air, and a book would slither from between its companions and drift down to Wycliff.

He held out his arms and before too long, he had a stack of some seven books. "Thank you, Lady Miles, that will be sufficient to make a start."

Back in his study, Wycliff set the books on conversing with the dead to one side. Then he gathered all his papers about his investigation and shoved them into a satchel. In the afternoon he would meet with Sir Manly to discuss his progress.

In his mind he kept seeing the woman sewn together like torn fabric. Doctor Husom had ascertained that none of the limbs were Beth's. Wycliff now knew who else's had been used—those of Nell and Tabitha.

Nell Watts had been a washerwoman, and immersing her hands in hot water all day had given her a terrible rash up her arms. Tabitha Chant had been a prostitute who had complained of stabbing pains through her stomach. Both had attended the charity surgery at the Royal Hospital to find relief from their ailments. Neither were seen again.

The autopsy had found that the hyoid bone in Beth's neck was fractured, something that occurred in cases of strangulation. The monster hadn't just patched together pieces from the deceased, but was possibly committing murder to obtain those pieces. Unless he found the torsos and necks of Nell and Tabitha, he couldn't say whether a similar fate had befallen them.

Which raised another issue: Where were the rest of their bodies? Did the unknown surgeon sort through his specimens and only use those that met certain criteria? Their remaining parts could have been consigned to the crematorium and no one would ever know. Especially if a known surgeon placed the remains on the cart to be disposed of.

Another image was burned into his mind—the ghost of Beth, clawing at her throat, saying it hurt, saying the doctor had given her medicine that made her sleepy. Nell and Tabitha attached to her by ephemeral ribbons. None of which he could tell Sir Manly without revealing how he was able to find and speak to the shades.

On a single sheet of paper Wycliff had written his short list of suspects, compiled after discussion with Miss Miles. A list that included all those men known to be working on a cure for the Afflicted, and who possessed some degree of medical knowledge.

At the top of that list was the name Doctor Peter Husom. A surgeon who experimented with galvanism to animate the deceased.

Below that, Sir Hugh Miles. The last person to be seen with Beth and who had quietly disposed of a man's torso with a kicking leg.

Both names caused him discomfort. He worked with these men. Both had provided crucial evidence to aid his investigation. Doctor Husom would surely be unlikely to provide proof of murder if it had been his own hands wrapped around the woman's throat. Or had he acted solicitously to remove himself as a suspect?

Two more names on his list were less likely—Reverend Jones and Lord Dunkeith. For the sake of completeness, they needed to be raised as possible suspects before he dismissed them.

He buckled the satchel and headed for the stables, hoping the ride might clear his head and allow the clues to make sense. By the time he trotted up the street in Whitehall, his mind seemed clearer—not that he liked the picture he constructed from the clues he'd gathered.

Standing in front of General Sir Manly Powers' desk, Wycliff had the satchel over his shoulder and the papers in his hands. As though giving a report on a recent battle, he began to read from his notes, starting with the hand that had crawled from the Thames. He moved on to his search for the rest of Mr Barnes, a secondary Afflicted, and the body snatcher's vague description of the "large medical man" who had taken delivery of the corpse.

Next he narrated the appearance of the woman found in Chelsea. He briefly covered the fact that she was dead, but pointing and muttering, and that the doctor had ascertained that none of the attached limbs were hers. He raised the cases of the missing women in the Chelsea area, in particular the two of a similar appearance to Beth and his belief that their limbs had been attached to the woman they had discovered. He speculated that their bodies might never be found if their parts had been burned.

Wycliff reached the end of his notes and folded the papers in half. "The woman, Beth Warren, was last seen with Sir Hugh Miles at a charitable surgery in the grounds of the Royal Hospital. She had gone to see a doctor about a sore throat. Doctor Husom found the woman had been strangled and then dismembered."

Sir Manly grunted and the ornate moustache, this week with whorls of ascending size, rose up and down. "Dreadful thing to do to a woman."

"Two others, Nell Watts and Tabitha Chant, also went to the charitable surgery to consult a doctor and were never seen again." Unfortunately, no one remembered them or knew who had been in attendance on the days they had gone to the Royal Hospital.

"Three at least? A true monster, all right."

"There is one more matter of concern." Wycliff shoved the papers back into the battered satchel.

"Spit it out, man," Sir Manly said.

"Doctor Husom revealed that two weeks ago, a man's leg and torso had been discovered, and the leg was kicking at anyone who approached. Sir Hugh dealt with the matter, but he has not made any mention of it to me, despite his knowing it might be pivotal to my investigation."

Sir Manly tapped his fingers against the leather inlay of the desk. "That's not like Sir Hugh. Why would he not mention the leg, especially if it matched the hand that was running through the mud?"

"Why indeed?" Wycliff had his theories, but what he needed was more evidence—and to pin the large man down to extract some answers. Sir Hugh had dealt with the matter all right: by keeping it to himself. His silence on the discovery spoke volumes. "We must ask if his secrecy implies culpability? He, presumably, destroyed the stitched-together torso that was found. He was the last known person to see Beth, although I have yet to ascertain if he treated Nell and Tabitha. He is known for his experimental surgical techniques. However, I have not yet ascertained whether Sir Hugh uses the cart bound for the crematorium."

Sir Manly continued to tap on his desk what could have been a secret message in code, for all Wycliff knew. "Tread carefully, Wycliff. Sir Hugh is well known."

"So well known that the scandal sheets have speculated for some time that he may be the Chelsea monster. While such gossip is not evidence suitable for presenting before a magistrate, what we do have is rather compelling." Even more so if he let it be known that Sir Hugh had given Beth a draft that made her sleepy.

"Let's review it again. Leave out nothing, no matter how small." The tapping stilled.

Wycliff held in a sigh. It would be a long afternoon. If he wanted a warrant to find more evidence, he needed to craft a most compelling case from what he had available.

# 18

Hannah found dinner that evening unexpectedly quiet. Lord Wycliff had not returned from London, and rather than feeling relief at his absence, Hannah kept glancing at his empty chair with a wistful air.

"I will ask Cook to leave a plate on the stove. He may be hungry when he returns," Hannah said as they finished their meal. Her father chuckled and exchanged a look with her mother. Hannah rolled her eyes. Her concern was merely to ensure that their boarder was fed; there was no need to read more into her actions.

To ward off further remarks, she grasped the handles on the bath chair and pushed her mother into the front parlour. There, Seraphina played a game of chess against an invisible opponent—a mage in Germany. Her father adjourned to his study, writing up his notes about the latest batch of mice they had infected.

Hannah was engrossed in *Mansfield Park* and the life of Fanny Price when the front door rattled under the force of someone banging upon it. Hannah nearly dropped her book in fright as the vibration caused a painting on the wall to bounce.

Seraphina tutted under her veil as she considered her next move. "Probably someone in urgent need of your father, and who thinks anyone living in the country must be hard of hearing."

Hannah glanced at the clock sitting on the mantel. Nearly nine. Too late for a social call, which left someone requiring the well-known surgeon.

"I'll go," she said to her mother as she hurried to the door. The banging continued at regular intervals.

Mary appeared in the hall and glanced at the front door. "Who is it, do you think?"

"I shall answer that question once I open the door." Hannah worried about the maid. Having Viscount Wycliff in residence appeared to have affected her nerves. Mary crept about the house as cautiously as a chicken learning to live with a fox.

Hannah pulled open the front door and froze on the spot. At least six men in bright red uniforms with white braid clustered at the door, bathed in the soft glow from the ensorcelled lights attached to the underside of the porch ceiling. The soldier who had been banging stepped aside, giving way to his commanding officer.

"In the name of the king, miss, we are here for Sir Hugh Miles." Remembering himself at the last moment, the officer removed his shako as he addressed her.

A military matter. No wonder the men were in such a hurry. She only hoped it wasn't an escape from the Repository, although that would require both her parents. "Of course. I shall fetch him."

Hannah didn't have to venture far. The noise had drawn her father from his study. "There are soldiers here for you, Papa," she said.

"I shall need my bag, Hannah. Would you fetch it, please?" Her father buttoned up his waistcoat as he approached the door.

"Sir Hugh Miles, you are hereby placed under arrest for the murder of Beth Warren and for committing crimes against God," the officer read from the warrant in his hand.

"What?" Hannah glanced from her father to the officer. "This is preposterous. My father has done no such thing."

Seraphina wheeled herself along the corridor. The brave soldiers on the porch recoiled at the sight of the veiled mage. Some shuffled to stand behind the others and the cluster of men contracted into a tight red ball. "What is going on here?" she demanded.

"It would appear these men are here to arrest me for murder," Hugh answered his wife.

"You can all go away. You have the wrong man." Hannah crossed her arms and stood between her father and the soldiers. No one was removing him from their home if she had anything to say about it.

Large hands settled on her shoulders from behind. "These men are only doing their duty, Hannah."

Hannah spun and threw her arms around his expansive middle, resting her head on his chest. "No! They cannot take you away. Mother, surely you will stop them?"

Seraphina rubbed her hands together and sparks leapt between her fingers. She whispered under her breath and formed the sparks into a large sphere that spun between her palms. The soldiers muttered among themselves and most shuffled away from the open door. One brave soul stepped into the house, his rifle clutched in his hands, his knuckles white and his eyes wide.

"Sera," Sir Hugh growled at his wife, "you will not use magic against these men. I will not be gone long. Truth will prevail."

"What is this commotion about?" Wycliff appeared in the foyer, still wearing his overcoat and clutching his top hat.

Hannah glared at him. "You! This is your doing! These men are here to arrest my father."

"That is ridiculous. I have just come from Chelsea, where I have been gathering more evidence. No decision was to be made until tomorrow. Who issued the warrant?" Wycliff tossed his top hat on the sideboard and held out his hand.

The officer passed over the piece of paper and the

viscount scanned the contents. "Contrary to what you believe, Miss Miles, this is most assuredly not my doing. I presented the evidence I have gathered to Sir Manly today, and he then directed me to continue my enquiries in Chelsea. I have been seeking anyone who last saw two other missing women. I was also assured that no action would be taken until I had spoken to Sir Hugh." He looked up. "This warrant was signed by Lord Ashburton, the magistrate."

Seraphina let out a bark of laughter that made the soldiers take another step backward and the ball of sparks flare hotter in her hands. "Ashburton has long had a grudge against Hugh, ever since a cannonball took off his son's arm and my husband's attempts to sew it back on failed. The spiteful little man probably leapt at the chance to have Hugh arrested."

Gently, Sir Hugh broke apart his wife's hands and the ball of sparks fizzled into nothing. "The man does like to collect grievances. But spite alone does not build a case, Sera. I shall go with these men. I am sure Lord Wycliff will soon have this cleared up."

Hannah held her position next to her father. "I would rather this were cleared up now. If Viscount Wycliff presented the evidence, he can have it dismissed." Soldiers were not going to haul him off because some man was silly enough to lose his arm to a cannonball.

"Matters are not that simple, Miss Miles. Once the magistrate has issued a warrant, only he can revoke it."

Wycliff handed the warrant back to the officer in charge.

"We have our orders, miss. Please step aside. We have no wish to harm you." The officer reached for Hannah.

"No one touches my daughter," the mage hissed.

The officer froze. Ice crystals formed on his eyelashes and his breath frosted over his lips. His outstretched hand never reached Hannah.

Her father pulled her into a hug. He spoke against her hair as she clung to him. "Let me go, Hannah, before this encounter takes a dark turn and these men are hurt through no fault of their own."

Hannah swallowed the lump in her throat. She did not want to see the men harmed for following orders. Her father was right—truth would prevail and he would soon be home. "I will fetch your warm overcoat. It is cold outside."

Sir Hugh smiled and stroked her hair. "There's my girl."

By the time she had fetched a heavy wool coat and a warm hat, her mother had removed the freezing spell on the soldier. The man stomped his feet on the porch as though his toes had fallen asleep.

Hannah fussed over her father and tied and retied his scarf several times until the soldiers started grumbling. "I'm sure you'll be back in time for dinner tomorrow," she said, hugging him again.

"Take care of your mother," her father whispered, and then kissed the top of her head.

Tears formed in the corners of her eyes as Hannah watched her father be led away by the soldiers and bundled into a plain black carriage.

Lord Wycliff leaned against the doorframe, his arms crossed over his chest as he watched events he had set in motion. "I'll not forgive you for this," Hannah said as she stalked back inside.

Hannah had a troubled night. Her mind played out a nightmare in which her father was tortured on a rack to extract a confession of murder. A mockery of a trial followed and his nemesis, Lord Ashburton, banged his gavel as he shouted, *"Guilty!"* As a crowd cheered, her father was hanged from the gallows, his lifeless body turning in the breeze. Then the angry mob, not satisfied with one dead body, turned their attention to his wife. Their house was surrounded by people chanting *Burn the witch.* Up in her turret, Seraphina launched her attack on the people below, just as Hannah awoke with a gasp, the sheet tangled around her body.

Dawn light brushed past her curtains and caressed the floorboards.

"It was only a bad dream," Hannah whispered as she rubbed her hands up her arms to dispel the chill from the brisk morning air. Despair formed in her stomach. What if her father was not vindicated? Her mother was a powerful mage, but she was still dead and was treated as such by English law.

After she dressed in a dark brown day dress, to reflect her mood, Hannah headed to the dining room.

She couldn't eat, but needed a cup of tea after such a terrible night with so little sleep. She scanned the newspaper and thought of the old saying that good news travels fast, but bad news travels faster.

*Sir Hugh Miles Is the Murderous Chelsea Monster!*

The article went into gruesome, and entirely fictitious, detail about the mutilated corpses found and speculated that there were far more murder victims that had not yet been discovered. It finished with an outlandish account of how her father conducted experiments out in the open by the light of a full moon.

Hannah snorted. "What complete rubbish. You cannot conduct experiments in an open field. What do they think he uses as a light source?" She threw the paper to the table.

"Nothing will stop people from gossiping, Hannah," her mother said. "I could arrange a lightning strike to find the writer, but I don't think your father would approve."

"It's not fair. What will we do if Father is not cleared of these charges?" Hannah searched her mother's veiled face, desperate for some reassurance that everything would be all right.

Seraphina reached out and took her hand. "Whatever happens, we have each other and we will vindicate Hugh."

Hannah tried to smile. She didn't want to become

an outlaw, seeking justice for her deceased father while she and her mother were hounded from location to location. Their life was quiet and modest and she rather enjoyed it just the way it was. "When might I visit Father?"

"This afternoon, apparently there is paperwork that must be completed before they will admit you. I suspect Ashburton wants wards put around your father to ensure he doesn't escape."

"I cannot believe Lord Ashburton issued a warrant, when the charges are so blatantly untrue." She glared at her tea. Why did nothing work in their favour?

Her mother poured more tea into Hannah's cup. "What is obvious to you and I escapes the notice of others. Follow the evidence, Hannah, and the truth will prevail."

A dark presence entered the room, one that had stolen the joy from the house. To think she had almost missed him at dinner last night. That was comparable to missing a cholera outbreak.

Lord Wycliff bowed and then turned to the buffet. Apparently he still had an appetite. "Quite so, Lady Miles. While I understand that you believe me responsible, Miss Miles, I merely presented the evidence to Sir Manly. It is unfortunate that the magistrate drew his conclusions without seeking further clarification on some points."

"I will see Father released. Now, if you'll excuse me, I have chores to do before I can see Father and must tend to the mice and Mr Barnes' hand." Hannah rose from her seat. She couldn't stomach being in the same room as the man who had kicked the foundation stone out from under their lives.

Seraphina stopped her daughter as she walked around the table to avoid Wycliff. "I have done as you requested. There is an enchantment on the house that will allow the hand to roam freely, but he cannot go beyond any outside door or window." Then she drew a small object from her pocket, placed it in Hannah's palm, and curled her fingers around it. "I also made this for him. I am sorry it took so long, but mage silver is tricky to brew and takes its own time to form."

Hannah tightened her grip on the magical ring. At least one creature would be freed from its prison. "Thank you, Mother."

"If the appendage is to be let loose, might I suggest you find a better name for it? It seems wrong to refer to the piece by the name for the whole." Her mother pushed her bath chair away from the table.

Hannah had been pondering that question. It didn't seem right to give the hand a name better suited to a pet. "Perhaps in this instance we could drop the mister and refer to him simply as Barnes?"

"An excellent compromise." Her mother followed her from the room and they left the traitor in their midst to dine alone.

As Hannah took the stairs downward, she pondered her plan. The easiest way to clear her father was to identify the true monster. There was one person, or *piece* of a person, who had seen him. She had established a rudimentary communication method, with the hand able to respond yes or no. Now all she need do was pose a simple series of questions to find the murderer.

In the cool laboratory, Hannah tackled her usual chores first. She cleaned the cages and gave the living mice fresh straw, food, and water. The Afflicted mice were given their sliver of mouse brain, which they fell upon with ravenous hunger.

Next she took down the cage containing the hand and peered at its resident. "I have excellent news, Barnes—you are to be freed from this cage. However, my mother has placed a ward around the house so that you cannot cross any threshold or windowsill. She also made you a special ring to wear." Hannah pulled the item from her pocket and held it up.

Light glinted on the silver, which seemed to contain fire within. This ring was fashioned as an oar—a reference to the ship tattooed on his wrist. "I hope these terms are an acceptable compromise."

The hand tapped twice on the metal bottom of the cage and held his pinkie aloft.

Hannah slid the ring onto the finger and the mage silver changed shape to perfectly fit the digit. The hand waved the finger as though he preened at the jewellery.

With agreement reached, Hannah lifted the hand out and set him on the table. He sat for a moment as though taking his bearings. Then he leapt down to the floor and scuttled out the open door.

"Oh, dear. I should have tried asking my questions first, or at least have warned Mary." It only now occurred to Hannah that the maid might not appreciate the bodiless hand's exploring the house. "I shall formulate my questions and then find Barnes, he might be more cooperative after a bit of freedom and I still have a few hours to fill before I leave."

With the laboratory creatures fed, Hannah wiped down the shelves and surfaces. Her mind wouldn't settle long enough for her to continue the examination of slides and samples. Instead, she climbed the stairs with heavy feet. A scream from upstairs roused her to move faster.

On emerging into the main hall, Hannah found the hand at one end, Timmy at the other, and Mary trying to climb the wall halfway between the two.

"What is it?" she screamed at Hannah.

"I would have thought that rather obvious, Mary. It's a hand. Formerly he was attached to a Mr Barnes, but he has lost the rest of his body and is now known simply as Barnes." Hannah ignored the shaking maid and walked up to the hand.

Timmy stared at it with wide eyes. "Blimey. Never knew they could do that."

"They don't usually." Hannah picked up Barnes and raised him to her eye level. "No more scaring Mary. It is ungentlemanly. Perhaps you should apologise."

Mary let go of the painting she had pulled over her head, but she kept her distance. "Will it be wandering around the house?"

"Barnes is free to explore the house. I assure you he means no harm. Think of him as a type of spider." The hand did resemble one, with the fingers acting like legs to carry him along the ground and allowing him to climb.

"I'm scared of spiders." Mary inched along the wall.

*Of course you are.* Hannah sighed. *Rat* wouldn't work as an analogy, and was insulting to Barnes besides. "What if we referred to him as a Romanian hamster?"

The maid screwed up her face and darted from the safety of the wall to stand behind Hannah. "What do they look like?"

Given Hannah had made up the idea, she felt poetic license was allowed in describing the fictitious animal. "Let us say they look like this hand, although much hairier in colder climates."

Mary peered at Barnes from over Hannah's shoulder. "Sounds exotic, miss. I'm going to call it that if anyone asks."

"Where's the rest of him, though?" Timmy asked. There was no fear in his face, only open curiosity as he came over to see.

An idea struck Hannah. "Would you like to touch him and see if your gift tells you anything? Father and I are trying to ascertain why Barnes here is so lively. You might be very helpful to us." She needed to do something to replace the memory of her father being led away by soldiers. What she really needed to do was find the true culprit. This could be another step in that direction.

Timmy screwed up his face. "Would he mind?"

The hand waved a finger back and forth.

"That means no, Barnes does not mind. Why don't we go into the library? Barnes hasn't explored in there yet." Hannah carried the Romanian hamster to the library and let Barnes run around the floor. Today her mother worked in her turret room, so they needn't worry about Barnes being run over by the bath chair.

They sat on the rug before the fire and Hannah called Barnes over. She created a platform with her outstretched hands and held him out to Timmy.

The lad hovered one hand over the severed limb. "He won't bite, will he?"

"Barnes does not possess teeth, Timmy. Although I suppose he could pinch if he were so inclined." She bit back a laugh that drove away a tiny piece of the despair within. If this in any way helped to find the true murderer, it would be worthwhile.

Timmy lowered his hand until his fingers settled over the stump of wrist jutting up. He closed his eyes and hummed a quiet tune under his breath.

"Does the tune help?" Hannah asked.

He opened his eyes. "When I touch someone, the

magic starts jumping around inside me and it can be scary. The tune calms me down."

"Can you discover anything about our new friend?" She wanted this to work, not just for her father but for Timmy. The lad needed to grow his confidence in his gift.

He shrugged. "He's mostly dead, like y—" He swallowed the rest of the words and his eyes widened, then he muttered, "Sorry, miss."

Hannah flashed him a reassuring smile. "There is a reason for Barnes feeling mostly dead. Can you discern anything else? I am more interested in whether you sense anything about the rest of him, like a sore head or an aching toe."

He closed his hands again and this time silence fell. Only quiet breaths filled the space between ticks from the clock. At length, the lad opened his eyes again. "There's nothing there. Like empty space where his body should be."

Hannah considered a different approach to the issue. "Hmm… What about concentrating on the hand? Is there anything that feels different from other hands? Apart from his being dead."

Timmy nodded and his eyes brightened. "It stung. He ran away because it hurt so much."

That wasn't what she had expected. "What stung? Did he encounter something while exploring the house?"

"No. It's old and doesn't hurt so much now—it's more like an itch. At first, though, it hurt all over, like when you stick your hand in a patch of nettles. I'm sorry I'm no good at this." The lad frowned and dropped his hand back into his lap.

Hannah smiled at the lad and patted his shoulder. "Quite the contrary, that is extremely helpful. None of the Afflicted have ever reported a stinging or itchy sensation, which means there is something different about what happened to Mr Barnes."

"Oh." His face lit up in a smile. "I hope it helps."

"You have given me information. Now I need to determine what it means. It could be dark magic, a potion, or another process." *It hurt all over*. What if the hand had experienced an electrical charge—could galvanism account for the pain Barnes had felt? If only she could take Timmy to Doctor Husom's laboratory and have him touch a limb that had endured electricity coursing through it. Then they could compare whether they felt the same.

"Now, Barnes, you are free to explore, but I want you back in the library later today. You and I are going to try to figure out what happened to you."

The hand nodded a finger yes, then hopped down to the rug and scuttled to the bookshelf.

"I'll follow him, miss, and make sure he doesn't scare Mary again." Timmy leapt to his feet and chased the Romanian hamster.

"Thank you, Timmy," Hannah called.

While sitting on the floor, an idea came to her: an automatic writing board with its carved letters of the alphabet and numbers. It was perfectly designed for a finger to move the planchette to spell out words. She was sure her mother had one stashed away somewhere in the library. She could ask Barnes to describe his killer and finally she would have the evidence to free her father.

# 19

Hannah's idea to have Barnes spell out what had happened to his body didn't quite go as planned. She held in the disappointment and tears that heated behind her eyes. The hand sat on the planchette and used the thumb to spin himself around the wooden board like an ice skater on a frozen lake.

"Whatever are you up to?" Seraphina asked as she wheeled into the library.

"I thought to use the board to have Barnes tell me who did this to him, but it didn't work." Hannah threw up her hands as Barnes whirled around the alphabet.

"Does he not recall?" Seraphina conjured a handkerchief that fluttered into Hannah's lap.

"The issue is rather more fundamental. Mr Barnes was illiterate." She dabbed at her eyes with the embroidered square of cotton and felt foolish that she had expected Barnes to spell out the name, or at least a description, of the true murderer.

"Oh. That is a rather large impediment to finding the culprit." Her mother muttered under her breath, and small icicle-covered trees popped up around the edge of the board. Barnes now skated in a tiny winter wonderland.

"I am trying to devise a series of yes and no questions to learn more, but it is frustrating. I even tackled the issue head-on and asked if Papa had done this to him. But he doesn't know." Tears spilled down her cheeks as Hannah was consumed by her inability to help her father.

"I have asked Old Jim to hitch up the horses. I need you to visit your father, dearest. I have done what I can, but I am not allowed in the prison. Those in charge think I will magic your father away." A sigh heaved through Seraphina's draped body.

Hannah rose to her feet and wrapped her arms around her mother. "We will bring him home and prove him innocent of these charges. Now, I shall fetch a spencer and bonnet."

In her room she chose the short navy blue spencer and a straw bonnet with matching blue ribbon. Hannah shrugged on the spencer and tucked stray ends of hair under the bonnet as she descended the stairs. She encountered Wycliff in the hall.

"You may be intent on seeing my father hang, but I assure you, my lord, I shall prove you wrong. My father is innocent of these most heinous charges." Hannah curled her gloved hands in her skirts to contain her anger, lest she shake a fist in his face.

How she wished she were a man, that she could strike him and call him out!

"And I assure you, Miss Miles, that I bear no malice toward Sir Hugh. Like you, I merely want to find the guilty party who is murdering, cutting apart, and then stitching back together citizens of London." That black gaze bored through Hannah and stole her breath.

How dared he sound so reasonable.

"You had Papa arrested," was all she managed to whisper. She bit her bottom lip to stop the tears that burned behind her eyes. He had had her father torn from their household. She would never forgive that.

He placed his hands behind his back and stiffened his posture. "Unfortunately, there is evidence that points to your father's being the one experimenting in rejuvenating rotten Afflicted bodies, by sewing on healthy limbs."

There were times that Hannah wished her mother used her magic with a little less discrimination, and would turn the viscount into a topiary figure, or a goldfish. Or any small, easily squashed creature.

She tried to marshal her thoughts that so often scattered before him as though he were an autumn wind. "You know that I assist my father. I can attest that he has not performed any such procedure here."

Wycliff arched one eyebrow. "Exactly. He has not done such procedures *here*. Meaning he may have done them elsewhere. Your father admitted to discussing such a possibility with your mother, but we do not know how far they took that conversation. Did you also know that only two weeks ago your father destroyed a torso with a leg that was kicking out, but failed to inform us? It could have been more of Mr Barnes."

Now Hannah was the one transformed into a goldfish. Her mouth opened and closed, but she couldn't make words emerge. The viscount was mistaken. If her father had found more of Mr Barnes, he would have told her. Hot, angry tears filled her eyes. She hated this man because he made her doubt her parents, the two people she loved most in the world. With nothing more to say, Hannah fled across the hall, from the house, and to the escape offered by the waiting carriage.

The sun broke free of the clouds and shone down upon the city. Despite the growing warmth in the air, Hannah huddled into the standing collar of her spencer, the chill originating from the inside, rather than the outside. Through the carriage window, Newgate prison loomed grey and dull and sucked the life from the air around it. And no doubt stealing the lives of those within as well.

As she left the carriage and walked toward the first gate, the tingle of magic crept over her skin. This time it wasn't the familiar tickle of her mother's magic, but the nettle-like sting of the workings of another mage. Layers of magic ensured that those imprisoned stayed there and even aftermages with magic in their blood were unable to escape.

Hannah took the dim corridor to the turnkey's room.

"Miss Hannah Miles to see Sir Hugh Miles," Hannah said to the dour-looking man.

"What do you have there?" He pointed a pencil at the bundle in her arms.

Hannah held the bundle tighter to her chest. "An extra blanket, a few trinkets from home, and a meal to share. Surely you would not deny a man a few reminders of his family's love for him?"

The guard narrowed his eyes and looked as though he might strip her of the package for her father. Then he blew out a sigh. "Let her through," he yelled to a man stationed at a wide door made entirely of bars.

The next guard unlocked the door and swung it open to admit her. "This way, miss. I'll take you to your father," he said once he had locked the door behind her. "My brother owes his life to Sir Hugh. He saved him after a Frenchie blast took his lower leg off. We were ever so grateful to have him home and he still does fine work as a cobbler."

"Many men owe my father a great debt. He was an excellent field surgeon." She hoped the guard's good opinion meant her father was better treated, just as he had ensured a higher level of treatment for soldiers under his care on the battlefield.

At least her mother had managed to secure a cell for him on the State side of the prison, where they paid for his food and lodging. Poorer prisoners were consigned to the Common side, where they had to fight the rats for scraps.

"Here we are, Miss Miles." The guard stopped at a

solid door with only a small barred square at face height. He drew out his chain of keys and selected one to fit to the lock. "I'll give you one hour, then I'll come back to fetch you."

"Thank you," Hannah murmured as she stepped inside.

"Hannah!" Sir Hugh jumped to his feet and held his arms wide.

Hannah dropped her parcel to the floor, ran to her father, and buried herself in his large and comforting embrace.

"Oh, Papa. Mother and I are ever so worried about you." Tears moistened her eyes even though she had vowed not to cry in front of him. What if he were found guilty of murder and hanged? She screwed her eyelids tight to force the tears away.

Sir Hugh rubbed her back. "There, there, Hannah. Everything will be all right. I will be found innocent and you will prod the viscount in the direction of the true culprit."

Hannah swallowed down all her doubts and reservations. To find the true murderer, she needed a full and honest discussion with her father, and she would at least feel warmer with her mother's gift activated.

The cell did not look completely unbearable. There was a bed pushed against one wall under the high, barred window. A table and two chairs sat against another wall. It could have been a monk's room in a monastery or a holding room in the Repository of Forgotten Things, except the latter building was far warmer and didn't have moans and screams echoing around the halls.

Hannah slipped from her father's embrace to fetch the parcel from the ground. "I brought a bundle from Mother. First, an extra blanket because she says your feet get cold at night."

Sir Hugh huffed a laugh, took the folded blanket, and placed it on the foot of his bed.

"Next, I have some cold meat, cheese, and bread. Last, I have a glow mushroom to save on candles." Hannah set the squat rounded object on the table and tapped the top. The mushroom emitted a soft yellow light. "This one also gives off warmth when you are seated near it."

"It's almost pleasant, is it not?" Sir Hugh pulled out a chair for Hannah and she sat. She emptied the basket of its contents and set them before her father.

For herself, she cut a small slice of cheese and nibbled on it while she considered how to begin. Viscount Wycliff had sown doubt in her mind and she needed to cut it down. "If I am to find the true murderer, I need you to tell me all you know, Papa. It is time you were truthful with me."

"Truthful about what?" he asked as he cut a slice of bread and layered it with meat and cheese.

"Viscount Wycliff said you were known to be sewing healthy limbs onto the Afflicted to replace their rotten limbs. He further said there was a torso found with a kicking leg, which you concealed." There—she had made the horrid allegations out loud. Let the viscount's suspicions fester and rot in this place without infecting their home.

"Ah." Her father took a large bite and chewed slowly.

Each grinding motion of his teeth increased Hannah's agitation and a storm brewed in her stomach. "You mean his accusations are true?"

He swallowed the sandwich. "Somewhat, yes. After your mother and her friends were struck down and the other ladies dismembered by soldiers, I watched as their limbs attempted to reattach themselves. I wondered if an Afflicted body would accept a substitute limb. I discussed at length with Seraphina the possibility of attaching healthy legs to her."

"Oh, Papa." Hannah swallowed the lump of cheese and it almost stuck in her throat. She had thought her father devoted and determined, but never demented.

"Do you know what I would do to make your mother whole again?" he whispered. "When you love someone, you will do whatever is in your power to make them healthy and happy."

"Did you attempt such an operation?" Since her mother was still confined to her bath chair and had nothing below her knees, it was safe to assume that any attempted procedure had ultimately failed.

Her father cut more bread and layered meat and cheese between the slices. "Not on your mother, no. She refused. But there was an Afflicted who had lost an arm to rot, and she was eager to try the procedure.

While it succeeded in part and she regained the use of a hand, it came with an...emotional toll."

Hannah took a piece of bread to peck at while she stomached the news that her father had undertaken research without her. "What emotional toll did it take?"

"When we attached another person's limb to her body, it came with more than mere flesh and bone. She said the hand gave her memories of things and people it had touched. Songs it had played on the piano. Flowers it had plucked from a meadow. She knew they were not her memories and she likened it to having a lodger in her body. At times the hand even seemed to obey the commands of a body that no longer possessed it." Her father dropped his sandwich to the table and fell silent.

"But a limb cannot retain memories." Or could it? Barnes the hand displayed independent thought without a body, no matter how often she told herself it was quite impossible.

"Do you know that, or do you merely hypothesise that it is impossible? Five years ago I would have thought it impossible that my dead wife would continue to live under my roof, and make me smile every day." Hugh picked up the sandwich again and leaned back in his chair as though they talked over a late supper in their own dining room.

Hannah pondered the new information. "Science and magic still have so much to teach us. Let us continue on the assumption that a limb that retains life also retains memories in its muscles and nerves. Who then would create a being made from multiple donors?

I can only imagine the distress of so many memories that are not your own. What a horrible price for immortality, if it comes with insanity."

They ate in near silence, the cries and shouts of other inmates penetrating even the thick stone walls of the prison. Hannah imagined them as cobbled-together monsters, their minds overwhelmed with memories of lives they had never lived. The surgeon responsible needed to be stopped, if only she could find the clues to unveil him.

"Some men are so focused on the end result, Hannah, that they do not see the effects of the method or how it impacts others." Sir Hugh poured water from a pitcher into two roughly made wooden cups.

Hannah took the offered water and stared at it suspiciously. Secrets left undisturbed could poison a family like a body in a well. "If the torso and leg were not your work, why did you send it to the crematorium and not tell Lord Wycliff?"

He drained his cup and lowered it to the table with a soft thud. "Because I thought it was the work of someone else whom I, rather foolishly, sought to protect."

Hannah set aside her water untouched. She couldn't eat or drink as new information kept coursing through her mind. She edged closer to the truth. "Who are you protecting, Papa?"

He dropped his head to his chest and was silent for several moments before he looked up at her again.

"Peter Husom. There are ties between a student and his teacher that bring a sense of responsibility."

"He was your student?" Hannah softened her tone. She could well understand her father feeling protective of a brilliant former student who had perhaps made the wrong choice.

Her father stood and paced the small square cell. "No. I was Doctor Husom's student over thirty years ago. The man has not aged a day since I first entered his lecture room as an eager lad of sixteen."

Hannah leaned back against the stone, needing its cool touch as her mind overheated. "Are you sure it is the same man? Perhaps he looks similar to his father."

"It is the same man. I wondered at first, for he had been gone from the city for many years, but he said things that gave him away. He may fool others, but not the likes of you and I." Hugh held up his finger and the light flashed over the mage-silver ring.

Apart from being a type of tracker and a way to signal Seraphina, the ring also conveyed a level of protection against certain spells. "Do you think he uses a glamour of some sort?"

Hugh rubbed the ring as he paced. "I believe so, to slightly obscure his features. I asked him about it directly once and he laughed and said the answer was in his name, if anyone looked closely enough."

Hannah pondered what that meant. His name made it clear? Did it have something to do with being a doctor? "Do you believe he is some sort of Unnatural creature, that he has not aged?"

Her father shrugged. "Or he ages so slowly that the passage of thirty years has not touched him. I do not know. That is his secret."

There were so many strands to this conversation that Hannah wished she had brought her notebook in which to write them all down. If Peter Husom were a type of immortal, why did he seek to create immortality? Or was he trying to make immortal companions? That led Hannah down a rabbit hole of pondering what he could be. The only sort of creature she knew to be resistant to ageing was a vampyre, and they didn't need electricity to create more of their number.

She shook her head to clear all the voices and to focus on just one. "Let us start from the beginning. Who has the required knowledge and access to equipment to dismember bodies and sew together new ones? Not to mention some method of reanimation. It does seem the only possible candidate is Doctor Peter Husom."

Hugh stopped pacing and peered out the small window in the door. "Galvanism seems the most likely method with which to bring a deceased person back to life. Not that his attempt worked during the meeting—we both saw that the effect was short-lived. You must also consider Reverend Jones."

Hannah frowned. She had already discounted the reverend. "He is a man of the cloth, relying on the power of prayer."

"A man of the cloth who originally trained as a surgeon. It was only after he graduated that he decided to pursue an ecclesiastic career. He has the required skill and we know he is devoted to proving that the Afflicted were created to show God's hand at work."

Hannah struggled to imagine the devout man committing murder. That aside, there was another name that Hannah had to mention. "There is also Lord Dunkeith."

Her father turned and paced back. "Better to investigate and exclude him, I'd say. He has no medical training that I know of, although his family did employ an aftermage apothecary to tutor him."

Resolve crept through Hannah. She would dig further into the movements of the other three men. She would not rest until she uncovered who had murdered Beth Warren and those who had been stitched to her. "Very well. I shall undertake my own enquiries, even if Lord Wycliff will not listen to reason."

"There is one other thing, Hannah. Our situation is somewhat delicate. If I should fail to be cleared of this charge—" Hugh curled his large fingers around the back of the chair and faced his daughter.

She jumped to her feet and cleared away their meal. "No! Do not even consider such a possibility. I will find the culprit and you will be home before you know it."

He walked around the table and stilled her hands. "Hannah. I cannot protect or provide for you and your mother, should anything happen to me. You know the law—the dead cannot inherit. What if you—"

Hannah threw her arms around his strong neck to

silence his words. She didn't want to contemplate the last unspoken truth that worried her father. Even when he was incarcerated, his concern was for her and her mother. She kissed his ruddy cheek. "We will free you. The alternative is not acceptable. Besides, Mother is a formidable mage. Do you think the spells attached to these walls would stop her from reclaiming you?"

Hugh laughed and hugged her tightly. "Your mother is indeed most formidable. If only you had seen her as a young woman. So many underestimated her and thought to use her as a puppet, and she showed them all."

Hannah smiled. How she wished she had seen her mother when she had erupted upon a startled court. But she would have many years to sit by her father as he told the stories. She would make sure of it.

# 20

Wycliff prowled back and forth in his modest study, barely managing two full strides before he encountered the wall. He turned and took another two steps, only to be blocked by the opposite wall. He had never intended to see Sir Hugh Miles, the man who had opened his home to him, thrown into prison on a charge of murder.

Wycliff's investigation sought to determine who had murdered Beth Warren, Nell Watts, and Tabitha Chant and then turned them into a patchwork woman. As he paced his confines, he raged at the magistrate, Ashburton, for issuing the warrant prematurely, before all the necessary evidence had been obtained.

How could he find a way through the mess created by the magistrate? He wanted the murderer brought to justice, but he had not intended to create an untenable situation for Lady Miles and her daughter. If Sir Hugh were hanged, they would be two women alone in the world and already burdened by Lady Miles' deceased status. Honour demanded he put things right. Somehow.

To that end, he had the kernel of an idea. During his time in the household, he had come to appreciate Miss Miles' quiet presence. He even somewhat enjoyed her occasional passionate outbursts that made her eyes sparkle with life. But there was another, deeper reason. He was lost on a strange sea, and he might have put in jeopardy the one place that offered him safe harbour.

How to broach the subject that had taken root in his mind? He settled on approaching Lady Miles in the first instance. If the mage decided to smite him where he stood for his impertinence and for having her husband arrested, at least he would have the satisfaction of having tried.

He rapped sharply on the door and then pushed it open, not waiting to be invited to enter. His feet needed to move and the library offered more freedom to pace.

Lady Miles sat at the desk. Images danced before her as they obeyed commands given with the swipe of a hand. "Wycliff." As she lowered her hands, all the figures fell like marionettes with their strings severed.

"Lady Miles. There is a matter of some delicacy I would broach with you." He stopped before the desk and clasped his hands behind his back.

"Oh?" She looked up, her face hidden behind the thick veil. Today a dark red metal diadem encircled her brow. Small tassels of blood red and gold hung from the main circlet and brushed the linen covering her head.

"Firstly, I would reinforce that I did not intend that Sir Hugh be arrested and removed from your home. I presented what evidence I had gathered and was given instructions by Sir Manly to continue my enquiries in Chelsea, before any such decision was to be made."

The mage dismissed his concerns with another wave of her hand. "Ashburton is a spiteful little man. I have no doubt he rubbed his hands with glee, ignored Sir Manly's directives, and issued the warrant regardless."

He nodded, satisfied that the mage held no ill feelings toward him. Or none that she chose to display. He might still find himself turned into a toad. "Secondly, I wish to discuss the possible implications of Sir Hugh's arrest—your condition, and the situation of your daughter."

Now that he had vocalised the main points he had argued in his head, words failed him. He didn't need to see the mage's eyes to know she stripped him bare and examined him from the inside out. His gut churned as though she was stirring him up with a stick.

"My condition?" She spoke the words in a slow and measured tone, yet they sparked a warning in his brain.

"The matter I would discuss is connected with your being Afflicted." He was at risk of losing control of the interview. Perhaps he should state his intention plainly, but he was unsure how the words would sound out loud. To date he had only whispered them in his head.

He continued his pacing in the hope that movement would restart his stalled thought processes.

Lady Miles clasped her gloved hands in her lap and tilted her head. The action made the tassels sway and drop to one side. "Tell me, Wycliff, is your objection to the Afflicted merely that they continue to go about their lives after death, or does being near them provoke another reaction you cannot fathom? I suspect you lash out because you do not understand what you have become."

He halted in his tracks and, behind his back, dug his nails into his palms. "What I have become? I'm sure I have no idea what you mean."

She snorted and the veil drifted out and back. "When will we drop this silly charade you insist upon? You returned from the war a changed man and cannot resume the life you once led. The sooner you reconcile yourself to the change, the better. You need to find an anchor before you are lost for eternity."

*Lost for eternity.* A hollow, bottomless void opened up inside him. He swallowed a dry lump in his throat. The mage saw too much. They danced around the topic of his changed condition, but neither spoke of it outright. Perhaps she was right. Would it not be better to rip off the bandage and press a hot iron to the wound to deal with it once and for all? "I have taken your advice on board about finding an anchor. But I do not see the need to learn anything about my *condition.*"

"I took you for an intelligent man, my lord. I hardly think ignorance is the best course of action in your situation." She wheeled herself to one side of the library shelves that stretched up above their heads. She reached out and one book wriggled free of its space and glided down to her. "Since you are not yet ready to take my advice or instruction, perhaps you will at least read a book I recommend." She held out the slender volume.

Curiosity got the better of him and he took the book. The cover was a worn bronze colour and the lettering a faded gold—*Selected Greek Myths*.

"I think there is a particular tale in there that may resonate with you, and begin to answer some of the many questions you claim not to have."

He grunted. He failed to see how fairy tales and myths would be of any assistance. "This was not the particular matter I wanted to discuss with you."

"Then I assume it concerns Hannah, given how you have been glaring at her across the table for weeks." She wheeled the chair backward until she stopped beside the desk.

He clutched the book much as a man might cling to a piece of wood when adrift on the ocean. He needed an anchor and one might yet be found in this house. "I will preface my remarks by repeating that I bear no ill will toward Sir Hugh and am cognisant of the favour you do me by allowing me to dwell under this roof."

"If I thought you bore any malice, you would not be dwelling under this roof, sir—at least, not in your current form. You follow the evidence, as a good investigator should. I know Hugh is innocent and time will reveal that truth. But Hugh's arrest has reminded me of the delicate nature of our lives here." She dropped her hands into her lap.

"That has also preyed upon my mind. Should anything happen to Sir Hugh, you and your daughter would be two women alone in the world." It would seem they had both been thinking of their circumstances.

"Our lives are more complicated than you realise." Lady Miles fidgeted with the linen of her gown, making little waves in the fabric between her fingers.

"Complicated in what way?" The lives of a dead mage and a spinster were not complicated, but sad and lonely. Not that he had any issue with solitude; he much preferred his own company to that of anyone else. Society, for whatever reason, had overlooked Miss Miles, in the way a plant that grew in the shade was overlooked by the sunlight.

Lady Miles smoothed the small ocean of waves she had made, until they lay flat once more. "As you are aware, a mage is awarded a position in society equivalent to that of a duke. That position is not hereditary and is lost upon death. Further, English law states that the dead cannot inherit, hold property, or marry."

None of this was new information. For centuries, mages had been elevated to the highest ranks as a reward for making their magic available to the monarch. "I am aware of the Unnaturals Act, under which all Unnaturals are beholden to the same laws as all other Englishmen. I would assume that Sir Hugh inherited your estate on your demise."

The red tassels on the diadem swayed in agreement. "Yes. And should Hugh die, Hannah is his only heir."

"This all seems straightforward. I am not seeing any complications." From the surroundings, he assumed the estate to be a modest one. Adequate to keep the family, but they certainly didn't live a lavish lifestyle. The offer he planned to make was not to secure an heiress, although any contribution to repair his ancestral home would be most welcome. Rather, his offer was a matter of honour, to ensure they were not left without a protector because of his actions.

Lady Miles rapped her knuckles on the desk and the phantom puppets rose to resume their places. "Why do you think Hugh and I devote all our time and resources to finding a cure for the French curse that created the Afflicted? Do you think parents would invest so much time to cure themselves?"

Yes, he had assumed they sought to cure the mage and wrest her back from death. Odd that she brought his attention to their being parents. How would that impact their effort—

A lightning bolt slammed into his brain. A parent would do anything to save a beloved child. Particularly the child who was the sole heir.

"Impossible," he whispered. He had spent much time in the company of Miss Miles and could vouch for her being entirely alive. She carried no whiff of decay or sign of rot. He had personally witnessed a most becoming blush to her cheeks on more than one occasion.

With a slice of the mage's hand, the puppets dissolved into thin air. "How I wish it were untrue. I love my daughter and would do anything to ensure her a long and happy life. In this instance, to do that I must first betray her greatest secret."

"She is Afflicted?" He swallowed the burst of bile that rose in his throat. He had been about to offer for the woman, but if she were dead, there could never be any marriage.

"Two years ago, Hannah's dear friend Lady Elizabeth Loburn thought to cheer her up by giving her a gift. A jar of expensive and much sought-after face powder."

His mind still couldn't process her words. "But Miss Miles is not dead. I see the life in her eyes. She breathes."

A new scene took form on the desk top. A tiny diorama of a ghostly bedroom and a young woman lying under the blankets, her parents by her bedside.

"There are some benefits to being a mage, especially a dead one. When Hannah fell ill and the other ladies died, Hugh and I realised there was only one thing we could do. I used my magic to pause the curse within her, and Hannah became a frozen moment in time. She is the space between heartbeats. A body that has inhaled but does not yet realise it will never exhale. Should my spell fail, the curse will resume its progress throughout Hannah's body. She would die within a day or two and arise as one of the Afflicted." Lady Miles' words were softly spoken and each one was tinged with sadness.

Now he understood the precarious and complicated nature of the Miles family. "If she dies, she cannot inherit. I assume some distant relative would be named the heir?"

"Yes. A very distant cousin who is a butcher and, I am informed, has a dim view of the Afflicted in general and of me in particular." She huffed a soft laugh.

He appreciated the irony. He had once held the same opinions. But contact with Miss Miles and her mother had rubbed some of his prejudices away. "Without Sir Hugh's protection, you would both be thrown on the streets. It would seem, Lady Miles, that in this matter we are of one mind. This was the original matter I wished to discuss with you. I came here to offer my name and protection to Miss Miles, and by extension, to you."

"You are an honourable man, sir, but consider your offer carefully. In Hannah's frozen condition she can never conceive. Nor will she ever know motherhood in the event my magic fails and death claims her. There is a strong possibility that there might never be an heir for your title."

He curled his hand into a fist. No heir. His line would end with him. Or perhaps that was for the best. What if he passed on more than financial woes, and any children were tainted by what he had become? "I have little enough to offer your daughter, I would not pass the burden of a bankrupt title to any son. It would be a marriage in name only."

"If you are certain. I can give no guarantee that we can reverse this most dreadful curse and save Hannah. It may be that time will steal her from us regardless of our efforts. Would you continue to protect a dead barren wife, or would you set her aside once you inherit?" The scene on the desk changed—the bed became a coffin as two figures grieved beside a freshly dug grave.

His spine locked rigid and he stiffened at the suggestion that he pursued their property. "I may be financially bankrupt, but not morally. If I merely sought a fat purse or a broodmare, I assure you I could have enticed some rich merchant's plump daughter with my title, if not my person."

A third figure joined the ghostly mourners on the desk. "Your offer is altruistic, then...or do you harbour a secret and all-consuming love for my daughter?"

*Love?* Wycliff inhaled too sharply, which resulted in a fit of coughs and splutters.

"No need to choke on the idea," the mage said tartly. "Hannah is as worthy of love as any woman."

The ground seemed to tilt and sway under his feet. He trod dangerous territory and needed to find his balance. "No. I am not consumed by passion for your daughter. She does possess admirable qualities, such as her quiet intelligence. I believe my offer to be the correct course of action and it is not entirely unselfish. You told me to find an anchor, and while I do not understand it completely, something inside of me says that this family, and Miss Miles, may provide that."

"Just as I thought," Lady Miles muttered under her breath.

Now that he had voiced his offer, the void inside him closed up. He had made a step in the right direction, but still he clung to the book, wondering what answers the stories within would yet provide. "I promise you, Lady Miles, that once given, my loyalty is irrevocable. Dead or alive, with or without children, your daughter shall have the protection of both my name and body. Miss Miles will always have a roof over her head and the sustenance she needs."

She made a *harumph* noise and tapped her gloved hand on the desktop. "There is one other thing. As you know, the dead cannot marry. Hannah must be wed now, before the spell fails."

"Very well. I have no objection. I only hope there is a satisfactory conclusion to my investigation that exonerates Sir Hugh." A little more of the weight holding him down lifted.

The graveyard on the desk disappeared and was replaced by a tempestuous ocean. A small boat, such as a child might make from paper, was tossed back and forth by the waves. "Perhaps now you will see why it is imperative that you speak to me about the other matter. Understand that, and you will understand the source of the loyalty you would give to Hannah. You are correct —she will be your anchor, but never to hold you back or weigh you down. Hannah will become your safe harbour, and your connection will ensure you never become lost in the eternal night."

Her words echoed through him and settled in his bones. He held up the slim volume. "I will read this while I digest all we have discussed. May I speak privately to Miss Miles?"

"No. Not yet. I must speak with Hugh first and seek his agreement." She waved her hands and ethereal music filled the library.

He took that as his cue to leave. As he pushed the door closed, the book fell open in his hands and the title of the myth caught his eye.

*Cerberus.*

# 21

All through the night, Hannah tossed and turned in her bed as she made plans and discarded them. She needed to determine whether Doctor Husom, Reverend Jones, or Lord Dunkeith could be responsible, but how? She couldn't just barge into their houses and demand answers to her questions. But she knew someone who would do exactly that. All she had to do was ask for his assistance.

The next morning over breakfast, she stared into her cup of tea, working up the courage to ask. While she held the viscount personally responsible for her father's being in jail, they both had the same ultimate goal—finding the true culprit.

"Lord Wycliff, I wondered if we might find a quicker resolution to this horrible matter if we joined forces." Hannah addressed her cup of tea, rather than the man himself. It seemed easier to talk to the silent brew than the silent brooding person.

From across the table came a quiet clink as he laid his cutlery on the plate. "You wish to assist my investigation?"

Assist? She wanted to direct his path, not take notes and apologise in his wake. "I spoke to my father yesterday. He had some insight into possible suspects, but I am unsure as to how to proceed."

Dark brows shot together. "Do you so easily dismiss the evidence against him?"

"I have heard my father's explanations and I intend to pursue other suspects. I trust that you will follow the evidence, which I believe will reveal my father to be innocent of these charges. If not, then that is a consequence I will have to live with." She suppressed the shudder that wanted to run through her body. No good would come of imagining a future where her father met his end on the gallows, and all the inevitable repercussions that would follow.

"Let us discuss this further in my study. I have everything there," Lord Wycliff said.

Hannah followed him down the hall and into his study with its view over the front garden and to the fields beyond. One wall held scribbled notes and drawings attached to a large map of London and the surrounds. Red thread ran from a drawing to the Royal Hospital and then across to a spot in Chelsea near the Physic Garden.

"Where Beth Warren was found," she murmured as she followed another strand. This one led from the docks to Bunhill Fields and then down to Neat House

Garden. "This, I assume, is the known path of Barnes. What do these pins mark?" She pointed to pins pushed in around Chelsea.

He leaned a hip on his desk and watched her, like a hawk perched in a tree. "Three mark the homes of Reverend Jones, Doctor Husom, and Lord Dunkeith. The other pins are sightings of the Chelsea monster."

Hannah studied each slip of paper pinned to the wall. With each note she read, calm settled over her. The viscount was nothing if not thorough. He had investigated the background of each man who had performed in the SUSS resurrection challenge and there was nothing targeted at her father.

A list of names with ages and descriptions caught her attention. Two were circled—Nell Watts and Tabitha Chant. "Who are these women?"

"They disappeared around the same time as Beth Warren. Nell Watts was a washerwoman and I believe her legs were stitched to Beth's torso. Tabitha was...a lightskirt and I believe she contributed her arms." He crossed his own and now appeared more defensive than predatory.

Hannah turned from the board and caught his profile. The morning light struck the hard angles of his face and cast half in shadow. "How did you deduce that? Have you found their remains?"

"No, they have not been found. I cannot reveal my source, but I believe the information to be correct." He uncrossed his arms and clasped his fingers around the edge of the desk.

Next to the list were several drawings of the unfortunate woman, or women, that made up Beth Warren. Hannah glanced from the sketches to his notes and hastily drawn lines. "Do these strike you as similar? All three appear to be in their twenties, with a similar build and long, dark hair."

He pushed off the desk and stood behind her. "I did notice. Almost as though the surgeon was searching for pieces that would fit together."

There was a gruesome puzzle—finding bits of different people that appeared the same.

"Are these drawings entirely accurate?" She tapped a sketch of Beth that showed her as she had been found. Hannah cast a critical eye over the surgery performed and one thing stood out in her mind.

"Yes. The artist was most particular in ensuring a correct representation." Lord Wycliff leaned closer and the smell of fragrant wood drifted over Hannah.

Hannah traced a fingernail down a line of stitches where the arm was joined at the shoulder. "This is not my father's work."

"How can you be so sure?" His shoulder brushed hers as he leaned in to peer at the small detail.

She snorted. How was it not obvious? "My father is a renowned surgeon who worked diligently during the war to patch up our soldiers. While he might look like a butcher, I can assure you that he has such skill with a needle that my mother said he made a better seam than the most expensive modiste."

"How does this prove your father is not responsible?" He held his position, and heat flared over Hannah's side closest to him.

She concentrated on the drawing and tried to ignore the man radiating more heat than the coal fire. "These stitches are large and irregular, as though the person responsible is not overly familiar with stitching flesh. Father's stitches are small and neat, even when under enemy cannon fire. He never falters, nor would he ever make such crude stitches. Smaller stitches result in cleaner scars."

At last he moved and his attention roamed the pictures, lingering over the lines of stitches used to patchwork multiple bodies into one. "If you think this person is no surgeon, would that also eliminate Peter Husom?"

"Possibly, unless the crude stitches are deliberate, in which case both Doctor Husom and my father are suspects once again." Her father had said Doctor Husom had not aged in thirty years. What secret did he conceal? Quite apart from the things he kept in his laboratory. "Doctor Husom has a limb strung out in a frame in his private laboratory, and also a cat, both awaiting his galvanism experiment."

The viscount moved sideways and rested a finger on the pin that marked the doctor's residence. "He lives close to the Physic Garden and also near where Beth was found."

"My father also said that he has not aged in thirty years. Once Doctor Husom was Papa's teacher and mentor." The words did not come easily to Hannah's tongue as she revealed a portion of the doctor's secret.

"He is immortal? Could he be a vampyre? Although I have seen him out and about during the day." Wycliff grabbed a pencil from his desk and made notes on a clean sheet of paper.

"Vampyres can endure the sunlight, but they do not like it, as it weakens them. But if he were, why undertake such butchery? Surely it would be beneath him?" Hannah was no expert on vampyres, but she thought they appreciated the beauty in life—art, poetry, and fine clothing.

Lord Wycliff circled something on the page and then pinned it to the wall. "Or perhaps an immortal life makes a human life less valuable and he sees us as playthings."

There was a horrible thought. A little of Hannah's admiration for Doctor Husom was rubbed away. Other ideas flowed through her head and she spoke them aloud. "Papa also said that Reverend Jones trained as a doctor before deciding to join the clergy. Lord Dunkeith studied with an apothecary. Whoever did this is either unused to working with a needle and human tissue, or he has no care for his patients' appearance or scarring."

Wycliff tossed the pencil to the desk and stood before the wall of evidence. "There is a third option. What if whoever did this was not familiar with living tissue, such as the supposed Chelsea monster?"

Hannah considered the possibility, but it didn't sit

right with her. People were terrified of the looming monster spotted in the shadows and who, supposedly, had been seen at the site where the body was discovered. But no one had yet seen him attack or injure anyone. If anything, he fled when discovered, as though afraid. On impulse, she burst out, "What if the monster is the result, not the cause?"

"You think this supposed monster is a stitched-together creation, like the poor woman we found? Beth did not long survive what was done to her. I find it unlikely another such creation has existed for longer when she could not." Dark brows pulled together.

That was an inconvenient flaw in her hypothesis. Without knowing what the mind behind them had used to animate the limbs, there was no way to determine why one lived for longer than the other.

"My mother said that just as no two people are alike, no two spells are the same," Hannah said. "There is a possibility that the person responsible used magic that worked differently each time. The most obvious solution is to find the monster." That would also, surely, prove her father innocent, since he languished in Newgate.

Viscount Wycliff studied his map and the pins denoting sightings. "There have not been any recent sightings of the monster, but should a man be wandering the fields at night, he will encounter the militia set to watch for it. Your time might be better occupied visiting Doctor Husom's laboratory again and ascertaining the origins of the limb you saw."

"Yes. I did not think to ask at the time." Hannah chewed her lip as she tried to make sense of the trail of clues stuck to the wall. The limb hanging in its copper frame and spiderweb of wires was as good a clue to follow as any. Perhaps she could also drop a few subtle questions in order to ascertain if Doctor Husom were a vampyre, such as asking if he had anything to drink.

"I will visit Reverend Jones and Lord Dunkeith later today. Now, if you don't mind, Miss Miles, I have plenty to do before I interview those gentlemen." Wycliff walked to his desk and seated himself.

Hannah stared at his broad back and on impulse, stuck out her tongue. Despite his protestations that he followed the evidence, she suspected he sought to tighten the noose around her father's neck. If he would not help, she would do it on her own.

Decision made, she marched from his study. She couldn't enact her plan until nightfall, and there was plenty to fill her day before then. Firstly, she wrote a note to Doctor Husom asking his permission to visit his laboratory again. The idea of going there alone gave her some trepidation. The man had been her father's teacher. What power or magic halted the ageing process for him? She handed the note to a local lad to be delivered, and then tackled her other chores, tending to the creatures in the laboratory and making her notes on their condition.

Next she searched the house for Barnes, whom she found with Timmy. The lad was in the kitchen, practicing his reading as Barnes pointed to each word.

There was hope yet the hand might learn to read and spell out his story, but not in time to help her father.

After dinner, she announced her intention to study in her bedroom and trod the stairs with growing excitement. After considering her wardrobe options, she thought the undertaking better suited to Sir Hugh's assistant, and fetched her boy's attire from the trunk.

With her hair braided up under a cap, Hannah crept back down the stairs and across the yard to the stables.

"Oh, bother," she whispered to the horses. She hadn't thought through this part of her plan. At best, she was an adequate rider, and only aside. She glanced down at her trousered legs. This adventure would have to be astride. How on earth did people ride with a leg to each side of a horse?

Hannah patted the nose of the placid and stout horse that pulled the gig. "We shall have to make the best of things."

Tacking up the quiet horse wasn't so difficult and Hannah allowed herself a moment of satisfaction at having done the job herself. She led the horse to the mounting block and clambered into the saddle. It felt odd to have a leg on either side and she worried she would wobble off with no pommels to grip.

As they turned left onto the main road, Hannah kicked the horse and urged it through the uncomfortable trot into a rocking canter.

"Oh!" she cried out at the odd motion, and clutched the front of the saddle to keep herself secure.

She would simply have to keep her seat. She couldn't walk all the way to Chelsea, that would take far too long.

As the moon rose, Hannah relied on the horse's eyesight to spot any holes in the road as she guided him through Knightsbridge and down toward Chelsea. Small roads and lanes intersected one another as she neared the Royal Hospital.

Halting the horse presented a new problem. The few times she had ridden sidesaddle, Hannah had never dismounted unassisted, for a groom or her father always helped her down. The best approach seemed to be holding onto the horse's neck and lowering herself to the ground.

Once her feet were on the dirt, she scratched the horse's neck. "We made it. Now, I should like you to stay here while I set about finding this monster." Hannah tied the horse's reins to a tree with a wide canopy that would shelter the animal, and there was lush grass for it to crop.

Now that she stood in the dark and cold, a little of her initial bravery evaporated. Perhaps this wasn't her smartest idea. At least she wasn't entirely alone. Chelsea was a growing area and dots of light shone from the widely spaced houses that bordered gardens and fields.

She wasn't sure how one hunted a monster and she had little to protect herself with except a few of her mother's spells in her pockets. Another pocket held a miniature glow mushroom, but she didn't want to activate it and attract the attention of the armed men who patrolled the night, keeping the residents safe.

The peacock-feather ring on her smallest finger tingled, and Hannah caressed it with her thumb. Her mother would know she had escaped from the house. She only hoped she would be allowed the latitude to investigate.

A bird fluttered to a branch nearby and cocked its head at Hannah. A coincidence, or a spy for the mage?

"I will be careful, and yes, I will let you know the instant I feel unsafe," Hannah said to the bird. If it were her mother eavesdropping, that should satisfy her maternal urges.

Hannah gave the horse one last pat, more to reassure herself than the beast, before she slipped across the road to the tree-dotted field. Did the monster roam the area looking for victims, or was it seeking dark spots to hide the failed experiments?

She decided on a path dictated by the surrounding trees. With one in sight, she walked to it and rested against its bark while she chose the next tree. The moon tried to shine down but clouds drifted across its face, obscuring its features like a heavily veiled woman. Only the occasional shaft of dull silver managed to penetrate the growing clouds.

Time drifted by as the night grew chillier and stars played hide and seek behind the clouds. Hannah's feet began to ache in her slightly too-large boots and she wondered how far she had walked.

Just as she was halfway to the protective branches

of the next stand of trees, a larger shape detached itself from the shadows and moved through the grass.

"There's someone over here!" an unseen voice yelled.

*Blast!* The militia had spotted the prey at the same time as Hannah. To add to the growing cloud cover, mist decided to roll in off the Thames and wash over the ground. The weather conspired with the night to hold tight to its secrets.

More voices called out, muffled by the thickness of the air. Time had run out for Hannah to learn all she could about the creature. Was it man or monster? It certainly couldn't be her father, unless Sir Hugh had escaped his prison cell. This was an opportunity she couldn't lose. She stopped to survey her surroundings. Where had the shape gone? The surrounding fog was so thick one could lose sight of a barn in daylight. It turned the evening into a nightmare landscape full of hidden terrors.

Hannah tripped over a large rock. As she threw out her hands to steady herself against it, a voice screeched in her mind that something was amiss. The rock was warm, despite the chill bite in the air, and somewhat softer than expected. She studied its pitted grey sides to try to determine what pulled at her mind.

Then the rock groaned and changed. It rose up out of the ground and sprouted limbs. The watery moon-light was blocked as it towered above her. Before her stood a monstrous man. A creature of misshapen clay, as though a blind person had tried to fashion a man from the description of another.

Hannah reached into her pocket and pulled out the mushroom. She tapped the cap and a soft yellow light came from her hand. The creature drew in a sharp breath and recoiled.

"I'll not hurt you. I want to help," she whispered. How odd that it should fear her, when it was easily twice her size and built like an oak.

She held out the light and curiosity overrode fear. The first thing she ascertained was the rise and fall of its chest. It either breathed and drew air into its lungs, or it pretended to breathe, which didn't seem likely. Only the Afflicted adopted the pretence to appear alive in social gatherings. The creature bore a jagged line that ran from his throat down his chest, to disappear under its torn and dirty shirt, as though the unknown surgeon had autopsied the poor fellow and pulled open his chest. As Hannah inspected the flesh that was uncovered, she found similar crude workmanship at its exposed wrists.

"Who did this to you?" she asked in a gentle tone, as though it were an injured kitten and not a seven-foot-tall behemoth.

She stepped forward and the creature took a step back.

"Watch out, lad!" a man yelled from behind.

"It does not mean us any harm," she called. Honestly, men assumed anything bigger than they were must be a threat. The militia had chased the creature through the night, but it had run from them. Despite the rumours, she had seen no evidence of violence from it.

"Back away, lad. Let us deal with it," a familiar voice called.

Lord Wycliff had discovered her whereabouts.

"No. You stay back," she called over her shoulder, keeping her attention on the living thing before her. Or was it living?

The creature emitted a low-pitched whine and clawed at its throat.

Hannah lifted the light. What wouldn't she give to conduct a thorough examination under bright sunlight. How many scars did the creature's body bear, on the inside and out? "Can you speak?"

Yellow eyes stared down at her and a single tear formed at the corner of its eye.

"Speak," it mumbled, as though its tongue didn't belong to its mouth. The monster reached out a hand toward her.

The men behind her shouted and a shot whizzed past Hannah and thudded into its flesh.

"Hold your fire, you imbecile!" Wycliff shouted. "I will see to it that you are court martialed for firing so close to that boy."

The creature pulled at its shoulder, where a dark stain spread over its shirt. The action exposed a tattoo that appeared to be some sort of barrel with a rope coming out of it that formed a heart. There was a word inside. She peered closer...something starting with *M*?

The creature cried out again. As it spun away, something fluttered from its grasp. In only a few steps, its retreating form was swallowed by the enveloping dark and mist.

Hannah peered down to find what had fallen from the creature's hand. Scanning the ground with the help of the glow mushroom, she found a large white daisy.

The creature had offered her a flower.

Hannah picked it up.

"You should not have come out here unaccompanied, Miss Miles." Wycliff loomed out of the dark to appear next to her, as men ran through the night to pursue the creature.

"You gave me the distinct impression you did not require my assistance. So I thought to conduct my own investigation." She twirled the daisy between her fingers.

"You are fortunate I spotted the *lad* riding off on one of your father's horses. Are you unharmed?" Lord Wycliff asked.

"I do not think it meant any harm. It had picked a flower for me." She held out the daisy.

Lord Wycliff took off his overcoat and draped it over Hannah's shoulders. "Did you recognise him?"

"No. I can confirm he is not the madman, only the sad culmination of someone else's mad work." She inhaled the warm aroma that clung to the wool of the coat.

What demented mind thought to piece together a human? Hannah recalled her father's words about the experiment he had once tried, and the Afflicted woman assaulted by memories of the hand sewn to her body. Was the monster tormented by the things remembered by its disparate parts?

"Let's get you back to the house and warmed up. You are damp from the mist, and shaking." Lord Wycliff placed a hand at her back and steered her toward the road.

On impulse she leaned into him and, for once, his unnaturally high temperature gave her comfort, rather than annoyance.

# 22

No doubt due to the hours spent stalking the fields around Chelsea, Hannah slept like the dead. The actual dead who slumbered undisturbed for eternity in their tombs, not the undead who attended parties and balls and danced all night.

She arose later than the rest of the household and found the dining room deserted. The tea was lukewarm and the toast damp and limp. She chewed without tasting as loneliness crept through her bones and chilled her body. Without her father's large presence to fill the house, it seemed empty, both physically and in spirit. At least she had found the monster and could confirm that what the people feared was not her father.

Something scratched and niggled at the back of her mind when she considered the monster's appearance. A memory tried to wriggle free, but it couldn't break out of the tired mist pressing on her.

The ring on her finger tingled in a silent summoning.

"Time to face Mother," she whispered as she pushed her plate away.

Hannah opened the library door to find Lord Wycliff standing by the fireplace, his hands clasped behind his back. Wearing his customary black coat, a charcoal grey waistcoat, and a sombre expression, he appeared to be a mourner at a funeral.

If he could mourn anything.

Lady Miles sat in her bath chair next to the sofa.

"Good morning, Mother. As you can see, I am unharmed by my excursion last night and I have learned crucial information that might free Papa." Hannah crossed to her mother and ignored the dark presence.

"Hannah, I am pleased you suffered no harm, but less pleased you stole out without telling me where you were going." Her mother tilted her face as Hannah leaned down to kiss her veiled cheek.

Wycliff had barely spoken to her on the ride home the night before. He had taken the reins of her horse and led it from his as though she were a naughty child on a lead-rein. It looked as though the two of them were going to reprimand her for running off into the dark on a monster hunt. Hannah decided upon a pre-emptive strike.

"Did Lord Wycliff tell you we found the monster last night? It is a marvellous discovery, for it proves it is not Papa. How soon will he be home, do you think?"

Hannah glanced from the viscount to her mother as she dropped onto the sofa.

"Hannah." Lady Miles uttered her name as a sigh. "An encounter in the dark does not provide much in the way of evidence to free your father."

Hannah turned to Wycliff. This was his doing, surely. "You were there, my lord. You saw him. The monster cannot be my father and he must be released now."

He rested one hand on the mantel. "You are the only one who saw the creature up close, Miss Miles, and the soldiers did not find him. We have no proof to exonerate Sir Hugh, especially that which is provided by his daughter. Further, since there has not been a murder or a body discovered in the days since your father was imprisoned, some are taking that as proof he was responsible."

"No!" Hannah turned to her mother. "This isn't fair, Mother. I saw him. He is a giant creature, sewn together like the woman Beth Warren. He meant no harm and even offered me a flower, but I couldn't learn anything before the soldiers frightened him off."

If Wycliff had stayed away, Hannah might have succeeded in determining who had done that to the poor creature. At least it could speak, unlike Barnes. She might even have persuaded the monster to accompany her home. This impasse was all the viscount's fault.

She couldn't comprehend that people took the lack of bodies popping up in the fields like gruesome mushrooms as proof her father was the madman. Hannah bit down on her crooked finger to hold back her tears. What would they do if her father were hanged? She swallowed the lump in her throat. They were not yet defeated. There must still be a way to prove him innocent.

"What will we do, Mother?" she asked, her voice a raspy whisper as she sought to control her rioting emotions.

"Miss Miles, I am well aware that I have contributed to this situation and that my actions have placed you and your mother in a perilous position. Honour demands I remedy that." Lord Wycliff took a step away from the fireplace and stood with his back ramrod straight and his hands clasped at the small of his back. His shoulders were rigid, his jaw tight.

Well, it *was* all his fault. He needed to stay inside the house while Hannah mounted a second search for the monster. Perhaps she should take something to show she meant no harm, just as he had tried to give her a flower. A toy soldier, perhaps? No, not a soldier. A wooden horse? Oh! Barnes. If she took the hand, it might show the monster that she meant no harm to such creations.

"Hannah. Lord Wycliff has something important to say to you about our family situation." Lady Miles reached out and took Hannah's hand, pulling her mind away from Chelsea and back to the library.

Hannah glanced at her mother, but nothing was revealed from under the thick veil. The churning in her stomach gave a warning shot as to what concerning their *situation* he wished to address. Hannah could only pray her instincts were wrong. "I assume, Lord Wycliff, that to *remedy* the situation, you pledge to prove my father innocent? How went your interviews with Reverend Jones and Lord Dunkeith?"

He frowned, as though he had not expected her to throw that gauntlet at his feet. "Reverend Jones faints at the sight of blood, which is why he abandoned a medical career. Lord Dunkeith was not at home when I called. But that is not the matter I wish to discuss."

"Fainting at the sight of blood does not necessarily clear the reverend of involvement. A dead body has no circulatory system and therefore does not bleed." Although congealed blood did smear over things. Did that trigger a fainting attack or did it have to be fresh, flowing blood? Perhaps they could set a trap for the reverend to determine his reactions.

"Hannah, do try to pay attention," Seraphina said. "Your father's arrest has shone a light on the perilous nature of our existence. I have spoken with your father overnight and we are of one mind in this matter. Now, Lord Wycliff has something important to say."

All the thoughts in Hannah's mind dropped at once, like a curtain descending at the end of a play. An idea more monstrous than what she had encountered in the dark the previous night climbed from the rubble. She stared at her mother and mouthed, "No."

Lord Wycliff coughed and cleared his throat, as though his words stuck in his craw. "You have been most passionate, Miss Miles, in your condemnation of inconstant men. I pledge to you that I am not such an individual. My loyalty, once given, will remain in place until I no longer walk this earth."

A chill flooded Hannah's spine and raised goose-flesh along her arms. No matter how hard she rubbed, she couldn't dispel the cold. "You will need to speak plainly, my lord, and not in riddles. I thought my mother called me here to reprimand me for gallivanting about in the dark, and you speak of loyalty. I do not see how the two matters are related."

Or rather, she had an inkling how they were related and didn't want to venture any farther down that road. Her mind stuttered and froze and she cast around the room, desperate for a way to escape.

He coughed again, as though the damp air of the night before had taken up residence in his lungs. "Regardless of what happens to your father, you and your mother will always have my protection and a roof over your heads, if you will agree to take my name and my hand in marriage."

"No," Hannah whispered. One hand went to her breast to guard her heart, as she gripped her mother's hand tightly. Realisation dripped through her being like melting ice from the tip of a frozen branch.

"No," she said again, this time to her mother. Hannah's eyes were wide as she shook her head and mouthed, "No, no, no," until it became a quiet moan torn from her throat.

"Hannah, you know that should anything happen

to your father, we will be alone in the world. There is also your *condition*, which would prohibit you from inheriting your father's estate. Lord Wycliff offers us a way forward should the unthinkable happen." Her mother tightened her grip on Hannah's hand.

The viscount's forehead had furrowed at Hannah's refusal. "Lady Miles apprised me of the impediment to your inheriting your father's property. I make my offer to relieve you of that burden. I understand this also means there will be no heir for my estate and I accept that."

"No heir?" Hannah's heart tore into tiny pieces and each one *whooshed* from her chest and lodged in her throat. Tears pricked behind her eyes. She tried to pierce the thick veil covering her mother's face to see her eyes. "You told him? I am your only child. How could you? Why, *how*, could you betray me like this?"

She swallowed back the cry building in her throat and let go of her mother's hand to wipe the heels of her palms against her face. She wouldn't cry in front of him, no matter how much she wanted to. Her heart fractured at her mother's cruelty, and her veins crackled with the pain of betrayal as though she were a limb attached to Doctor Husom's galvanism equipment.

Lady Miles reached for her, but Hannah scuttled along the sofa cushions and out of reach. "I love you, Hannah. Never doubt the lengths to which your father and I will go to ensure you remain protected in this world. Did I betray your secret? Yes. Because I am aware that we teeter on a precipice that could collapse beneath us if your father is found guilty. I will not see you cast out in this world, existing on the charity of others, like the late Lady Albright. Viscount Wycliff is an honourable man who would stand beside you throughout all the years to come."

"You have all been discussing me and my condition *behind my back*?" Hannah leapt to her feet. Once her sanctuary, now the library felt like a torture chamber. Had he laughed when he'd found out she was infected? She dared a glance at his chiselled face, but found his features unreadable.

"I believe there is some urgency to marry before your condition...deteriorates," Lord Wycliff intoned as though he delivered a sentence of death upon a prisoner.

Hannah screwed up her eyes and forced back the tears. Her quiet existence had turned into a nightmare and she struggled to draw breath into her lungs. Her gasps turned into sobs that she couldn't control. She pressed her hands to her stomach as the pain overwhelmed her in waves.

Once, she had dreamed of marrying for love such as her dear friend Lizzie had found with her duke. When Hannah had dabbed the cursed face powder upon her skin, she never realised such a dream was cast forever beyond her reach. How cruel was Fate, to first snatch her life away and now, to condemn her to a cold marriage with a man who considered her kind an affront to his God.

Hannah rose to her feet and screwed her eyes shut for a moment. She drew a deep, steadying breath and found a small portion of strength to cling to.

Her mother rubbed her hands together and whispered over them, then held them open and blew. A fine mist formed into the ghostly image of Sir Hugh, pacing his small cell. He rubbed his hands over his face and his shoulders were slumped.

"I am certain we will yet prove your father innocent of the charges against him, but this incident has reminded us of the fragility of our position. Should anything happen to him and when the spell over you fails, we will both be cast into the streets. Lord Wycliff has agreed to marry you and give this family much needed stability, while we continue to find a way to reverse this terrible curse."

Her parents were right, of course. The dead could not inherit or hold property. Once the Affliction permanently stopped Hannah's heart, she would no longer be her father's heir. The house and all their worldly possessions would belong to a distant cousin who had a dim view of mages and Unnatural creatures. He would not extend any charity to them.

The world dissolved into mist as tears blurred Hannah's vision. Her determination fled as her heart tore apart. Those she loved most in the world had turned on her. She cast one last look at her mother. "You betrayed me," she sobbed, then ran for the door. Hannah's feet pounded the floorboards as she hurtled through the house and out the back door.

She let despair free and as it racked her body, she stumbled blindly into the welcoming embrace of the forest. Only among the dense foliage did she slow her pace. She held out her hands to shield her face from the scratch of branches. When she collided with a large elm, she slid down its rough bark to the base. Hannah drew her feet up and hugged her knees as she wept.

Her mother had told *him*! How could she? Her Afflicted state was a family secret. With his gift, Timmy had uncovered it when he'd touched her hand, but the lad had kept it firmly to himself. The monthly rite her mother performed kept Hannah frozen in time and stopped her body from realising death would grab her with the next breath. Day and night, her parents laboured to find a cure to save their child, and the dozens of other people struck down by the French curse.

"I will never marry him," she wailed to the silent trees and ferns. "We will find a cure." Once she was cured, there would be no impediment to her being her father's heir and she would always look after her mother. The woman who had once been the greatest mage in England would never be thrown into the street or forced to live under a hedgerow. Hannah had no need of a husband, so long as they could turn back the hands of time and prevent her death.

Blues and greens swirled in a pattern through her tearstained vision. Percy the peacock picked his way through the leaves and stopped before her. His ornate tail feathers fanned out over the ground. Hannah studied the pattern Nature had drawn upon him, tracing the circles and swirls to calm her mind and bring the tears under control.

The iridescent feathers shimmered from bronze, to green, to blue as he moved. Why was the male bird so beautiful, while those in his harem were so plain?

"Life is not fair. Why are you painted in such beautiful colours, while the little peahens are dipped in tones of brown? Did you ask God to tattoo you in such vibrant hues?" Hannah asked her silent companion.

The word *tattoo* bounced around in her mind. Lizzie had whispered that Harden might get a tattoo to celebrate their wedding. Last night she had seen a tattoo on the stitched-together man. Someone else had a tattoo. Who was it?

The modiste's son! Hannah remembered the story the woman had told of her initial horror at finding out her son had drawn on his body a needle and spool of thread, the loop of thread forming a heart and the word *Mère* inside.

Last night, the Chelsea monster had revealed a tattoo when it clutched at the gunshot wound and pulled the ragged shirt to one side. Hannah had thought it was a barrel and a rope, but what if it were *a spool of thread*?

There was the chance it was a common tattoo. For all she knew, all sons of seamstresses might have such a design inked into their skin. But how many had French mothers? How many sons were gentle giants who had died in the last few weeks? It was too coincidental.

Hannah needed to talk to the modiste and find out more about her son's death. This could be the clue they needed.

"I will prove Father innocent and we will find a cure for this horrible affliction. Then we can forget all about that terrible conversation," she said to the peacock.

Percy cocked his head and trilled, then flicked his tail upright and fanned. Dozens of magical eyes regarded her, and each one reflected her mother's betrayal.

# 23

Hannah picked dry leaves from her skirts and considered her options. The woman within who longed for a love match wanted to hide in the forest forever. The child who desperately wanted to clear her father of heinous accusations forced her to stand. She gathered up the shattered pieces of her heart and locked them away inside, where they were safe.

She wanted to mourn the loss of trust in her mother, to rage at a secret exposed, to sob that she was offered only a cold and practical arrangement. But Hannah was nothing if not pragmatic. Her father sat in prison with terrible charges levelled against him. She would have time to cry later, when he was safe at home. Then she could berate him for his collusion in revealing her Affliction to Wycliff.

As much as it pained her to admit it, she needed help...and in particular the assistance of Viscount

Wycliff. She took up a mental broom and swept every syllable and glance of the morning's awful interview under the proverbial rug. She would not think about it until later. Now was not the time to indulge in tears—she had a murderer to unmask.

With each step she took back to the house, Hannah buried her disappointment, wiped away her tears, and poured steel into her spine. Despite all this, her courage almost deserted her as her fist hovered over the viscount's study door. It took three attempts before she could make herself rap on the dark wood.

"Enter," a deep voice commanded.

She flung the door open and let the words burst free before she turned tail and ran back to the comforting embrace of the forest. "We are missing a vital clue. I need your help to question a modiste."

"A modiste? I require a little more information than that." He laid down his quill and turned, but otherwise remained immobile.

"The Chelsea monster had a tattoo on his chest. Here." She tapped the space above her heart. "It is a spool of thread and a needle enclosing the word *Mère*. There is a French modiste whose son died a few weeks ago. He had such a tattoo."

The viscount leapt from his chair and grabbed the coat and hat on the rack by the door. "You can tell me more on the way."

Hannah was silent for a moment as she watched him tug on his coat. Just like that, he believed her, with no argument or bluster or, thankfully, a repeated offer of marriage.

"I shall harness the horse myself while you fetch a coat." Then he shooed her from his study.

Hannah ran up the stairs, gathered the items of clothing she needed, and ran back down and out of the house. This time she ran toward the viscount, not away from him. In no time the two of them were in the gig and trotting along the road. Having a purpose helped her shake off the sorrow that wanted to chill the very marrow in her bones.

On the way, Hannah elaborated on their mission. "My friend, Lady Elizabeth Loburn, has engaged a French seamstress to make her wedding gown and trousseau. Our conversation turned to tattoos—"

The viscount nearly pulled the horse to a halt as he whipped around to stare at her. "You were talking about tattoos?"

"Yes, my lord. Do you think polite ladies only talk of embroidery, music, and dinner menus?" For a man of the world, he seemed to have a very narrow understanding of women.

He laughed out loud and urged the horse onward again. "We may not have been associated for long, Miss Miles, but I have come to realise that despite your demure manners, you are in fact quite a rebel and do not conform to what society expects. Please continue with your tale of tattoos."

Had that been a compliment? One didn't have to

scream and shout that one was not following the expected conventions. Many like herself went about quietly doing as they pleased. Marching to their own drum, as it were.

"The modiste told us that she was horrified when her son had been tattooed to honour her. Then she began to cry, wishing she could see it once more. It transpired that he had a heart condition and died suddenly a few weeks ago. She described him as a lion of a man with the soul of a lamb. I believe he may be the Chelsea monster. If we can discover what happened to him, we may yet find the missing clue we need."

"Unless he too was buried, and his mortal body dug up by grave robbers and sold, unbeknownst to his grieving mother." Lord Wycliff's attention was on the road and the increasing number of horses and other carriages sharing it.

She didn't want to contemplate that option. Her day was miserable and she needed a tiny ray of sunshine within it.

The horse took a corner a little too fast and the gig lurched to one side. Hannah slid into the viscount and he shot out a hand to steady her.

Not for the first time, Hannah found herself pondering how caring a gentleman he could be. Despite their differences, he listened to her opinions and treated her as an equal. The tiny, practical voice in the back of her mind whispered, *Would it be such a terrible thing to accept his offer?*

She didn't want to even contemplate the possibility, but like Pandora's box, once she peered within, she couldn't quite clap the lid back on again. Thoughts escaped against her will. He knew her painful secret and promised loyalty that would extend beyond death. He vowed to care for her family always. And that was no insignificant thing to her. Certainly she had no other prospects on the horizon.

She might even discover his tragic secret. Though hoping for a full confession on their wedding night might be too fanciful.

Hannah gripped the side of the gig more tightly and tried to concentrate on their present mission. She directed the viscount down a series of roads and lanes to the street that contained the dress shop. The modiste lived above her shop, and a narrow set of stairs wound up the side to her apartment.

Wycliff tied the reins to the front of the gig and jumped to the ground before offering a hand to Hannah. The shop was closed and she led the way up the steep stairs and knocked on the red painted door at the top.

The door opened and the seamstress beamed upon seeing Hannah. "Miss Miles, we do not have an appointment I have forgotten, have we?"

Hannah flashed a reassuring smile as the other woman's smile was replaced by worry. "No. Forgive me, Madame Fontaine, but I am here on a matter concerning your son. I need to know if he was under the care of a doctor before he died?"

Grief washed over the modiste's face at mention of her son and she clasped her hands together. "Oh, *oui*. Sir Hugh Miles—"

Hannah nearly cried out loud in despair. Her brain refused to accept the evidence that mounted against the father she loved.

The older woman continued, unaware of Hannah's distress. "—recommended he see Lord Dunkeith. He brewed a potion to help with the heart of *mon cher* François. He is ever such a gentleman, that one. When the potion did not work, he insisted on paying for my son's funeral and made all the arrangements." She dabbed at her eyes. "All his friends came. They called him Frank, as you *Anglais* do."

"Lord Dunkeith?" Hannah was not interested in the deceased's friends. She turned to Wycliff, seeking verification that she had heard the correct name. Had her father not been involved at all except as a reference?

"*Oui, c'est ça.*" The seamstress nodded and looked from Hannah to the viscount.

"Thank you, madame, you have been most helpful," Wycliff said. He took Hannah's arm and urged her back down the stairs.

"Lord Dunkeith brewed a potion and took care of the funeral arrangements." Hannah repeated the words, waiting for them to filter through her mind. It couldn't possibly be true. He was a gentleman. But then, so was her father, and he languished in gaol.

Perhaps she wasn't such a good judge of character after all.

Wycliff helped Hannah back into the gig. "Dunkeith was last known to be treating her son, but we do not have any evidence that he was responsible for his death."

Now that Hannah had grasped the idea, her mind leapt into action, piecing together the bits she knew. "Lord Dunkeith paid for the funeral and made all the arrangements. Shall we locate his grave and see if Frank occupies the coffin within? I'll wager he does not. I am certain that it is Madame Fontaine's son who roams the fields."

"We still have nothing to connect Lord Dunkeith to the mutilation and reanimation of these people." Wycliff turned the horse in the narrow street and then navigated the growing traffic on the road.

Once Hannah overcame her reluctance to see Lord Dunkeith as the responsible party, the ideas flowed from her mind. "My father recommended that Frank see Lord Dunkeith for a potion for his heart. What if he likewise suggested that Beth see him for a potion for her cough?"

Wycliff swore under his breath. "Of course. It makes sense now."

"You know something, my lord?" Hannah gripped the side of the gig as the horse dodged around a larger carriage.

He stared straight ahead for a long moment before

saying, "Beth was given a potion for her cough that made her sleepy."

Hannah didn't remember seeing anything to that effect pinned to his study wall. "How do you know that?"

"The source is not important, but I believe it to be accurate. That would make *two* individuals who were sick but not fatally so, until they took one of Lord Dunkeith's potions. To extrapolate further, Nell might have seen him for a lotion for her itch and Tabitha might have sought relief from her stomach pains with a draught."

"All the pieces of the patchwork Beth may have been to see Lord Dunkeith." Hannah said the words, but her mind struggled to believe them. Why would the handsome peer do such an awful thing?

"If Beth was murdered for her parts, what if she were pointing to Dunkeith's house? It is across the road from the Physic Garden. I *knew* something smelt wrong there." He flapped the reins against the horse's flank and it broke into a canter.

Events of the day drifted through Hannah's mind. As she thought of love and marriage, she remembered a devoted lover who sent his dead fiancée a bouquet every week. "Lord Dunkeith loves Lady Diana Morgan. They were to be married, but she was struck down two years ago and became one of the Afflicted. I believe he searches for a way to restart her heart so they might yet wed."

Hannah wanted a man who would love beyond

death, but how could such a beautiful thing become so twisted, and result in the death and mutilation of so many others? The gig bounced into every pothole as they sped along the road. Hannah clung to the side to keep from tumbling out as Wycliff urged the horse onward.

"How many other people are involved, do you think—all those whose limbs we found, but not the remainder of their bodies? Did they all visit Lord Dunkeith for a remedy to soothe an ailment, only to be given eternal sleep?" Hannah voiced the ideas in her head, mainly to distract herself from the image of bouncing out of the gig and being smashed upon the road.

"We might never know. But if we can prove he killed Beth Warren and Frank Fontaine, at least charges for those crimes can be brought against him." Lord Wycliff slowed the horse to a trot as he steered it into the drive before Lord Dunkeith's house. He jumped down, ran to the door, and rapped hard upon it.

Hannah scrambled from the gig without assistance, her knees knocking together after the harrowing ride, but grateful that her feet were on firm ground.

The butler opened the door and narrowed his eyes at them. "His lordship is not at home, my lord."

"Can you sense if he is here and using his magic?" Wycliff asked Hannah as she joined him on the front step.

"I—I don't know. I've never tried that before."

Hannah could distinguish between her mother's magic and that of others by the feel of it. She never went searching for magic in use; usually she simply walked into it.

Wycliff pushed the butler out of the way and gestured for Hannah to enter the house. She stood in the tiled foyer and turned in a slow circle. If his lordship were here, surely he would be in the conservatory? She peered in that direction, but felt nothing.

She closed her eyes so she did not rely upon them, and let her body tell her whether magic was being used nearby. As she was about to open her eyes and say no, a faint tingle ran over her scalp.

"Upstairs," she said, and pointed to the ceiling.

Wycliff bolted like a hound after a rabbit and took the stairs two at a time.

"You cannot go up there, my lord," the butler called after the retreating form.

"I'm ever so sorry for the intrusion," Hannah said to the butler as she picked up her skirts and hurried after the viscount.

At each floor, Wycliff stopped and waited for Hannah. "Which way?"

It took her a moment or two to catch her breath and wait for the tingle. With each flight of stairs, the tingle turned into a prickle, but it still ran over her scalp, indicating they should proceed upward.

At last they reached the top storey of the house. Still the sensation ran through her hair. Hannah turned in a slow full circle, willing the reaction to indicate a door coming off the hallway. Instead she ran a hand over her itchy head. "I'm sorry, I must be wrong..."

"The attic. The stairs will be hidden from view." He peered at the panelling and Hannah was certain he...sniffed.

"There's a seam here." He gripped a piece of moulding with his fingertips and pulled. The wall split apart to reveal a narrow staircase leading higher.

The prickle in Hannah's scalp ran over her body, as a low moan tumbled down the stairs and washed over them.

Lord Wycliff disappeared into the narrow opening and Hannah followed him. The walls closed in on them and she almost couldn't see around him in the dim stairwell.

At the top was another door. Lord Wycliff grabbed the handle, but the door held fast. He grunted, and then put his shoulder to the door and burst through it into the attic room. Hannah spilled through behind him.

She took in all she could at a glance. In the middle of the floor was a large slate table such as her father and other surgeons used for surgery and autopsies. The hard surface was cut on a slope to drain away fluids. Buckets sat at each bottom corner to catch what ran off the table. On the cold surface rested a woman's naked body. Long, dark hair draped over the end of the table. Two arms waited on a trolley at its side. Legs had been laid in place, but were not attached to the body.

The Chelsea monster huddled on the floor, rocking

with its knees to its chest as it moaned. The low, keening noise made a ghastly musical accompaniment to the mad surgery about to be performed.

Next to the autopsy table was what appeared to be a large, claw-footed bath containing a yellow liquid. Draped in the water were copper wires that ran upward to the ceiling, where they twisted into a solid cable before disappearing through the roof.

"He has tried to copy Doctor Husom's galvanism equipment," Hannah whispered.

As she surveyed the scene in an instant, a single word leapt to her mind to describe it—*chaotic*.

Every surface was covered with books, papers, and bottles. Vials of varying shapes and sizes stood everywhere. Some were plain clear glass, others made of cut glass in beautiful hues. They had been tossed aside with no regard to their value or contents. Some were upright, others listed against their neighbours, and a few had tipped over, their contents oozing onto the floor below. Some bottles had wax seals, others were open and emitted a variety of clouds. One even seemed to have a fine drizzle falling *upward* from its open top.

Quite frankly, surveying the laboratory made Hannah's skin itch with the overwhelming desire to start cleaning and tidying up. How on earth could any serious scientific research be conducted in the midst of such a *mess*?

Lord Dunkeith wore an apron over his fashionable clothes, and clutched a needle in one hand from which dangled a length of catgut. He was frozen in time as he took seconds to grasp the meaning of their intrusion, and they stared at each other. His eyes widened and his mouth made an O shape.

Then Lord Dunkeith dropped the needle on a tray and snatched up a vial. "Stop them!" he yelled as he hurled the vial to the ground at Wycliff's feet.

The viscount jumped backward as glass shattered and a green haze exploded.

Hannah coughed and held her sleeve over her face as the details of the room, along with their quarry, disappeared. The trickle of sensation over her scalp became an enraged ocean that crashed down her throat. She gasped as her lungs caught fire. Her entire body hurt as the magical gas enveloped them.

Gritting her teeth, she wrapped her fingers around the ring on her smallest finger and rubbed the mage silver. She whispered a few words passed on by her mother, and the familiar maternal touch flowed up her hand, along her arm, and through her body. Her mother's warding spell repelled the magic trying to incapacitate her.

Hannah wondered how Lord Wycliff would be able to function, when she had her mother's spell to counteract the green haze. A coughed racked her lungs —she burped a cloud of green smoke—and it was gone, expelled from her body.

Through the dense fog came a roar. A yellow burst of smoke erupted from where Wycliff stood and collided with the green fog. The colours swirled and then dissolved in a puff of sulphur.

The monster charged at Wycliff, who growled and ran at the stitched-together man. He drew back his right arm and threw a punch to the creature's middle.

Hannah cast around, looking for some way to help, when she spotted the hidden door in the wainscoting.

It stood open a few inches. "He's getting away!"

"I am somewhat preoccupied, Miss Miles." Wycliff threw punches that the creature batted away as though a mosquito annoyed him.

"Oh, this is pointless," Hannah muttered under her breath. There was no use in her running after Lord Dunkeith—she could do nothing to apprehend him unless she threw herself at his ankles. And wealthy lords were long accustomed to escaping the clutches of desperate maidens.

The modiste had said that despite his large size, her son had a gentle soul. That called to mind how he had picked a flower for her when the men had shot at him. Watching Wycliff battle the seven-foot-tall man, she observed how one-sided the fight seemed. The reanimated corpse never aimed a blow at the viscount, when it would have been a simple thing for him to thump the smaller man on the head.

That gave Hannah an idea. She only needed to determine how to implement it.

The monster blocked the door where his master had fled while Wycliff pounded at his middle. It appeared neither would listen to her entreaties to cease.

Taking a deep breath, Hannah threw herself between the combatants just as the viscount drew back for another punch. She watched his fist descend and threw her hands up in front of her face, braced for the blow.

# 24

Wycliff threw the punch with all his might, aiming for the monster's chin and hoping it would be a weak spot on the behemoth. Miss Miles darted between him and the monster and in a second, he realised he couldn't stop himself from hitting her. As he pondered what the furious mage would do to him for striking her daughter, he discovered his fist had failed to connect with her slender form. An enormous hand wrapped around his and absorbed the blow, halting his fist a mere inch or two from Miss Miles' face.

She peered at him from between her fingers and pressed herself into the creature.

"Miss Miles! Get out of the way before you are hurt," he commanded. Shock at what he had almost done collided with concern for her safety, and the urgent need to pursue his quarry.

With a seven-foot protective monster at her back,

the woman was bolder than usual. "No, not until you stop. He is not fighting you, my lord, merely deflecting your blows and preventing us from following his master."

He wanted to snatch her away from it, but he had to admit that the thing sheltered the woman better than any gentleman could. "How can you be so sure?"

She smiled up at the ugly thing as though it were a lost puppy. "Because he has a tender heart. Do not judge him by his outward appearance, but by his actions. He has not made a single aggressive move toward you."

Wycliff lowered his fists and gestured to the obscured doorway. "Very well, but Lord Dunkeith is getting away. Ask your creature to move, please."

Miss Miles turned and placed both hands on the monster's chest. She looked up into his eyes, where even the irises seemed comprised of patchwork. "Please move. We need to stop Lord Dunkeith so he cannot do this to anyone else."

"You. Stay?" the creature rasped.

Miss Miles patted his chest and then turned back to Wycliff. "I will stay here for now, but you must go and stop Lord Dunkeith. I'll follow as soon as I can."

He didn't have time to worry about her, but must trust instead to her sensible nature and the protections she carried from her mage mother. As soon as the creature shuffled to one side, he dove through the narrow door.

He chased a rabbit through a warren, he thought as

he hurtled down another dark and twisty passage, the air close and stale. There were a bevy of passages concealed between the walls of the house, no doubt how Dunkeith managed to carry his victims to and from his laboratory. As Wycliff wondered if he would ever draw fresh air or see the sky again, he burst out through another section of panelling.

He paused in the unfamiliar hall for a moment, his head cocked to listen. A faint shuffle caught his attention and he swung in the direction. He ran toward a door that hung open and allowed a breeze to come through from outside.

Wycliff ran through the door and out of the house. He paused and drew a breath into his lungs, glad of its cool touch after the hot stairway.

"He can't have got far," Wycliff muttered.

He found himself in a cobbled courtyard. Across from the house stood a double height barn. To the other side was a lush garden with mature trees that would create welcome shade in summer. Which way would he have gone? Through the garden, perhaps—a more familiar environment for him?

A horse's neigh pulled his attention toward the stables. Why flee on foot when one had faster horses available?

He took off at a run across the cobbles. Anger surged through his body, turning his blood to molten steel. His quarry had committed murder while safe behind the expensive façade of his house. They might never know how many lives had been taken as

Dunkeith sought to pry one Afflicted woman from the grasp of death.

The rage took over as he dropped to all fours, heedless of curious servants running to see the cause of the commotion. As he sprang through the open doors, he welcomed the change. Let the monster in the barn deal with the beast.

Dunkeith stood in the barn aisle with a leggy bay. He struggled to place a bridle over the animal's ears as it whinnied in panic, the whites of its eyes showing. The animal danced sideways as Wycliff plunged through the open doors. The horse reared up, before galloping from the stables to the safety of open space beyond.

Dunkeith was knocked sideways as the horse bolted, and fell. "Damnation!"

Wycliff focused on the noble as he stalked closer.

Dunkeith looked up and his eyes widened. Already on the ground, he scrabbled backward, away from Wycliff. He held up his hands as he glanced from side to side. "Easy, boy. Nice doggy."

*Doggy?* Wycliff snarled and it came out as a puff of smoke. He opened his jaws and let saliva drip from his fangs, each droplet hitting the brick floor with a sizzle as he advanced on his prey.

Dunkeith scurried backward until he hit the solid wall of a stall. He turned his head and sobbed, "I don't want to die like this. I don't even like dogs."

As Wycliff trod loose hay on the brick floor, the tinder burst into flames beneath him. A fiery trail led to the murderer. Sparks raced along and licked at the wooden walls of empty stalls.

"Fire. Fire!" Dunkeith pointed and yelled, but he never moved from his spot on the floor.

The air shimmered beside the fallen lord, as though a cloud of smoke formed, sucked from the burning hay. It hung a foot from the ground and grew to seven feet tall and three feet wide. As Wycliff watched both the murderer and the strange shape, a tear split down the middle and peeled apart to reveal...nothing.

"What...what is that?" Dunkeith turned his head from Wycliff and stared at the snatch of night sky suspended inside the barn.

Except it wasn't sky. Recognition rumbled through Wycliff. The void called to him with a soft voice, urging him to feed it the evil, worthless soul cowering before him. Shadows moved within the inky space, whispering of the torment Dunkeith would face for eternity for his crimes.

How easy it would be to grasp the aftermage by the throat, toss him through the rift, and have done with him! But if Wycliff did so, there would be no public reckoning. With no confession, there was a slender chance the magistrate would not let Sir Hugh go free. He wouldn't risk that.

Besides, justice must be seen to be done. The families of the victims deserved to see Dunkeith unmasked as the true monster. The man had all of eternity to atone for his sins—after he was found guilty and hanged.

Wycliff placed a large foot on Dunkeith's chest and the fabric smouldered under his touch. The man sobbed and begged for mercy as a puddle formed under his trousers.

*Coward,* Wycliff thought. He called the beast under control and commanded it to heel. He shook his limbs as he regained his form and stood over his quarry, careful to avoid standing in the urine that flowed toward the central drain conduit in the barn.

The doorway to the underworld shimmered and then disappeared with a *pop* like the snap of a burning twig.

Dunkeith's hands waved in two different directions. "You...? What...what are you?"

"Justice." Wycliff wrapped his hand in Dunkeith's shirt and punched him hard in the jaw. He had the satisfaction of seeing the man's eyes roll up into his head as he fell over, unconscious.

He grabbed him by the shoulders and hauled him up to a sitting position. His head lolled to one side and his eyes seemed to point in different directions.

"Oh, is it over already?" Miss Miles ran into the barn and skidded to a halt before the line of ankle-high flames.

"Yes. I caught him as he was trying to bridle a horse. It didn't take too much to subdue him." Lord Wycliff stamped on the burning hay.

Miss Miles reached for a pitchfork leaning against a post and began separating the hay to put out the flames. "For a man who willingly committed murder to cure his love, I thought he might have put up more of a struggle."

Wycliff schooled his lips to resist the urge to laugh, but raised one eyebrow. "Did you want to see him pummel me a little, as Mr Rowley did?"

Her eyes brightened and he swore mischief danced in her gaze. Before she could answer, a man ran through the open doors with a bucket clutched in his hands. "Fire!" he yelled, before he tossed the contents at the smouldering tinder. Another groom was right behind the first and he also lobbed his full bucket in the same direction.

Unfortunately, Wycliff stood right next to the burning hay and was drenched from head to toe. His hair was plastered to his face and water soaked through his coat and ran down his trousers and into his boots. He shook himself and the water dripped onto the scorched hay.

He met Miss Miles' stare and dared her to laugh.

She couldn't hold it in. She dropped the pitchfork and burst into laughter.

"When you have finished, could you find me a length of rope?" he inquired.

She stopped the next man who ran in before he also tossed his full buckets. "The fire is out. May I please have some rope?"

A stable hand fetched a length of rope and Wycliff soon had Dunkeith trussed up like a Christmas goose, and bound hand to foot. His servants were not happy and muttered among themselves, but they stood back and waited to see what would happen.

Miss Miles leaned on the half wall of the horses' stalls and stared at the prisoner. "He has such a handsome countenance, yet it gives no clue of the monstrous workings of his mind."

Wycliff didn't see anything remotely handsome about the man. Was that the sort of insipid look she admired? "Imagine if we all wore the visible signs of our deeds. Almack's would become a place of fetid horror, much like visiting the rotten Afflicted in the Repository."

"Why did you kill those women?" Miss Miles asked as the noble showed signs of regaining his wits. "You devoted your life to healing others. How could you descend to such a dark place?"

"Because they resembled my love. You of all people, Miss Miles, should understand the importance of my work. We must find a cure for the Afflicted." Lord Dunkeith struggled against his bonds.

Wycliff rubbed his wet hair with a currying towel and then tossed it over the wall. "What do you mean, they resembled Lady Diana? Why was that relevant?"

Dunkeith's eyes were overbright and shone with madness. "It was all part of my plan. If I could not restart Diana's heart, I would find a body in which to house her mind. But it needed to be as perfect as she is."

Miss Miles clasped a hand over her mouth. "No.

You cannot justify murder in the name of love. What sort of poisonous love demands the lives of innocents?"

Lord Dunkeith rolled his head to rest it against the wall. "What would you do for love, Miss Miles? We cannot marry unless she is cured. Her heart is dead and mine is frozen without her."

"What you did goes against everything we believe in. To take the life of another by force makes you more of a monster than the stitched-together man hiding in your attic." Miss Miles wiped a tear against the sleeve of her pelisse.

"How did you make Frank Fontaine live?" Wycliff asked. How did one creature remain ambulatory while the others did not?

Lord Dunkeith laughed and it carried a manic pitch. "Magic. The body is immersed in a potion that recreates the amniotic fluid of birth. Then, if the weather cooperates, the fluid is charged by a lightning strike. He has been my only success. The woman did not live long before she failed. The stupid lump of flesh was supposed to dump her in the crematorium."

"You merged galvanism with your aftermage gift for the apothecary's arts. Fascinating," Miss Miles said. "When did the body with the Afflicted parts go into the bath? Before or after they were stitched together?"

Dunkeith leaned toward her. "You know of that? That was an early, and unsuccessful, experiment. I thought the body would be a suitable torso, but I discovered that Afflicted remains do not behave in the way I required."

Miss Miles stood on the bricks a careful distance from Dunkeith. "Afflicted limbs retain too much independence."

"Yes!" Dunkeith laughed. "When it didn't behave, I consigned the remains to the crematorium."

"Is that what happened to the other people you murdered?" Wycliff reminded the man of the lives he had taken. He suspected the bodies, and any evidence, had been consumed by the magically enhanced flames.

The noble snorted and looked away. "What does one usually do with rubbish one no longer requires?"

A group of soldiers arrived, no doubt alerted by Lady Miles, who tracked her daughter by the mage-silver ring.

"He doesn't look like the Chelsea monster," the lead officer said as he peered at the bound man.

"Monsters rarely appear as we think they should," Wycliff replied. "Sir Hugh Miles is innocent of any crime. This man murdered Beth Warren, Frank Fontaine, Nell Watts, Tabitha Chant, and possibly many more. His current unidentified victims are on his table in the attic."

Two soldiers picked up the fallen lord and ushered him from the stables. Hannah and Wycliff watched as he was loaded into a carriage without any windows.

"What will happen to him now?" she asked. The servants appeared confused, gathering in small groups to whisper.

"He will take your father's cell in Newgate Prison." There was one good thing—her father would be released and one source of tension in the household would be eased.

As the carriage rolled out of the courtyard, Miss Miles glanced up at the roof of the house. "We still have much to do. We will need to identify the women up there, so their families can bury them."

"We might never find the owners of the limbs, but I'll have the Runners spread word on the street with the description of the torso. I imagine that, like the others, she probably came to Dunkeith for a potion for some minor illness."

They headed back into the house and up the narrow, dark stairs to the attics. The monster still sat on the floor, leaning against the wall. The dead woman was now covered by a sheet.

"What would you do with him?" Wycliff had an inkling, given what he knew of her nature. He suspected the monster would join the Miles menagerie.

"There is so much we do not know about him, from what Lord Dunkeith put in the potion that reanimated his flesh, to how long the effects might last. We have much to do, studying Frank and the notes and bottles in this attic." Miss Miles gestured to the crammed workspace, where every surface was covered.

"Frank?" He swallowed a smile. She was already calling her latest acquisition by his first name.

"Yes. That is his name." She crouched and rested a hand atop one of the creature's hands. "Will you come with me? I will take you to a new home."

"Master?" The monster raised his head and yellow

eyes glanced from one side to another.

"You are not to worry about him any more. He will answer for the things he did. If you come with me, we will look after you." Miss Miles took Frank's hand and he held hers as gently as if she were a daisy. He followed her down the stairs and from the house.

Wycliff allowed himself a silent laugh at the sight. "He's not going to fit in the gig," he observed once they were out in the drive.

Even the placid horse snorted and rolled its eyes at the load it was expected to convey.

"Bother. We can't risk a panic by walking into Chelsea to look for a hackney." Miss Miles tugged at the torn collar on Frank's shirt, but it did nothing to conceal his gruesome appearance.

Wycliff was about to go find a hack, when the clatter of hooves made him look around.

"Old Jim!" Miss Miles called as the family's elderly retainer drove their carriage into the sweep.

The man touched the brim of his cap after he pulled the horses to a halt. "Miss Miles, your lordship. Lady Miles sent me. She said you might be needing the carriage."

Wycliff opened the carriage door, then bowed toward Hannah. "Your carriage awaits, Miss Miles. I'll stay here to ensure nothing is touched, and will make arrangements for the woman's body and the limbs."

Miss Miles rested a hand on his forearm. "Thank you. Come along, Frank. Let's take you to your new home."

## 25

Hannah took the creature home, where Mary took one look at him, screamed, and fainted. The gentle giant caught the distraught maid before she hit the ground.

"Do you really think she has a suitable constitution for this household?" Lord Wycliff observed when he returned, the ghost of a smile on his lips.

"Mary is part of the family. She simply requires time to adjust to change." Although perhaps she should not bring home any dismembered or reassembled body parts for some time, to give the maid a chance to recover her wits.

The next day, with the true monster in custody, her father was released from prison. Lord Dunkeith made a full confession and pleaded that he not be thrown into the pits of Hell. While waiting for his execution, he took to spending much time on his knees in prayer, trying to atone for the horrible crimes he had committed.

Hannah also spent much time on her knees—organising and sorting the clutter in Lord Dunkeith's attic under a warrant from the magistrate, while the Dunkeith heirs sorted themselves out. The family of the woman was found and she was given a decent burial. No one would be stitching her to other women to create an abomination.

"The man was a scatterbrain!" her father exclaimed one afternoon, holding up a stack of papers. "His notes are erratic and he didn't apply any sort of scientific approach to his work."

"That would explain why he couldn't replicate the first result. Perhaps he didn't know what triggered his success." Hannah picked up bottles and vials and placed them in a crate.

They took samples of the yellow liquid in the bathtub, which congealed and emitted a noxious smell like rotten eggs. Hannah drew a sketch of the arrangement of the copper wires and bathtub.

"How will we make certain this doesn't happen again, Papa?" she asked as they worked.

Her father dropped another stack of papers into a box. "The matter has been raised with the members of SUSS, and we have decided that no one will work in secret any more. We are all to open our laboratories to others. We are also amending our charter to include a requirement for *express consent* before experimenting on the dead."

"Will it be enough?" Could anyone stop a determined madman?

"It is a start, Hannah." Her father patted her head as she walked past to tackle another bench.

Once everything was packed up, tidied, and the floors swept, Hannah followed her father from the attic. He closed and locked the door, although no one would be recreating the terrible experiments in there now.

"There is still one matter outstanding, Hannah," her father said as the carriage bowled along in the direction of home.

She stared out the window. For a week now she had managed to forget that horrible interview in the library. "You are home. The matter is resolved."

"Hannah." He moved from his side of the carriage to sit next to her, and took her hand. "I am home...this time. But what if something strikes me down? If you succumb to the French curse like your mother, my estate will go to my cousin. He is a greedy and narrow-minded man who will have no qualms about seeing you and your mother thrown into the street."

Her heart grew heavy in her body and she wanted to slump under the woes she was forced to endure. "Is Lord Wycliff any better an alternative?"

"Yes. While he may be rude and abrasive, he is a man of honour. He vows to protect you and your mother. I believe he is the sort of man who, once he gives his word, will abide by it."

Hannah stared at her hand, dwarfed by her father's

larger one. There were days when she didn't want to grow up. Why couldn't she be a child forever, protected by her parents?

Thinking of being a child, she placed one hand over her stomach. She would never know the joy of motherhood. "Either frozen or dead, I cannot conceive and fulfil my duty to provide an heir."

Her father pulled her into a hug. "While it is true that children bring a particular type of love into your life, it does not mean you will have an empty life without them. You will find another way to bring joy into your days."

Hannah let out a sigh. It was time for her to grow up and assume her share of responsibility in looking after their strange family. Future events would impact not only her, but also Mary, Timmy, Barnes, and Frank.

Her father kissed her forehead. "Think on it. I know you will do the right thing."

She did think on it. Setting aside emotional considerations, there was a pragmatic merit to the offer. Yet still her heart ached for romance. She might have to take up reading more novels. Or she could do something more worthy, like offering a home and education to orphans like Timmy.

After another day had passed, it was time to address the matter. Hannah went in search of Wycliff, knocked on his study door, and waited for the call to enter. She stood in the middle of the room and clasped her hands in front of her.

"A few days ago, my lord, you made me an offer. Now that we have apprehended the true murderer and my father has been released, I likewise release you from a promise hastily given." There, she'd said it. Let them air the matter and put an end to it.

He stared at her for what seemed an eternity...his black gaze so like looking at a starless night. "I gave your mother my word and I will abide by it."

"There is no need, my lord. My father is restored to us and our situation is not so perilous. Given that you have made it clear you are repulsed by the Afflicted, I doubt you wish to be legally bound to one." How could he bear to stand next to her in church, when he had previously been most emphatic in his desire to see them all herded onto a funeral pyre?

He rested his hands on his thighs and spoke with slow, measured words, as though he feared spooking her like a nervous horse. "Your father is returned, for which I am thankful. But given that I am not aware that you have been cured, your situation remains perilous."

Hannah didn't need to be reminded of that. She tried to live each day to the full and to ignore the open grave that awaited her with her next breath.

He tapped his fingers against his thigh. "I owe you an apology, Miss Miles. I have been wrong in my assessment of the Afflicted, and you have opened my eyes to that. As you once pointed out to me, having the capacity to commit a crime and the intention to do so are two different things."

She stared at him. While she had expected him to say many things, an apology was not one of them. "Thank you, my lord, for admitting that. It does ease my concerns somewhat. But there is another delicate matter. I most likely could never provide you with an heir."

Hannah dropped her gaze, unable to look at him while raising such an issue, or rather the lack of issue. Silence was her only answer, until she glanced up to ensure he was still in the room.

He had fisted his hand and then uncurled his fingers against his leg. "I have considered my own circumstances, and believe it may be for the best if I do not have offspring. Ours would be a marriage in name only, should you accept my offer. Or is the prospect too horrifying?" He stood and tucked his hands behind him.

Her insides rolled, but now that she had spent a few days in careful consideration, she no longer found the idea of marriage to him horrifying. The loss of her dream of a love match and children saddened her, but she had always been a practical person. Her father was right: The man before her might be abrupt, but he was also honourable. He had shown that he could treat her as an equal, and did not expect her to submit to his ideas. Nor, it appeared, would she have to submit to his person.

Could a tolerable match grow from such small origins? "It would be a fortuitous marriage for you, my lord. If both my mother and I are deceased, you will inherit my father's entire estate, which I believe will be sufficient to revive the fortunes of yours. Once I died, you would be legally able to set me aside and find yourself a more fertile wife, such as Lord Albright did."

He ground his jaw and his nostrils flared. "You would compare me to that shallow creature? Do you consider me so scheming and devious that I would do this solely for financial advantage?"

Did his motives matter? Money, honour, boredom. What did she care? The end result would still be the same. Hannah's shoulders slumped as she contemplated the years ahead. Years of forced proximity and stilted conversation over tea until death finally released them. If she were lucky, perhaps he would take a portion of the funds and retire to his country estate.

*It doesn't have to be like that*, a tiny voice whispered in the back of her mind. What if they could find common ground? She had seen him smile and it stole her breath. He had shown moments of genuine kindness to her. His touch warmed her like no other had done. What if those aspects were nurtured to grow into something marvellous?

If she dared to take a chance, what might she reap in return?

Like any woman, she still had her pride. With a decision made, she straightened her back and met his gaze. "I will accept your offer of marriage, with one stipulation. Should my parents find a cure for the

Affliction and reverse my condition, you will grant me a divorce and renounce any claim to my father's estate."

He nodded curtly. "Very well."

He held out his hand and she took it. With one handshake, her future was sealed.

THE NEXT DAY, Hannah visited Lizzie and her mother, who were finalising the last few details before the society wedding of the year. Hannah stared at the gilt-edged invitation in her hand. The names blurred as the letters changed places, as though they sought to spell out a different name. The *E* kept running to the edge of the heavy paper, chased by the wayward *H* from Harden.

"Whatever is the matter, Hannah? You have been staring at that invitation for at least fifteen minutes. Have we spelt someone's name wrong?" A faint frown pulled at Lizzie's fair brow.

Oh, drat. Weddings were much on Hannah's mind, but not the wonderful society event being planned here like a military campaign. A far more hurried and private nuptials loomed on the horizon.

"I—" No, that didn't seem right. It had not been her decision. "We—" That didn't fit, either. "It has been decided—"

"Whatever is worrying you, Hannah? It is unlike you to be so distracted," Lady Loburn said from the end of the table.

Hannah set aside the engraved square and laid her hands flat in her lap. Better to confess and have the news out in the open. It was hard enough to keep one secret from Lizzie; she could not hold in two. "I am to marry Viscount Wycliff."

"No!" Lizzie's voice wailed like a cold wind through a graveyard. Her friend's eyes widened to the size of saucers and her jaw dropped. "Oh, Hannah, he hasn't compromised your virtue, has he?" Her friend's voice dropped to a whisper on the word *virtue*.

"No, perish the thought! It is nothing like that. Father's arrest and incarceration was a most worrying time for us, and highlighted the tenuous position of our family." Hannah chose her words carefully. Never would she burden her friend with the knowledge that her gift would be the cause of her death.

While her heart still ached at her mother's betrayal, Hannah had to agree with her parents. The marriage might give them protection, but it also ended her daydream of marrying a man who made her heart and mind race. Lord Wycliff certainly raised her pulse, but usually in agitation or anger.

"Viscount Wycliff has offered the protection of his name to me, and promised that he will always have a care for Mother and me." The words weighed heavily on Hannah, as though she had been selected as the sacrifice to appease some demon.

Lizzie glanced from her mother to her best friend. If she didn't stop frowning, she would mar her brow before the wedding. "But you do not love him, do you?"

Hannah let a sad sigh blow through her body. She loved her friend dearly, but they lived such different lives. "No, I do not love him, but I have found much to admire in him. On closer acquaintance, I have discovered him to be a man of both intelligence and integrity."

"This cannot go ahead, Mother. Hannah must marry for love and you must tell Lady Miles so." Lizzie turned to her mother, expecting her to the fix the problem, one mother to another.

Lady Loburn stared at Hannah for a long minute, and then turned to touch her daughter's hand. "You, my child, were blessed by angels on the day of your birth, and have lived a charmed life. But not all women live the fairy tale of falling in love with a dashing duke. Most, like Hannah and myself, make do with what life sends our way."

The frown deepened on Lizzie's forehead. "I know not every woman can marry a duke, Mama, but the least Hannah deserves is affection from her husband."

Under the table, Hannah dug her nails into her palms. She refused to cry. Lord Wycliff have proven himself capable of intelligent conversation and had acted honourably in clearing her father's name. Perhaps it might be too much to hope that affection could one day grow between them. But if a stitched-together man and a severed hand could take up residence in their house, anything could happen.

Lady Loburn gathered up the completed invitations. "I think it is a good match. Hannah will be a gentling influence on the viscount, and I believe he will embolden Hannah. While he is not a wealthy man, from all accounts neither is he a wastrel. The two of them will make do. And, you know, there is nothing wrong with being styled Lady Hannah Wycliff. It sounds rather well, I think."

Hannah was grateful for Lady Loburn's understanding of the situation, although intrigued by how she had *made do* with the marquis. Not for the first time, Hannah wondered why her friend did not favour either of her parents in looks. "While I am mindful that life intended me for spinsterhood, Lizzie, your mother is right. This is a good match. Besides, Mother has promised that if he proves to be a cruel husband, she will turn him into a goldfish."

Lizzie pouted and then a smile broke over her face. "Lady Wycliff! Once you are married, I can tell you all my scandalous secrets. When we go to the country, we can invite you both, and Harden can take Wycliff out shooting or something."

"See, every cloud has a silver lining. There is much we can do together as two old married women." Hannah managed to find a smile, if not for herself, then for her friend. The duke had a large enough country estate that Hannah could stay for a month and never set eyes on her soon-to-be husband save at dinner.

"La! Won't it be marvellous if we have daughters at the same time, to continue the friendship we and our mothers have." Lizzie beamed and clapped her hands.

Hannah bit her lip to stop herself from crying out.

There would be no children from her body, but she could share in the joy of motherhood if it blessed her friend and lavish her love upon them.

Lizzie rose from her seat and flung her arms around Hannah. "If Hannah cannot marry for love, then she can still have a wedding full of love. We will arrange it, won't we, Mother?"

Lady Loburn beamed. "Yes, of course. Hannah will be surrounded by her friends and family, who care for her deeply. She does not make this journey alone."

On a dreary morning, a small group assembled in the modest chapel where Reverend Jones had attempted to send Lady Jessope back to her God. This time there were more bodies to fill the pews. Lizzie and Lady Loburn insisted on being present, and would not allow Hannah to wed without her closest friend to attend her.

Lady Miles and Lady Loburn sat side by side and chatted as though they were both young girls again. The household staff sat behind them. Mary was actually speaking to the imposing figure of Frank, having recovered from her shock at the man's appearance. Timmy sat with Old Jim and his grandson, Young Jim. Barnes sat on Timmy's lap, the boy's hand holding tight to the leash.

"Are you ready, my dear?" her father asked Hannah as they stood on the porch.

*No*, she wanted to cry before she bolted from the church.

But she would do this for her family, and because she had to trust that her mother knew something beyond her understanding. It seemed a lifetime ago when she had asked her mother why she had requested that Lord Wycliff be included at Lizzie's engagement ball. Her mother had replied that he had to be in play in the chess match of their lives. Hannah only hoped the end result would be worth it.

Hannah wore the dark orange silk gown made for Lizzie's wedding. Her friend had insisted she wear it today. In her dark hair rested her mother's tiara with the pearl drop. A shawl in shades of orange and red was draped around her shoulders against the chill of the day.

"Yes, Papa, I'm ready." Hannah rested her hand on her father's forearm and the two of them walked down the aisle.

Lord Wycliff waited next to the reverend, with the Duke of Harden as groomsman. His black gaze locked on Hannah as she walked to meet him. His black attire was relieved only by the embroidery on his waistcoat, where flames licked at the edges much as they did the hem of her gown.

She was only vaguely aware of the words of the ceremony. She learned her about-to-be husband's full name was Jonas Broughton Balfour, Viscount Wycliff. Soon the reverend turned to her and said the vows for her to repeat. Hannah never thought the word *obey* would be an issue, as she had been an obedient child and had no doubt she would prove an obedient wife. It was the word *love* that tasted dry in her throat. She stood before God and promised to love a man she hardly knew.

And yet, a tiny ember of hope burned inside her.

She offered her own silent prayer as he took her hand. *Let us find some common ground between us to make the years ahead bearable.*

Lord Wycliff said his vows and took her hands in his. They were warm against her chilled skin as he slipped the plain gold ring on her finger.

"You may kiss the bride," Reverend Jones announced.

An awkward silence fell. Hannah stared at the man who was now her legal husband. Surely he wouldn't kiss her? Would he?

Hannah thought she might expire on the spot. She had forgotten the last part of the ceremony. Then another thought tumbled into her mind. She was his wife and legally his property. He could do whatever he wished to her and she could not refuse.

Hannah glanced at her mother, hoping the mage was ready to turn the viscount into a goldfish if he took liberties with his new acquisition. She closed her eyes as he leaned forward and to her relief—and a tiny bit of disappointment—his warm lips brushed her cheek. The brief action made warmth bloom through her body. How unexpected. He hadn't kissed her on the lips. Did that mean he didn't wish to, or was he merely being polite?

Thoughts swirled in her mind as she took his arm. To the applause of her friends and family, and the pealing of the church bells, they walked down the aisle and out to the waiting carriage.

They returned to Westbourne Green, where the wedding breakfast was laid out in the large dining room at the house. Her father popped champagne and poured glasses for everyone, including the staff. Mary pressed one into the large hand of Frank, but he simply stood and stared at the bubbles.

Lord Wycliff stood awkwardly, his hands behind his back. "I have a gift for my bride."

He held out a King Charles spaniel puppy with long silken ears. The dog had rich chestnut markings against a white coat. It squirmed in his grasp and its tail wagged back and forth.

"Oh! How marvellous." Tears pricked behind Hannah's eyes as she took the squirming pup and it licked her face.

"It is female, if that aids in selecting a name, and I can take no credit for her appearance. Your mother handed her to me on my way into the room." His gift delivered, the viscount claimed a glass of champagne and stood to one side.

Hannah held the silken ball of fur and blinked back the tears. "I shall call her Bethsheba, or Sheba for short. In memory of Beth Warren and the other women who lost their lives to Lord Dunkeith's madness."

"A lovely tribute, dearest." Lady Miles held out a glass of champagne to Hannah.

"I'll take Sheba." Timmy took the squirming puppy from Hannah.

With her friends and family gathered around her, Hannah enjoyed the meal, and they chatted long into the afternoon. At last it was time for Lizzie, Harden, and Lady Loburn to climb into their carriage and return to London.

It seemed the rest of the family, Barnes included, evaporated into the woodwork until Hannah sat alone with her husband in the parlour. Or not entirely alone, since the puppy appeared to have gone to sleep on her feet.

Hannah contemplated her first night as a married woman. This had all come about because her mother had revealed a terrible secret. Now only one lingered in the room.

"As we embark upon our married life, my lord, I believe you have me at a disadvantage." Hannah curled her hands into her skirts, fisting the delicate fabric to steady her nerves.

"How so, Lady Wycliff?" Black eyes turned to her.

*Lady Wycliff.* Her heart and mind froze. Her mother had used magic to pause her in time, but two words from the viscount could turn her to stone. She was now his wife, until death parted them. Would he truly prove honourable and stand by her even if her mother's magic failed? Or, if she became one of the Afflicted, would she become like the late Lady

Albright—set aside and existing on what charity she could find?

She cleared such thoughts from her mind. "You are privy to my secret, but I do not know yours."

"No. You do not." He rose from his seat. "As you are aware, this is a marriage in name only, so I will say good night." He strode from the room without another word.

Hannah glanced down at the slumbering puppy. "It may be a marriage of convenience, but that doesn't mean it is also a marriage of secrets."

If her husband thought she would be so easily deterred, then he didn't know her at all. She scooped up the sleepy Sheba and climbed the stairs to her room. A small green velvet cushion had appeared next to her bed and Hannah laid the spaniel on it.

After she had taken off her wedding clothes and donned her nightshift, Hannah climbed alone between the warmed sheets. She stared at her left hand and on impulse, removed the gold ring and held it to the light. As she turned it, she realised there were letters inscribed within.

*Together, beyond death.*

The words sent a shiver over her skin, but was it from trepidation...or excitement at what lay ahead?

There was much more to her husband than there appeared. The smallest of smiles bloomed on her lips as she slid the wedding ring and its unseen promise, back on her finger.

THE END

The third instalment in Hannah and Wycliff's journey together continues in GOSSIP and GORGONS...

## ABOUT THE AUTHOR

Tilly drinks entirely too much coffee, likes to watch Buffy the Vampire Slayer and wishes she could talk to Jane Austen. Sometimes she imagines a world where the Bennet sisters lived near the Hellmouth. Or that might be a fanciful imagining brought on by too much caffeine.

To be the first to hear about new releases and special offers sign up at:
www.tillywallace.com/newsletter

*Tilly would love to hear from you:*
www.tillywallace.com
tilly@tillywallace.com

Printed in Great Britain
by Amazon